The Detections of
FRANCIS QUARLES

The Detections of
FRANCIS QUARLES

Julian Symons

edited by John Cooper

Crippen & Landru Publishers
Norfolk, Virginia
2006

Copyright © 2006 by Kathleen Symons

Introduction copyright © 2006 by John Cooper

Cover painting by Carol Heyer

Lost Classics design by Deborah Miller

Crippen & Landru logo by Eric D. Greene

Lost Classsics logo by Eric D. Greene
adapted from a drawing by Ike Morgan, 1895

ISBN (clothbound edition): 1-932009-44-2
ISBN (trade softcover edition): 1-932009-45-0

FIRST EDITION

Printed in the United States of America on acid-free paper

Crippen & Landru Publishers
P. O. Box 9315
Norfolk, VA 23505
USA

Email: Info@crippenlandru.com
Web: www.crippenlandru.com

CONTENTS

Introduction by John Cooper	7
Red Rum Means Murder	11
Death in the Scillies	16
Poison Pen	21
An Exercise in Logic	26
Summer Show	31
The Desk	35
Mrs Rolleston's Diamonds	40
Murder—But How Was It Done?	45
Ancestor Worship	49
Iced Champagne	53
No Use Turning a Deaf Ear to Murder	57
The Duke of York	61
Double Double Cross	66
Tattoo	71
Jack and Jill	76
The Conjuring Trick	79
Happy Hexing	83
No Deception	88
The Second Bullet	93
Preserving the Evidence	97
Death for Mr Golightly	102
A Man With Blue Hair	107
The Two Suitors	112
Airborne With a Borgia	116
Art Loving Mr. Lister Lands a Fake . . .	120
The Collector	124
Ghost from the Past	128
The Swedish Nightingale	132
The Barton Hall Dwarf	137
The Pepoli Case	142
Nothing Up His Sleeve	147
A Present From Santa Claus	152
The Link	156

Little Boy Blue	160
Affection Unlimited	164
The Whistling Man	170
Party Line	174
Who Killed Harrrington?	177
Murder in Reverse	182
The Vanishing Trick	186
The Impossible Theft	191
Final Night Extra	195
Appendix: The Casebook of Francis Quarles	199
Afterword by Mrs. Kathleen Symons	203

INTRODUCTION

Julian Symons (1912–1994) was a multi-talented author who produced first class crime fiction, biographies and poetry as well as being a fearless critic and social historian. His approach was intellectual and his style polished.

He wrote notable biographies of Charles Dickens, Edgar Allan Poe, Thomas Carlyle, Horatio Bottomley and his own brother, A.J.A. Symons. He had a passion for social history which led to his writing about the General Strike and life in the 1930's. He was also an accomplished poet and in 1937 he founded, and for three years edited, the magazine *Twentieth Century Verse*. After the war, he worked in London as an advertising copywriter. On the suggestion of George Orwell, he was asked to take over writing the column "Life, People and Books" for the *Manchester Evening News*.

In 1958, Symons started to review crime fiction for *The Sunday Times* of London. He was an able and confident critic of his fellow crime writers. At one stage, some authors disliked his comments and tried unsuccessfully to have him removed from the Crime Writers' Association, of which he had been a co-founder in 1953. He was appointed chairman of the CWA in 1958 and from 1976 to 1985 was president of the Detection Club.

During 1959, *The Sunday Times* produced *The Hundred Best Crime Stories* edited by Symons. In 1962, Longmans Green published *The Detective Story in Britain*, Symons' first critical volume. Later, in 1972, Faber published the very important *Bloody Murder* (U.S. title *Mortal Consequences*), the best overall view of the history of crime/detective fiction ever written. Moreover, as a learned and respected critic, he acted as an editorial consultant to Penguin Books for their crime list. Collins also made use of his expertise, asking him to select and introduce various titles to celebrate the Golden Jubilee of the Crime Club in 1980.

Julian Symons, the crime novelist, rarely failed to entertain in his twenty-nine novels producing a wide range of characters, settings and plots. He was always interested in the psychology that motivated his characters and their crimes, finding evil and confusion just below the surface of what appears to be a refined society. Some of his outstanding crime novels are *The Thirty-First of February* (1950), *The End of Solomon Grundy* (1964), *The Man Who Killed Himself* (1967), *Death's Darkest Face* (1990) and the excellent *Playing Happy Families* (1994). Several of his books won awards including the CWA award for the best novel of 1957 to *The Colour of Murder*. In 1960, *The Progress of a Crime* received an Edgar Award from The Mystery Writers of America.

Besides that superlative detective, Francis Quarles, Symons created several series characters, but each appeared in only two or three novels. The aptly named Inspector Bland of Scotland Yard features in Symons' first three detective novels: *The Immaterial Murder Case* (1945), *A Man Called Jones* (1947) and *Bland Beginning* (1949). The Queen's Counsel, Magnus Newton, appears in *The Colour of Murder*, *The End of Solomon Grundy* and *The Progress of a Crime*. The actor Sheridan Haynes is in two Sherlockian novels, *A Three Pipe Problem* (1975) and *The Kentish Manor Murders* (1988) and one short story, *Sherlock's Christmas*. Two other Scotland Yard policemen each have two cases. Inspector Crambo features in *The Narrowing Circle* (1954) and *The Gigantic Shadow* (1958; U.S. title, *The Pipe Dream*). Detective Superintendent Catchpole appears in Symons' last two novels, *Playing Happy Families* (1994) and *A Sort of Virtue* (1996).

Julian Symons was held in great esteem by his fellow crime writers. He was made a Grand Master by the Mystery Writers of America in 1982 and a comparable honour had been bestowed in 1977 by the Swedish Academy of Detection. In 1990, the CWA presented him with its highest award, the Cartier Diamond Dagger, for outstanding contribution to the genre of crime writing. This was more than justly deserved.

In Britain, the detective short story reached one of its highest peaks of popularity in the 1950's. In this period, the London *Evening Standard* newspaper regularly featured detective stories, especially written for the paper, by acknowledged leading writers of the genre.* Subsequently,

---

* In the year 1950 alone, the following authors had stories in the *Evening Standard*: Adrian Alington, Margery Allingham, Josephine Bell, John Bonett, Leo Bruce, Victor Canning, Edmund Crispin, Freeman Wills Crofts, Michael Gilbert, Cyril Hare, Richard Hull, Michael Innes, Selwyn Jepson, Milward Kennedy, Ronald Knox, E.C.R. Lorac, Philip MacDonald, Gladys Mitchell, E.R. Punshon, Clayton Rawson, John Rhode, Julian Symons, Roy Vickers and Clifford Witting.

various authors had collections published of their own contributions to the *Evening Standard* (sometimes revising the original stories). Freeman Wills Crofts, *Many a Slip* (Hodder & Stoughton, 1955), Edmund Crispin, *Beware of the Trains* (Gollancz, 1953; U.S., Walker 1962) and Julian Symons, *Murder! Murder!*, (Collins Fontana paperback 1961) all had their origin in the *Evening Standard*. Some *Evening Standard* stories also feature in two Michael Innes collections—*Appleby Talking* (Gollancz 1954; U.S. title, *Dead Man's Shoes*, Dodd, Mead 1954) and *Appleby Talks Again* (Gollancz, 1956; Dodd, Mead, 1957) as well as Julian Symons' *Francis Quarles Investigates* (Panther paperback, 1965). In 1950 and 1951, Gollancz also published two excellent collections of stories from the *Evening Standard*.

Julian Symons contributed stories to *The Evening Standard* right through the fifties and into the early sixties. Some of them were illustrated by artists such as Caswell and Mackenzie. Many of the stories were published under series titles—"London Alibi,", "Deckchair Detective," "A Thriller A Day," "Follow Francis Quarles," "New Detective Story" and "Francis Quarles Finds Out." The collection which I have the pleasure of presenting here, spans the period 1950 to 1964.

The majority of Symons' stories in the *Evening Standard* feature the private detective Francis Quarles who has eighty-seven known investigations in his casebook. According to Symons's "A Note on Francis Quarles," prefacing the collection *Murder! Murder!*, little is known of Quarles' background apart from the fact that he was probably educated abroad, spent some years in the Far East, was involved in mysterious war-time activities and never married. "It is reasonable," Symons remarks, "to suppose his silence hides some sort of secret."

This private detective is a large man with black eyes, standing six feet tall and weighing almost thirteen stone (one hundred and eighty-two pounds). Quarles always dresses smartly and has a penchant for silk shirts and brightly coloured ties. He is described as being perceptive and urbane but with a deceptive air of sleepy laziness. He is prepared to accept almost any case for an adequate sum of money. His office in Trafalgar Square was established in the mid-1940's. During the course of the stories, he has two secretaries, the neat, attractive blonde Molly Player and, briefly, a Miss Inchborne. Inspector Leeds of Scotland Yard features in over twenty cases with Francis Quarles. He is a brisk, burly figure with greying hair, and he has a rasping voice. Fortunately, he has no objection to Quarles' giving him a helping hand.

Francis Quarles's investigations usually involve murder in its various forms. To quote him, "There are no humdrum murder cases, and no insoluble ones either. In every unsolved crime there is always a human error, a clue which, if we could understand its meaning, would point straight to the murderer." The murders that Quarles investigates in this collection of stories take place in a variety of locations. Scenes of the crime include an aeroplane flight to Rome, a village bazaar, a beach holiday, a city hotel, a cruise ship, an English village, a country show, the Isles of Scilly, a weekend house party and even a bookshop. The final story in this collection even uses the *Evening Standard* itself as a major clue.

Although, in his critical writings, Julian Symons argued that the detective story has given way to the crime novel, his clever tales about Francis Quarles show his mastery of classic orthodox detective stories with all the clues given to the reader (although, as in "Final Night Extra," the fairness has sometimes disappeared in the passage of half a century). I have very much enjoyed discovering and putting together *The Detections of Francis Quarles*, a book which proves (if more proof were necessary) what an outstanding contributor to the genre Julian Symons was. None of the cases has previously been collected in an anthology of the author's work. I hope readers obtain many hours of pleasure pitting their wits against Francis Quarles, detective.

John Cooper
Westcliff-on-Sea

RED RUM MEANS MURDER

"WE'RE going to see George Mortimer. He's been murdered," Inspector Leeds said to Francis Quarles in the police car.

"George Mortimer the bookseller?"

"George Mortimer the blackmailer. Oh yes, he was a bookseller, too. Had a perfectly genuine business. But he ran the biggest blackmail racket in England, had done for twenty years. We never caught him, because he wasn't greedy. Sounds odd that, but it's greed that brings down most blackmailers. They ask for too much money or ask for it too often, squeeze the poor devil they're blackmailing until he cries out. Mortimer never took more than one bite and he always made it what his victim could pay. Not comfortably, I don't say that, but he could pay it. And after the payment was made Mortimer gave back or burned the evidence."

"The blackmailer's code of ethics."

"Call it that if you like. Anyway, he was sensible. I've met two or three people who, I knew perfectly well, had been blackmailed by him, but I could never get anything out of them. Here we are."

GEORGE MORTIMER'S body lay on the floor of his elegant little Mayfair bookshop. He had been shot from the front, right between the eyes. The bookseller-blackmailer was a plump, elegant, grey-haired man in his fifties. Quarles remembered him as a friendly figure with a slightly perverse sense of humour.

Sergeant Halse was reporting to the Inspector. "He had a wall safe. It's been opened with his own key and cleared out. No fingerprints. Must have let the murderer in himself; entry wasn't forced. Doctor says death occurred between 7 and 8 o'clock last night, though it wasn't discovered until this morning."

Quarles ceased to listen. He looked round the books on the shelves, modern first editions, leather-backed sets of the standard authors, an interesting collection of books on sport. He glanced at the books on Mortimer's desk, presumably ready for sending out—Florence Nightingale's *Notes on Nursing* and some others. Then he looked through a small pile of receipted accounts and whistled.

"Here, Inspector. Look at this invoice to George Congerton, Esq. Galsworthy's *Island Pharisees* first edition, £100. *Habits of the Conger*, by Plumley, £37 10s Maugham's *Liza of Lambeth*, first edition, £75. And so on. Anything strike you about that?"

"The prices seem pretty steep."

"They're ridiculous. Nobody in his senses would pay them. Unless he were paying them as some form of blackmail. Do you see what I mean? Mortimer was clever. If his cheque from Congerton was queried at some time he could say quite truthfully that it was a business transaction.

"There's no law to stop a man paying ten times what things are worth. I should guess that Mortimer chose the books himself. He had a queer sense of humour—he once sent me in an account in the form of an acrostic on my name. It would be just in his line to send *Habits of the Conger* to a man named Congerton."

He went rapidly through the pile of invoices, and picked out half a dozen of them. "The others are genuine, but all these are invoiced at fantastic prices. You'll find they were people he blackmailed, if you can get them to talk. And there's the same humour, if you'll notice. He's invoiced a book called *Done Brown in Chicago* to a man named William Brown."

"I don't doubt you're right." The Inspector jerked his thumb. "But where does it take us? These have all paid up. We want a man who hasn't paid."

"Yes." Quarles looked thoughtfully again at the books on the desk, and took a piece of paper out of the topmost one. It was a list of their titles and prices, and he cried out as he read it. Florence Nightingale, *Notes on Nursing*, £75; George Orwell, *Burmese Days*, first edition, £25; Trollope, *The Fixed Period*, first edition, £75; W. H. Auden, *First Poems*, £25; Preece's *Gentle Art of Fly Fishing*, £50.

"Total £250, and the whole lot worth perhaps a fifth of that. He was putting the screw on somebody. Who was it?"

Sergeant Halse had shared in Quarles's excitement. Now, he said: "Might this be useful, sir? It's a note in his diary for today. It says: Fill book orders, Wyce, Rutherford, Paton, and gives their addresses."

"It certainly is useful. Inspector, do you realise the man who killed Mortimer is probably one of these three?"

The Inspector grunted. "They may all be perfectly genuine customers. I agree they're worth looking up, but let's see what we can find out about them first."

Quarles was looking down at the five oddly assorted books. "You know, I feel these ought to be telling us something."

That afternoon the Inspector and Quarles read the notes obtained about Ralph Wyce, Arnold Rutherford and James Paton.

Wyce was a semi-retired stockbroker in his late fifties, reputedly wealthy and respectable. His name, unlike those of the other two, appeared half a dozen times in Mortimer's books. Rutherford was an unmarried lawyer, and Paton an accountant who had recently married. They were both men in their early thirties.

This happened to be one of Wyce's working days, as he explained when they saw him in his office. The Inspector told him about George Mortimer's death and Wyce tut-tutted. Yes, he had seen it in the paper. Yes, he had bought books from Mortimer in, the past. What kind of books? Old topographical works mostly, of which Mortimer had a fine collection.

The Inspector leaned forward. "Have you an order outstanding now?"

Wyce passed his hand over a bald head. He looked somewhat bewildered. "Why, yes, there are half a dozen books about the history of Essex that he's getting hold of for me."

"You haven't ordered any of these?" Quarles showed him the five books that had been on Mortimer's table.

"I certainly haven't. Fly fishing and modern poetry—they're a queer lot, if I may say so, gentlemen."

"We got little change out of him," the Inspector said as they climbed the stairs to Rutherford's chambers. "And I guess we shall get just as little out of this one."

He was right. Rutherford was a dark, intense-looking young man who at first replied cautiously to their questions. He agreed that he had ordered books from Mortimer. "I'm interested in nature study, and Mortimer was getting hold of some rare books on birds and flowers for me. Yesterday he told me that he'd got them, and was sending them off to me."

"Have you got the letter?"

"He rang up. Does it matter?"

The Inspector did not answer. They discovered that Rutherford, like Wyce, had only a very tentative alibi for the time of the murder.

They went to have a cup of tea after leaving Rutherford. The Inspector was a little discouraged. "I don't see that this bright idea of yours is leading anywhere," he said. "If one of these chaps is guilty, of course, he's ready to be questioned, and has his answers pat."

14   JULIAN SYMONS

QUARLES was staring at the five books in front of him. He seemed not to hear. The Inspector grunted, and turned to the crossword. After five minutes' silence he said: "Red rum turns criminal in six letters. What do you suppose that is?"

"Murder," Quarles answered absently and then sat up with a jerk. "Of course, that's it. It was in front of our noses, that's why we couldn't see it. Come on."

A bewildered Inspector followed him. "You know who did it—through the books?"

"That's right."

They found Paton at home with his wife, who went out and left them alone with him. The accountant was short, stocky, and inclined to be curt. Like the others he agreed that he had ordered books from Mortimer—some out of print text-books which the bookseller had been trying to find for a week or two.

"Had he told you they were ready?"

There was a moment's hesitation before Paton said, "No."

Quarles showed him the five books. "Do you recognise these, Mr. Paton?"

"No."

"Suppose I told you that your name is on this sheet of paper, with the blackmail prices you were to pay for the books." Quarles took the sheet out of the top book. "You burned everything you could lay hands on, but you never thought to look inside the books on the table."

"Just a minute now," Paton cried. He was across the room and out of the door before either of them could move. The key turned. The Inspector was half-way to the door when they heard the shot.

"Paton had an extravagant wife, and an invalid mother whom he kept in an expensive nursing home," the Inspector said afterwards. "For once Mortimer put the screws on too tight, and he paid for it. But there was no name on that piece of paper. How did you know it was Paton?"

"Look at these five books—an absolutely arbitrary collection they seem to be, don't they? No reference to the victim's occupation, no surface link at all. But there are other verbal tricks, if your sense of humour runs that way. I should have remembered that Mortimer sent me a bill in the form of an acrostic. Just look at the author's names, in the order they stood on the desk."

"Nightingale, Orwell, Trollope, Auden, Preece."

"How do the initial letters read?"

"N-O-T-A-P." The Inspector gasped.

"That's it. Invert the letters and you've got Paton's name. A little joke, but the kind that amused Mortimer. I might not have thought of it. Inspector, if you hadn't reminded me that red rum means murder."

DEATH IN THE SCILLIES

IN late spring there is a peculiar translucent quality in the light on the Isles of Scilly. That light is deceptive, for it carries with it a suggestion of warmth—whereas, as Francis Quarles reflected, it is often very crisply cold.

It was cold now in the hotel motorboat that plied every day between St. Mary's and the other principal islands.

In the Scillies you go out for the day when it is fine. You ask your hotel to pack up lunch and go with anything from six to twenty other people to Tresco or Bryher or St. Martin's or St. Agnes.

During the day you bathe, you fish, you wander about. In the early evening the motorboat brings you back to St. Mary's.

Quarles, who was taking a holiday after clearing up that strange case of the Disappearing Politician (the full story of which has never yet been told), found himself enjoying this idle and simple life. He felt at peace with the world and with his companions in the motorboat. There were six of them, and he knew all except one by name.

FIRST of all Miss Gwen Farquhar, who sat trailing a thin blue-veined hand in the cold blue water. Miss Farquhar, white-haired, faintly aristocratic, and in her seventies, came out every day with her wicker-work lunch basket.

Then Miss Murrell, a neat spinsterish schoolmistress.

Then Springer, a fair-haired young man with an Australian accent, who occasionally made the 20-minute trip by air to the mainland.

These three had been staying for some days in Quarles's hotel. But he knew also the Playfairs, the young couple who always held hands in the boat, and got out every day at Tresco. The sixth person in the boat, a red-faced man in a porkpie hat, had arrived at the hotel on the previous evening.

There were only murmurs of conversation as the boat drew away from St. Mary's. Lunch baskets had been put in the bottom of the boat and covered with a tarpaulin. The boat made its way towards a small island out of which rose two moss-covered hills.

"Hullo," said Quarles, "Somebody is landing on Samson."

Springer turned round with a smile. "That's me," he said. "Always wanted an island to myself."

The island of Samson is a curiosity in the Scillies. It is uninhabited, with no harbour, and those who want to land there have to go ashore in a dinghy. Springer had just stepped into it when Miss Murrell said: "I think I'll go to Samson, too. You won't mind, will you, Mr. Springer?" She dived under the tarpaulin for her lunch basket, as he had done.

Springer assented rather hollowly. The two were rowed ashore and disappeared together along the beach. From Samson the boat went to Tresco where the Playfairs were deposited, and from Tresco to St. Martin's where Quaries and Miss Farquhar got off at the little landing quay, together with the red-faced man in the porkpie hat who strode off purposefully.

MISS FARQUHAR smiled at Quarles. With a very reasonable mimicry of Miss Murrell she said. "I think I'll go to St. Martin's, too. You won't think I'm throwing myself at your head, will you?"

Quarles laughed. "Let's walk over the hill to St. Martin's Bay if you feel like company."

Three-quarters of an hour later they were in a sheltered bay on the other side of the island. The sun shone brightly.

"My," said Miss Farquhar, "I feel hungry." She undid the strap of her nearly new wicker basket with its initials, G.F., painted inside, and peeped at the contents.

She made an exclamation of annoyance. "Well now, that's too bad. I like egg and anchovy sandwiches. But today I asked for meat as a change, and what have I got?" She raised her hands in mock despair. "Egg and anchovy sandwiches." She got out her flask, poured some tea into a metal cup, and drank.

"I hope the tea's—" Quarles began, and stopped.

Miss Farquhar's face contorted into an expression of agony. Within a minute, under Quarles's horrified eyes, she had died.

Round the hill at the corner of the bay there appeared, striding as purposefully as ever, the man with the porkpie hat.

He was named Greenaway, and he was a sergeant in the Metropolitan Police Force, on holiday.

IT was with the help of Greenaway that Quarles carried out the grim duty of getting Miss Farquhar's body back to the landing quay. By midafternoon a doctor in St. Mary's had examined her.

The tea in Miss Farquhar's flask had been loaded with cyanide of potassium. How had it got there? As Quarles and Greenaway traced it back that became very difficult to explain.

The maid who had poured the tea into Miss Farquhar's flask had watched Miss Farquhar pack the flask in her lunch-basket with its initials G. F. on the inside of it. She had seen her walk down to the quay a few yards away.

The cyanide had been inserted on the boat, then? But that was impossible. Quarles himself could testify that there had been no chance of tampering with the interiors of lunch-baskets lying under a tarpaulin sheet.

Investigation of Miss Farquhar's room revealed from her bankbook that she was surprisingly well off.

Quarles asked the maid: "Did you pack the sandwiches for Miss Farquhar?"

"Oh no, sir. The chef did that."

Quarles asked the chef: "Why did you pack egg and anchovy sandwiches for Miss Farquhar when she asked for meat?"

The chef was indignant. "They were meat, sir—roast beef. I packed them myself."

"Did anyone else order egg and anchovy today?" The chef thought a moment, and then shook his head. "But Miss Farquhar generally had them?"

"That's right, sir. She'd had them three days running."

"Were any of the other baskets like Miss Farquhar's? Would there have been any chance of mistaking one for another?"

"There they are, sir." The motorboat passengers had all returned, and their baskets lay in the kitchen. None was in the least like Miss Farquhar's. Springer's was an old and battered affair wrapped in a loose oil-proof case. Miss Murrell's was a neat attache case with fittings inside. Greenaway's was a leather satchel. The Playfairs used only a large biscuit tin.

Quarles's stare at these things was prolonged. Then he turned away. "Yes, I see," he said.

Later that evening he talked to the boatman, and later still to Miss Murrell.

THERE were only four passengers on the motorboat next morning. Playfair said: "Where's Mr. Quarles today?"

"I think he took the airplane over to the mainland," Miss Murrell said in her precise voice. "He was up very early. I'm going to Bryher today, Mr. Springer." Springer did not reply, and she added coyly. "Are *you* coming to Bryher?"

"No, Samson again." His tone implied plainly that he was looking forward to a day on it alone. When the boat reached Samson he sprang into the dinghy, eager to be ashore.

"Pick you up about five," the boatman said, and Springer nodded. He made for one of the springy moss-covered peaks and scanned the island through a pair of field-glasses. Then he made his way briskly down to the valley Close to a large boulder he uncovered something in the grass.

He heard no approaching foot-steps and was surprised when Quarles's voice said: "Drop that, Springer." Springer looked up. There was a revolver in Quarles's hand, and at one side of Quarles stood Greenaway.

Springer dropped the thing he was holding. It was a wicker lunch basket, with the initials G.F. on the inside. Quarles said "This will hang you, Springer."

"HE was poor old Miss Farquhar's nephew," Quarles said to Greenaway afterwards "He lived in Australia. She'd been corresponding with him and had been foolish enough to tell him that she'd made him her heir. She had no other living relatives. Springer was planning to return to Australia, and then return in a few months to claim his inheritance."

"I don't see how you knew it was Springer."

"The apparent method of murder was by dropping cyanide into Miss Farquhar's flask. In most cases there would no doubt have been half a dozen times when that could have been done. Unfortunately for Springer in this case it was shown to be impossible. There was only one conclusion then, that the case with the poisoned flask wasn't Miss Farquhar's. And that was supported by the evidence of the sandwiches. Springer noticed that she had eaten egg and anchovy sandwiches for three days running. He prepared them for the substitute case which he had had made on one of his trips to the mainland. He changed cases on the boat and took Miss Farquhar's intending to burn it on Samson. But that man-hunting Miss Murrell pursued him, and he was only able to get away from her long enough to hide it. He went back to-day to dispose to it."

"But why Springer?" persisted Greenaway. "It might have been any of them?"

Quarles shook his head. "None of them would have dared to bring down openly a case exactly like Miss Farquhar's. It would have been remembered afterwards.

"But we didn't see Springer's case. It was concealed under a loose oilproof cover, and when he made the substitution he simply slipped the cover from one case to another under the tarpaulin.

"That was clever. But not," Quarles said thoughtfully. "Quite clever enough."

POISON PEN

MOST poison pen stories end with the discovery of the writer, but this one begins with it.

It was established to the satisfaction of everybody in the village of Rokewell that old Mrs. Hewitt had written the unpleasant letters that had been sent to the vicar, Dr. Moberly, Jennifer Waterlow and a number of other people.

Discovery of the writer was really very simple, after suspicion had been cast on Mrs. Hewitt by the fact that some of the letters were posted in a pillar-box near to her cottage.

She was sold some marked stamps provided by the police, and a watch was kept on her cottage. Mrs. Hewitt was something of a recluse and she had not been outside her front door for two days when just before 8.30 on Saturday morning she put some letters in the pillar-box and went back indoors.

Sergeant Needham, who was in charge of the investigation, opened the pillar-box at once and found two anonymous letters lying on top, with the marked stamps on them. A quick comparison of handwriting was inconclusive, as it often is, but there could be no doubt about Mrs. Hewitt's guilt, since she had been caught in the act.

The vicar, Dr. Moberly and Sergeant Needham called on Mrs. Hewitt and confronted her with the facts. Naturally she denied writing the letters and said that what she had put in the pillar-box were letters to her stepson in London and her married daughter in Wigan. No such letters, however, were found in the box.

That was on Saturday. On Monday Mrs. Hewitt was found in her sitting-room. She had been killed late on Sunday night by several blows from a poker.

FRANCIS QUARLES was taking a holiday at a friend's house near by. A telephone call from his friend, the Chief Constable of the county, took him to Rokewell with Inspector Abel, who had been assigned to the case.

"It's happened before and it will happen again," said the spruce little Inspector. "The old lady invented a whole lot of dirt, and stumbled on a piece of truth by accident. Somebody thought she knew too much for their good, and killed her. That's about the size of it, eh, Needham?"

Red-faced Sergeant Needham said reluctantly: "Looks very much like it, sir."

"Well, perhaps," Quarles was looking through a pile of some 30 anonymous letters, handed in by their recipients. "If any of the things she says about various respectable citizens were true, they had a variety of motives. She's accused the vicar of embezzling Church funds and Dr. Moberly of having distinctly unprofessional relations with some of his patients. For a recluse she seems to have had a remarkable interest in what went on. Had she got a telephone to gossip on?" Sergeant Needham said she had not. "What about relations, this stepson and daughter?"

"The stepson was the only one who came down much," said the Sergeant. "Name's Lester Wilson, lives up in London. Comes down sometimes at weekends. Fond of his stepmother—she brought him up as her own son—and doesn't believe she wrote the letters."

"What about the crime itself?" Quarles asked.

Abel snorted, "Very little that's useful. The poker was wiped clean, there was no struggle. It was someone she knew, she must have let him in herself. Somebody who received one of these." He smacked the pile of anonymous letters. "Or somebody who's not come forward yet to say that they received a letter. This case is going to mean some real hard plodding."

"I'll leave you two to that while I go out and look around." said Quarles. "I'd like to borrow this letter. It was sent to somebody I know." He picked up one of the two letters found in the pillar-box. Inspector Abel hesitated, then nodded.

QUARLES looked around. He gossiped with the village grocer, greengrocer, and its three publicans. He looked round the church and had a chat with the vicar. He had long conversations with the postman and the milkman.

He looked at Mrs. Hewitt's cottage, which stood twenty yards away from its nearest neighbours. Then he talked to those neighbours.

He was surprised by the faithfulness with which the poison pen writer had followed local gossip. It was all distorted, of course, and twisted to the most malicious meaning, but there seemed to be a seed of truth in almost everything that had been written.

It was almost as if the poison pen writer had hovered above the village doings, like some evil deity.

That was interesting, Quarles thought. But he learned nothing to suggest that any of the letters might have driven their recipients to the point of murder.

Perhaps the Inspector was right, Quarles thought, as he climbed up the hill to The Grange, where Jennifer Waterlow lived. Perhaps the murderer was somebody who had not admitted receiving a letter. He was still pondering this point as he rang the bell and introduced himself.

He remembered Jennifer Waterlow as a remarkably pretty girl, from a time when he had worked on a case with her father, the famous pathologist, Sir Geoffrey Waterlow. She greeted Quarles warmly. Behind her hovered a tall young man, who was introduced as Jack Belton. "Jack and I are going to be married," said Miss Waterlow.

Quarles offered his congratulations. "I wanted to see you about this." He held out the letter he had taken with the Inspector's permission.

Jennifer blushed. "Beastly things. That was the fourth. All of them insinuated things about Jack, and my going around with him."

"Yes. This was found on Saturday morning in the pillar-box, and it mentions a dance. When did you go to the dance?"

"On Friday night."

"Friday night," Quarles said in surprise. "Did anybody know you were going to it beforehand?"

Belton answered, "Nobody. We only decided to go at the last minute."

"What time did the dance begin?"

"We left here about a quarter past eight and got there about nine. Left about twelve and got home before half-past. It was at Wexmore, five miles away."

"It suggests in the letter that Belton here made love to you and says, 'I suppose you got your pink dress crumpled.' Were you wearing a pink dress?"

"Yes. As a matter of fact it was the first time I'd worn it. I suppose somebody passed on the news to Mrs. Hewitt."

Quarles thought for a moment and then said softly, "I see."

"The baffling thing is that there was nobody from the village at that dance," said Jack Belton. "Was there, Jennifer?"

"Nobody at all. It's almost as though there were some—some evil spirit—brooding over the village that knew everything people do and say."

"Come, now," Quarles said patiently, "you met somebody. Think."

They thought, and shook their heads. "Perhaps it wasn't at the dance. It might have been on the way there, or coming back. I could mention a name, but I don't want to."

Still they could think of nothing. "It took you three-quarters of an hour to get from your home to Wexmore. Why were you so long?"

Jennifer put a hand to her mouth. "The car, Jack, the car that had broken down—you remember?"

He remembered.

SPRUCE Inspector Abel and beefy Sergeant Needham listened to Quarles with interest.

"The evidence seemed conclusive, and yet I was never quite convinced that Mrs. Hewitt had written the letters," said the private detective. "For one thing she was a recluse, who wouldn't be likely to have the extensive knowledge of village scandal shown by the writer. For another, it seemed very foolish of her to post the letters in the nearest box. So I was on the lookout for anything which might indicate that she had been made a scapegoat, and then killed because she realised who the letter writer was.

"And in fact that's what happened. The letter writer chose Mrs. Hewitt as scapegoat because she was thought to be a bit queer and foolish. But in fact she put two and two together, and realised what had happened. Then she was killed."

Inspector Abel moved restlessly. "Let's have some facts man."

"Yes. The key to the case was the letter sent to Jennifer Waterlow found in the pillar box at 8.30 on Saturday morning. It referred to the dance she'd been to on the previous night and mentioned a new pink dress she'd been wearing. Jennifer Waterlow thought somebody from the village must have seen her and told Mrs. Hewitt. But that was impossible, because there was a watch kept on Mrs. Hewitt's cottage all night. Nobody went in or out during the night or in the early morning. She had no telephone. So Mrs. Hewitt couldn't have written that letter."

There was silence. "At first Jennifer and her companion, Jack Belton, said they'd met nobody from the village on the night of the dance. Then they remembered that on their way they had stopped to help a car that had broken down. Somebody else had stopped too, and had got off his bicycle to lend a hand. That somebody saw Jennifer's pink dress and wrote the letter."

"But I don't see—" said Inspector Abel.

"You don't? The poison pen writer—and murderer—was the person who always knows what's going on in a village, the person who met Jennifer on Friday night, the person who put the poison pen letters in the pillar-box when he opened it, and at the same time quickly slipped into his uniform the letters Mrs. Hewitt had really written to her stepson and daughter. The only possible person, in fact." And Quarles put a firm hand on the shoulder of Sergeant Needham.

AN EXERCISE IN LOGIC

MR. MORTIMER, the jeweller, was neither surprised nor alarmed when he heard the buzzer that acted as a signal for him to look out into his New Bond Street shop.

The signal was meant to indicate that a potential client was behaving in a suspicious manner, but then Fleury, who had pressed the buzzer, was a nervous little man, and in his six months at the shop had entertained frequent suspicions which had never yet been justified.

Nevertheless, Mr. Mortimer looked out of the panel through which he could see without being seen, and watched Fleury showing diamond necklaces and pendants to a big man who was wearing a brightly coloured tie and smoking a cigar. An American, obviously. Mr. Mortimer could see nothing odd, except that the American was looking at rather a lot of jewellery. Or perhaps Fleury was showing too many things, as he sometimes did.

Mr. Mortimer glanced towards the other end of the shop, where dependable, middle-aged Miss Robinson was busy with a fashionably dressed young woman who was looking at gold cigarette cases. The young woman had a Pekinese dog on a lead.

The American put down a necklace on the counter and pointed to another piece in a cabinet. Fleury turned to get it. There were seven or eight pieces of jewellery at his end of the counter and he took two of them, putting them back in their cases and replacing the cases in the cabinet.

He moved to put back some other pieces, but the American stopped him, indicating that he had not yet made up his mind about them. Mr. Mortimer frowned. Doubtless there was nothing wrong, but there were too many pieces on the counter. He stepped into the shop himself, a rubicund, blandly, smiling little man.

The American greeted him with the warmth and openness characteristic of Americans. His name was Walter Gayton, he was managing director of a steel company, and he wanted to take a few things back to his wife, Mimi, to show that he hadn't forgotten her during his tour of Europe. Mimi liked diamonds, he said, with a grin.

Mr. Mortimer, taking over from Fleury, soon realised that Gayton did not know much about jewellery and was willing to have his mind made up for him. Within five minutes Mr. Mortimer had made it up, and the American had agreed to take a necklace and a bracelet. The Pekinese dog somehow got off its lead and barked round Gayton's legs. The young woman retrieved it, apologising prettily.

At this point Mr. Mortimer became aware of Fleury at his side, muttering something. He made out the words, "Heart of Fire," and turned to see beads of sweat on his assistant's forehead. The Heart of Fire was a diamond pendant with a large and beautiful stone at the bottom, and it was one of the finest pieces in Mr. Mortimer's shop.

"What do you mean?" Mr. Mortimer said rather sharply.

Fleury had slightly protruding eyes. They seemed now to be almost popping out. "The Heart of Fire," he whispered.

"I showed it to this gentleman. It's not on the counter."

"Then it must be back in the cabinet." But it was not in the cabinet. The case that had contained it was on the counter, empty.

"It must have dropped down somewhere," said Walter Gayton when Mr. Mortimer explained what had happened to him. He looked on with an expression of slight amusement while Fleury and Mr. Mortimer crawled about on their hands and knees. Apologetically, they disturbed Miss Robinson and the girl. The Heart of Fire was not on the floor, on either side of the counter.

"You're sure you showed it to Mr. Gayton?" the jeweller asked Fleury.

It was the American himself who answered. "Why yes. I remember it. A lovely thing, but way out of my price range. It must be somewhere about."

But it was not somewhere about. At last Mr. Mortimer gave up searching and looked from one to the other of the four people in the shop, although as far as he knew Miss Robinson and the girl had not been within three feet of the Heart of Fire. His ruddy cheeks paled at the thought of his unpleasant duty.

"If you wouldn't mind stepping to my room at the back, Mr. Gayton—"

"For a search, you mean?" The American's friendliness vanished. He looked both tough and angry. "I certainly would mind. I'll go further and say that it's an insult. If you want to get in touch with me I'll be at my hotel. And you can forget about those things you were going to send. I'm not dealing with any man who treats me like a thief." He took two steps towards the door.

"Fleury," cried Mr. Mortimer. His assistant darted to the door, locked it and stood with arms wide apart barring Gayton's way. The American, who was half a head taller, looked down at Fleury for a moment and then carefully put out his cigar. With a bad grace he said, "Come on then, let's get it over."

They went into the back room. Mr. Mortimer searched Gayton, and did not find the Heart of Fire. He looked at Fleury.

"You want to search me?" the little man stammered. Mr. Mortimer nodded grimly. He searched Fleury and found nothing. They returned to the shop. More grimly still, Mr. Mortimer said. "I am afraid I must ask you to stay here while I telephone the police."

Now the young woman spoke for the first time since the loss had been discovered. "But that's ridiculous. I was never anywhere near those wretched diamonds of yours and I've got to meet my husband for lunch." She explained that she was Mary Forder, wife of the actor John Forder, then playing a leading part at the Orchard Theatre. She had come in to buy a cigarette case for her husband's birthday.

Mr. Mortimer was pale but resolute. "I am sorry, Mrs. Forder. I must ask you to stay. The Heart of Fire is somewhere in this shop, and nobody will leave until it has been found."

But in this last statement Mr. Mortimer was wrong. The police arrived and searched everybody in the shop, including Mr. Mortimer himself. A policewoman searched Mrs. Forder and Miss Robinson. Gayton and Fleury were searched all over again.

The police carefully examined everybody's shoes, in search of the false heels which are favourite receptacles for smuggled jewels, and would do as well for stolen one. They examined the Pekinese dog. They went through all the drawers, looked in all the cabinets, took up the rugs and the linoleum. They unscrewed the tops of silver sugar casters, in case the pendant should somehow have been dropped inside.

Even Mr. Mortimer felt bound to say that many of these measures were useless, because nobody in the shop had been near the sugar casters, or could possibly have raised the linoleum.

"Have you got any better suggestions?" asked Inspector Gregory, who was in charge.

Mr. Mortimer had no better suggestions. Gayton and Fleury were subjected to some rigorous questioning about the exact moment at which the Heart of Fire had vanished. Fleury said that he had gone to the cabinet two or three times to replace pieces Gayton had looked at, and to get out other pieces. It was his impression that the Heart of Fire had been on the counter just before he had last gone to the cabinet, but he could not be sure. Gayton could not be sure either. Had Mr. Mortimer himself seen the Heart of Fire on the counter? the Inspector asked. For the life of him Mr. Mortimer could not be certain. He could only say that he hadn't noticed it.

THE police telephoned Walter Gayton's hotel and discovered that he was well known there as an American business man. Then they let Walter Gayton go. They telephoned the Orchard Theatre and spoke to John Forder, who came down in a taxi and fetched his wife.

Mr. Mortimer watched all this gloomily. "But what about the Heart of Fire?" he asked.

"We shall find it," said the Inspector, and added ominously, "If it was ever here to find."

Mr. Mortimer, now almost in despair, telephoned to private detective Francis Quarles, who had the reputation of being able to see through a brick wall.

QUARLES was a big man, as big as the American. He listened with eyes half-closed while Fleury, Miss Robinson and Mr. Mortimer repeated their stories. "You're sure that's all? You've told me absolutely everything that happened?" He mopped his brow with a silk handkerchief. It was a hot day.

They said they had told him everything.

"Very well then. It was a simple exercise in logic, which can be solved with the aid of a hammer and chisel if you have them." In a slight daze Mr. Mortimer brought Quarles a hammer and chisel. "First of all, did the Heart of Fire pendant exist? Was it in the cabinet this morning?" Mr. Mortimer nodded. "You saw it. Did you handle it?" Mr. Mortimer shook his head.

"I saw it too," said Miss Robinson.

"Good. Gayton and Fleury saw it also. There is no reason why you should all be lying. Now, who took it? Not Miss Robinson or Mrs. Forder, they were never near it. Gayton? He could have taken it, but he didn't move about the shop or have contact with anybody to whom he could have passed it. If he had taken it, it must have been on his person. You, Mr. Mortimer? But Fleury thought that it was gone before you came into the shop. Besides, it was Fleury who called you into the shop. Why did you do that, Fleury?"

"I was suspicious," said the little man. "And don't ask me what of, I don't know."

"Or you wanted to rouse suspicion in your employer."

Fleury said with a sneer, "So you think I took it?"

Quarles's eyes were no longer sleepy. "Yes, you took it. You were the only one who moved away from the counter, when you turned your back on the others and went to the cabinet."

"And what did I do then? Make it vanish into thin air, I suppose."

"You put it back into the cabinet," Quarles said calmly. "You couldn't have done anything else."

"Then where is it, I should like to know?"

"Mr. Mortimer, will you let me have the cases Fleury put back into the cabinet after he had shown them to Gayton?" There were four of these cases. Quarles took the jewels from their velvet settings and began to break up the jewel cases. The second case split apart at the first blow, to reveal a false bottom in which a pendant sparkled.

"It was very simple. Fleury palmed the pendant when he turned round to put things back in the cabinet. He pressed a spring that opened the false bottom while he had his back turned to all of you, and put in the pendant. He put the case back in the cabinet and then pressed the buzzer. That was the only way it could have happened, that was the way it did happen. But what do you say about this?" He passed over the necklace.

Mr. Mortimer examined it, and exclaimed angrily. "An imitation."

"I thought so." Quarles nodded almost affectionately at Fleury. "He's an ingenious rogue. He had this copy of the pendant made, together with the false-bottomed jewel case. Then he stole the real pendant.

"Don't look alarmed, Mr. Mortimer, he can't have done that more than a day or two ago, and it shouldn't be hard to trace. He replaced the Heart of Fire with this imitation and at the first chance staged this sham robbery. He had to do that quickly, because once you looked at the imitation he was done for.

"The beauty of the scheme was that once it was carried out the imitation could stay in its hiding place until it was absolutely safe to dispose of it, and he'd given himself a perfect alibi by making sure that he was searched. It was neat, it was tidy, it was logical. In fact, it was too logical, because once you realised that a trick had been played, the only person who could have played it was Fleury."

SUMMER SHOW

"WHAT do you think of that little lot?" From under the bar counter Joe Grayson drew out six shiny broad beans, green and plump, well over a foot long. "Too late for entry in the show, but I reckon they'd have taken first prize."

The little group of farmers round the counter considered the beans solemnly. Francis Quarles looked at the poster behind Grayson's head, which told him that the Mannington Flower and Produce Summer Show was to be held on the following day, with sideshows, stalls. Punch and Judy, fortune teller, bowling for a pig, and prizes for local fruit, flowers and vegetables.

The men round the counter agreed that the beans looked good. Joe Grayson split one to reveal eight perfectly shaped beans, green and delicate, an equal distance apart in their soft furry beds.

"If they'd all have been like that you'd a won it," said one of the farmers. "What do you say, Mr. Ashley?"

A cadaverous, pale, dark-featured man with deep-set eyes, who had been sitting on a bench at the other end of the room, came up to the counter.

Quarles's host, a painter named John Tarn, whispered, "Here's the expert."

"SHOULDN'T look at these by rights, since I'm judging." Ashley said. "But as you're not entering them, there's no harm in it." He looked at the open bean, and nodded. Then most delicately, merely using his fingertips, he felt the others. Three he put aside with no comment, but at the fourth he said: "Soft in the middle."

He split the bean. It looked identical with the others, but inside there were only five beans instead of eight. "No good," Ashley said.

"You're a wonder, Mr. Ashley," said one of the farmers. "Have a drink."

"Tell me what that means," Quarles said to Tarn. "I'm baffled."

"They judge beans and peas like this. You make an entry of six bean or pea pods, and they should contain exactly the same number of beans or peas in them. Of course, there are other factors too—tenderness, ripeness, and so on—but the number is important. The judge opens just one pod and he tries to find a faulty one, as Ashley did just then.

"They do say Ashley's infallible, best judge in this part of the country. Queer chap, spent most of his life travelling round the world. Done all sorts of jobs by his own account, from selling vacuum cleaners and building bridges to working in a circus. Then settled down in England, made money as a nurseryman, and retired."

A big red-faced man pushed open the pub door. "Evening all," he said. "Pint of ale, please, landlord. Looks like a fine day for the show tomorrow."

There was a chorus of "Evening, Mr. Wayne." Ashley did not join in it. He thumped his glass of beer on the table still half-full, and walked out of the pub. There was an awkward silence for a moment, then everybody went on talking.

When they were on their way home, Tarn enlightened him as to the reason for Ashley's rudeness. "A bad business. Ashley's daughter, his only child, was more or less engaged to Wayne's son, and he threw her over. Treated her very badly. She took an overdose of sleeping tablets and died. Wayne's son's married and farming out in Kenya but Ashley and his wife have never forgiven Wayne—he was against the marriage, thought the two weren't suited. The Ashleys are fanatical about it. They've both got religion late in life, belong to some obscure sect, and they regard Wayne more or less as anti-Christ. There was trouble between them yesterday, when Ashley was helping to put up the tents. Wayne's dressing up as the fortune-teller, and there was a scene because he thought he'd been put rather out of the way. Bad to have that kind of thing in a village."

The sun was shining when Tarn and Quarles entered the large meadow where the show was being held, half an hour before it was due to open. Colonel Comstock, who had organised it all, greeted Tarn with a worried smile. "Ashley hasn't turned up yet to judge the beans and peas. Rang up and said he'd been unavoidably delayed. Ah, here he is now. That's good."

Ashley, grim and hollow-eyed, accompanied by a grey-haired woman, was ushered by Colonel Comstock to the door of a large tent. The two of them went in while Comstock stayed at the entrance talking to Quarles and Tarn. "This your first experience of a country show, Mr. Quarles?" Quarles said it was, "Lucky to get a fine day for it. Hope Ashley's not going to be long, all the judging should have been done this morning."

Ashley was not long. After a few minutes his head poked out from inside the tent flap. On tables inside the tent the entries of broad beans, peas and other vegetables were arranged on plates. One pod had been opened from each entry in the broad bean and pea section which Ashley was judging, and he curtly indicated entries to which he had given prizes.

Outside the tent there was a shout, and agitated voices. A young man wearing a steward's badge ran in.

"Is there a doctor here? It's the fortune-teller, Mr. Wayne."

"What's the matter with him? Taken ill?" asked Colonel Comstock.

The young man gulped. "No, Colonel. There's a knife—through his neck."

THE small fortune-teller's tent was next to the big marquee where Ashley had been judging. Wayne lay sprawled face forward across his table, his crystal ball just in front of him. His tall hat had fallen on the ground by his side. A thin shaft of sunlight through a gap near the top of the tent shone on the knife embedded deep in his neck. Quarles put a hand on the body. It was warm.

"Queer sort of knife," said Colonel Comstock. "Never seen one with a handle that looked as light as that. And the blade doesn't even look sharp."

Quarles touched the edge of the blade. "It's completely blunt. Does that mean anything to you?"

"Only that tremendous strength must have been needed to drive it deep into his neck like that. How long has he been dead?"

"Not more than five minutes."

"Then that lets Ashley out," the Colonel said. "He's the obvious suspect, but he was in the marquee judging. There's no other way out of it except the entrance where we were standing."

Quarles's face was grim as they returned to the marquee. He looked hard at the Ashleys. Mrs. Ashley, wild-eyed as her husband, returned his stare. Quarles thoughtfully examined the open bean and pea pods and then walked round the inside of the marquee.

When he had reached a point opposite the fortune teller's tent he got on to a chair and pushed at the apparently unbroken canvas. Suddenly a gap appeared where the guy ropes had not been firmly tightened. This gap was just opposite the larger gap in the fortune-teller's tent. Through it one could see the sprawled body of Wayne.

"You helped to fix these tents, Mr. Ashley," Quarles said. "You fixed them conveniently for murder."

"I don't know what you mean. You saw me arrive here. Since then I've been in this tent. You can all testify that I've had no time to do anything but judging—and also that I didn't leave the tent."

"That's right," said Colonel Comstock.

"Your wife could have opened these beans and peas and put the prize notices on them," Quarles said. "Because you're regarded as infallible your decisions wouldn't be questioned. You'd better open all those pods."

"Oh, I say now, I don't think we could do that." The Colonel's sense of propriety was outraged. "Ashley wouldn't make a mistake."

"But his wife might." In a tense silence Quarles broke open the pods of the beans given first prize. Two of the six were much inferior to the one on show.

Colonel Comstock's lips were tightly pursed. He broke open the beans awarded second prize himself and found a pod containing beans large hard, well past their prime. In one of the pea pods awarded a prize there were discoloured, brownish peas.

"You never judged these, Ashley," Colonel Comstock said harshly.

"You can think what you like." Ashley's voice was violent. "I did what I had to do."

"The Lord destroyeth evildoers," his wife said suddenly. "We are the servants of the Lord."

"What was your job in that circus, Ashley?" Quarles asked.

"I heard a voice that said, 'Kill'," Ashley answered his wife.

Tarn was looking puzzled. "Whether Ashley judged the entries or not I don't see how he could have killed Wayne. He never left the tent."

"He didn't need to leave the tent. Yesterday he helped to fix this marquee and the fortune-teller's tent. You remember Wayne was annoyed about the placing of it. He arranged things so that there was a gap in each tent to the point where Wayne was sitting. Then he threw a knife through the gaps into Wayne's neck. The two of them planned it together. I don't know whether any jury will consider them sane."

"But to throw a knife in that way would require extraordinary skill."

"It was a special kind of knife," Quarles said. "With a sharp point, a blunt blade, and a specially light handle to ensure balance in the middle. I recognised it as soon as I saw it, and I knew how the murder had been done. It's the kind of knife that's only used in a circus by a professional knife-thrower."

THE DESK

"THERE'S a subversive agent in this organisation." Sir George Claverty's eyes, cold, hard and blue, stared into Francis Quarles's black ones. "And I want you to find him." He said with emphasis: "I don't care who's involved."

In response to the detective's questions Sir George, managing director of Claverty's, revealed that his firm made a large variety of machine tools, including two or three secret ones that were about to go into manufacture. "Can't particularise," Sir George said. "But we're working on them with Government co-operation. And this Red agent wants to stop us." He pushed across the large desk in his office a postcard on which printed words taken from a book had been stuck. The card said: "You and your precious nephew aren't going to get away with making machines to help murder human beings. Stop manufacture immediately or take the consequences."

"My nephew, Ralph Rattray, has received a similar card," Sir George said grimly. "So have Baker, our head draughtsman; Williamson, who is in charge of the machine shop; and Grant, who's secretary of the company. They've all come during this week, and they were all posted in this district."

"Are all the men equally concerned with these new tools?"

Sir George shook his head. "Baker and Williamson are directly concerned with it, but my nephew Ralph deals with the administrative side of the business, and so, of course, does Grant. So whoever wrote these can't know a lot about our general set-up. Here are the other cards, all in much the same terms, you see." He pushed them over to Quarles, who was looking at them when the door opened.

"I say, Uncle—" said the young man in the doorway; and then: "Sorry, didn't know you were busy."

Sir George Claverty's voice had softened perceptibly as he said: "This is Ralph Rattray, my nephew and a junior director. Mr. Quarles is a private detective, Ralph. I was showing him those postcards."

"Oh, those." Ralph Rattray was a man in his late twenties, fair-haired and foppishly handsome. "I think you're making a lot of fuss about nothing, Uncle. Don't you, Mr. Quarles?"

Sir George said impatiently before Quarles could answer: "You don't know the effect this sort of thing can have. Williamson is as jittery as an old woman, and if he gets one or two more cards threatening him with death and damnation ..." He left the sentence unfinished. "Did you want to see me, Ralph?"

"It will keep," his nephew said, and gave his hand to Quarles. "Goodbye, Mr. Quarles. Hope you solve the mystery."

When Sir George turned again to Quarles his voice was as brusque as ever. "No use looking among the workmen for the joker who sent those cards. These tools aren't in production yet and they wouldn't know about them. What do you advise?"

"Nothing."

"What's that?"

Quarles shrugged his broad shoulders. "If this is a campaign to disrupt your output these cards are only the first step. By themselves they are meaningless. When we know the second step—then perhaps we can do something."

"But dammit, man, the second step, as you call it, may be a bomb blowing up my factory."

"No," said Quarles. "Five of you are threatened specifically. There is no threat to the factory or your workmen." Sir George got up. He was a tall man, and yet he did not look big when Quarles stood beside him to say goodbye. "But why those five?" the detective asked softly. "If we knew that, Sir George, it might be very helpful."

QUARLES employed the rest of that day in finding out something about the five men who had been threatened. Sir George Claverty, he discovered, was, in effect, the autocratic owner of the firm that bore his name. He was a hard employer, respected but not liked by those who worked for him. He was married but had no children, a fact which perhaps accounted for his indulgence towards his nephew. Ralph Rattray, who had recently been taken into the business as a junior director, had spent a good many of his twenty-nine years in pursuing women and trying to make his fortune by backing racehorses. He was regarded in the firm as a fool at his job. Baker, the head draughtsman, had been with the firm only a year. He had left a similar concern in the Midlands and come down south for the sake of his wife's health. Williamson was an employee of fifteen years' standing who had achieved his position in the machine shop through seniority and was said to be poorly thought of by Sir George. He lived at home with his mother and sister. Grant, the secretary, had also been with the firm for some years. He had married recently a woman much younger than himself. They had no children.

When Quarles had discovered all this he went home, drank two enormous mugs of tea and was making notes on the case when his telephone bell rang. Sir George's voice was almost unrecognisable in its hoarse emotion:

"Quarles? I've called in the police. Your second step's been taken. They've killed my nephew."

THE body of Ralph Rattray lay on the floor of the sitting-room in his small ground-floor flat. He had been shot twice through the body at fairly close quarters. The dead man lay face downward, with one arm flung forward in a dramatic gesture pointing towards a small desk that stood in one corner of the room. On a table near his body lay a card with the words "Number One" stuck on it, again in words obviously taken from a book. Rattray's personal attendant, a suave little man named Fisher, told his story to Quarles, Sir George and an attentive police Inspector.

"Mr. Rattray told me to be out tonight because he had a special visitor calling. No, sir, not a lady, nothing agreeable of that kind. I know Mr. Ralph wasn't looking forward to it because he shook his head and said to me: 'A nasty affair, Fisher. But there you are, I'm always getting into trouble.'" But what kind of trouble? Fisher had no idea.

So Ralph Rattray had been alone in his flat. At about nine-thirty that evening a man named Moorfield, occupant of an upper flat, had heard quite distinctly two shots. At least, he realised now that they must have been shots, although at the time he had thought they might have been a car back-firing. After a minute or two he had gone downstairs to investigate, found the door of Rattray's flat open. He went in and saw Rattray on the floor. Moorfield ran to Rattray and lifted him up. The young man was not quite dead. He tried to speak, but was unable to do so. A flow of blood came from his mouth. Then, with the last reserves of his strength, and with a strange expression on his face, Rattray pointed quite unmistakably at the small rosewood writing desk that stood in the corner. Still pointing, and making intense efforts to speak, he died.

"Plain enough," Sir George Claverty said sharply. "Ralph had some information about this scoundrelly saboteur, and it's in the desk."

The Inspector, a youngish man with a certain air of superiority, seemed nettled by Sir George's tone. "It's not as simple as that. The desk has been searched thoroughly and it contains nothing but a few bills and receipts and one or two business letters of no importance. Nothing that could bear on the case at all."

"Secret compartment?"

The Inspector's air of superiority increased. "Of course, we've examined it with that in mind, Sir George. There's nothing at all of that kind."

"Then there *was* a clue in the desk," Sir George persisted. "A letter or something like that. And the murderer removed it."

It was Quarles who said: "That won't do. Rattray would have seen the murderer remove anything from the desk. But at the moment of his death, when he was unable to speak, he pointed to the desk as a clue to the man who killed him. Doesn't that suggest something?" The Inspector and Sir George looked at him with equal blankness. "He didn't point at anything on or in the desk. *He pointed at the desk itself.* That was the clue."

The Inspector stared in bewilderment at the small old-fashioned rosewood writing desk. "But what kind of clue could the desk be? After all, a desk is simply—well, a desk."

"Not always," Quarles said, and told them what he meant.

THE faces turned towards Quarles as he sat in Sir George's office and in Sir George's chair varied in expression from the apparent boredom of the head draughtsman, Baker, to the intelligent interest of the secretary, Grant, and the patent apprehension of the foreman, Williamson. These three were flanked by a stony-faced Sir George on one side and by the Inspector on the other. Not looking at anybody in particular, Quarles began to speak.

"You have been called here together in this way to dispel any fear you may have that your own lives are in danger from a murderer or that there is any likelihood of sabotage in the factory. Sabotage was never intended, nor were your lives ever in danger from a murderer."

Baker looked interested for the first time. "Then what was the meaning of the postcards?"

"The postcards were a clumsy attempt to lend a political flavour to a private murder. We know now the motive for the crime—Rattray's pursuit of women—but even without that knowledge it was possible to discover the murderer."

Somebody shifted his feet. Quarles continued: "When I first heard about the postcards I said to Sir George that it would be interesting to know why those particular five people had been chosen as recipients for the cards, since only three of them were connected with the production of the tools in question. The other two, Rattray and Grant, had nothing to do with them. When we know, however, that the object of sending the cards was to cover Rattray's murder we can see that this motive would stand out too plainly if he was the *only* recipient who had nothing directly to do with the tools. So a postcard went to Grant, who also had nothing to do with them. We might expect, incidentally, that the murderer would send himself a card, partly with the object of averting suspicion from himself, and partly so that he would be sure of knowing what was going on. The postcard left by the body was intended to effect a similar deception. 'Number One', it said, implying that Numbers Two, Three, Four and Five were to follow. But in fact the murderer had achieved his object when he killed Rattray.

"Mr. Grant," Quarles said sharply, but the secretary's face was buried in his hands. "We have seen your wife and she has admitted her association with Rattray and told us of your jealousy. But if it is any consolation to you, it was Rattray himself who told us that you were his murderer."

Grant lifted his face then and said: "But when I left him he was dead."

"No, he was not dead. He was beyond speech, but he was not quite dead. He had sufficient strength to pull himself up and point to the desk in one corner of the room."

"To the desk? But I don't understand—"

"You don't understand how a desk can have anything to do with you? That is what you are thinking, no doubt. But there is a certain kind of old-fashioned writing desk which has a very clear connection with you. You have forgotten, Mr. Secretary Grant, that such a desk is also known as a *secretary*."

MRS. ROLLESTON'S DIAMONDS

SOMEBODY had strangled fat Mrs. Rolleston. Her body lay on the purple carpet of the sitting-room in her suite at the Excellence Hotel.

Francis Quarles had been telephoned by his friend, Inspector Leeds.

"Something that might interest you," the Inspector's gritty voice said. "Murder by a mystery man. Not much sense to it. That should appeal to you. Know the Excellence?" It was one of the most expensive hotels in London. "Want to come along?"

Quarles said he would come along.

HE found the Inspector, a grizzled, permanently angry man, in a suite of three rooms furnished garishly in purple and gold.

There was Mrs. Rolleston's own large bedroom with a bathroom leading off it, her maid's small bedroom and the sitting-room, from which the body had been removed.

In this room there were no signs of a struggle, except a little scuffing of the carpet.

The Inspector made a disgusted gesture towards the gilt cupids and striped purple wallpaper. "Can't blame the hotel. Her own choice. Shows you the kind of woman she was, eh?"

"She'd lived here a long time?"

"Five years. That's right, eh?" The Inspector turned to one of three men sitting on an enormous purple and gold sofa.

"Hotel manager," he explained to Quarles. "Name's Marshall. Last man to see her alive," he added with relish.

Mr. Marshall winced. He was a thin man with an anxious expression. "Five years, yes," he said. "She insisted that everything must be to her own taste." He shrugged. "She paid very well."

"She was rich?" Quarles's small black eyes stared curiously at the hotel manager's well-cut dinner jacket.

"If she were not rich she would not live here," the manager said simply. "Her husband died some years ago and I believe left her a large fortune. Her nearest relative is a nephew—his name is Delacroix."

Quarles raised his heavy eyebrows. "And he inherits?"

40

"Now, now," the Inspector said impatiently. "She was killed for her jewels. Here's the background to it.

"A fortnight ago Mrs. Rolleston broke the clasp of a big diamond necklace and sent it to the jeweller she bought it from to be repaired. The jeweller's name is Flair, and that," he pointed to another figure on the sofa, is Mr. Flair in person. The necklace was worth twenty thousand pounds and she wore it only on state occasions, as you might say. At other times she wore a good paste imitation. Now," he jerked a thumb at the third figure on the sofa, a large uneasy, baldish man in uniform, who twisted his peaked cap over and over in his hands, "this is Johnson the liftman. He's not very bright, but he tells his story straight enough. Tell Mr. Quarles about the mystery man, Johnson."

Johnson spoke in a slow, ruminative voice. "Not much mystery about it, sir. Just after half-past five it was that this gentleman gets in the lift and asks me what floor's Mrs. Rolleston, and I says second and takes him up."

"Description," the Inspector said, and the liftman made a ruminative protest. "Yes, I know you've described him already. Let's have it again."

"He was a gentleman about my own height—that's five foot ten—and he wore a dark grey trilby hat and a dark overcoat and black brogue shoes. Always notice shoes," the liftman added helpfully.

"Face," the Inspector said. "Let's see if you can add anything to that."

"About thirty-five I should say he was, and had a little dark moustache. Narrow lips he had—pressed to a line as you might say—and a thin nose. Can't say more, sir, I'm afraid."

"What kind of man was he?" Quarles asked. "Was he the sort of man you'd expect to pay a social call on Mrs. Rolleston?"

The liftman cogitated. His jaws seemed almost to be moving.

"No," he decided finally. "Wouldn't say he was a tradesman," he said, and Mr. Flair stiffened. "But wouldn't say he was Mrs. Rolleston's own style either. She was well-connected," he added solemnly.

"So he asked you her room number," the Inspector said, "And you took him along to her room."

"That's right, sir," Johnson said. "And rang the bell and she opened the door and said, 'Oh, it's you, Come in.' And he went in. And that's all."

"The necklace," the Inspector said, and Johnson clapped his hand to his forehead.

"She was wearing the necklace that's right, and he was staring at it. He didn't say a word, but he was staring at it."

"What you might call in your fancy way the Episode of the Mysterious Stranger," the Inspector said with heavy joviality to Quarles. "Johnson didn't see him again, so the stranger must have gone out down the stairs. But that wasn't the last time she was seen alive. Oh dear, no. Mr. Flair saw her, didn't you, Mr. Flair?"

The jeweller was a round, jolly little man with an unexpectedly precise voice.

"I called at 6.15 with Mrs. Rolleston's repaired necklace. She opened the door to me. She appeared quite composed. I showed her that the clasp had been mended, and fastened the necklace round her neck."

"So she'd taken off the paste necklace," Quarles said. "That implies that the mysterious visitor had left, since she must have put it on for him."

Mr. Flair coughed. "There was no sign of any other person in the suite."

"And when you left, was she still wearing the necklace?"

"She was." He coughed again. "She was—ah—very fond of jewellery."

The Inspector turned grimly to the manager. "Now, Mr. Marshall. When you went up at a quarter to seven she was still wearing the necklace?" The manager nodded. Quarles interposed.

"The real one or the paste?"

"I fear I am too little of an expert to know the difference," Mr. Marshall said deferentially.

"You went up to ask what she would have for dinner," the Inspector continued. "That's pretty unusual, isn't it?"

"Mrs. Rolleston was a valued patron," the manager said. "She always ate dinner in her own suite, and always at the same time, 8 o'clock."

"She ordered dinner for herself alone?" Quarles asked, and the manager agreed. "Was she in good spirits?"

"Excellent. And then at ten minutes past eight when the waiter came up with dinner she was ... dead." Mr. Marshall's anxious expression was intensified.

"There it is," the Inspector said to Quarles. "She died between seven and eight, and the presumption is that the mystery man came back and killed her. Not much struggle—she was fat but feeble. Took the necklace and rifled her jewel case. Nothing left at all. Then cleared out."

"H'm," Quarles said. "What about the missing woman?"

"Who's that?"

"The maid. Why isn't she here?"

"Her name's Helen Collins. Been with Mrs. Rolleston for three years.

Half-day off today, but she ought to be back by now. Of course she may be in it."

"And the missing heir. It's perfectly possible that the jewel theft is a blind, and that the criminal is—."

"Mr. Delacroix asking to see you, sir," a police sergeant said to the Inspector. After him stepped a neat, pretty little man perhaps 5ft. 4in. in height. His hands fluttered like leaves.

"MY poor aunt," he cried. "My dear aunt Jemima. Where is she?"

"Now, now," the Inspector said. "You'll be Mrs. Rolleston's nephew?" Mr. Delacroix flutteringly agreed. "Have you visited her this evening?" Equally flutteringly Mr. Delacroix denied. Without much hope the Inspector said to Johnson: "Is this—?"

Ruminatively the liftman shook his head. "Nothing like," he said decisively.

Mr. Delacroix drew himself up to his full, if small height. "I demand to know—." But what he demanded to know remained uncertain, for at this moment there was another interruption in the form of a large, bony woman wearing evening dress and carrying a large black bag, who entered struggling with a red-faced police sergeant. "Where is she?" she cried. "I must go to her."

The Inspector almost rubbed his hands. "Miss Collins, I presume? You're rather late."

"I've been to a dance," the big woman said defiantly. "She knew I was going."

"And while you were away she was murdered and her diamond necklace stolen."

"Her *diamond necklace*," Miss Collins screamed. "Not her *diamond necklace*," and her whole large body pitched over in a faint. The bag she had been carrying burst open, and the Inspector, the sergeant and Mr. Marshall were all down on their knees at once, staring at the cascade of bright, glittering stones that had fallen out of the bag on to the carpet.

"That seems to settle it," the Inspector said.

Helen Collins, who had been revived by smelling salts, screamed: "I had nothing to do with it. I only borrowed them for the dance. I haven't been here since lunchtime. I can prove it, I can prove it."

"Just a moment. Inspector." Quarles picked up the necklace and gave it to the rosy little jeweller. "Mr. Flair, is this the real or the paste necklace?"

After a brief examination the jeweller said shortly. "Paste."

Quarles sighed. "And you borrowed them when you left at one o'clock, Miss Collins? Of course, without your mistress's knowledge?"

She looked down at the floor. "She would never have let me take them for the dance."

"Then that does seem to clear up the case." Raising his voice Quarles said suddenly: "Stop him, sergeant."

The figure struggling in the sergeant's arms was that of the liftman, Johnson.

"THE best murders are the simplest," Quarles said afterwards. "If he'd been content to strangle her, take the jewels, and keep silent, he might have got away with it. But he spoilt it with the invention of that tale of the mysterious stranger, and caught himself out in a foolish lie. The story itself was meant to provide a red herring, of course. No more than that, but it was a fatal red herring for Johnson."

"But what was wrong with it," said little Mr. Flair. He was still looking at the necklace as though it were bewitched.

"Johnson took his mystery man up at half-past five—so he said. And at that time Mrs. Rolleston was wearing the necklace. Now, what necklace? Not the real one, for Mr. Flair didn't bring that back until a quarter past six. The paste one, then? But as we learned when we saw Miss Collins, she borrowed the paste necklace without permission at one o'clock. So Mrs. Rolleston couldn't have been wearing a necklace, and therefore Johnson was lying."

Quarles said meditatively: "It's an odd thing that the fact of her maid borrowing Mrs. Rolleston's necklace should help to hang her murderer."

MURDER—BUT HOW WAS IT DONE?

"IF I were to commit a murder," Francis Quarles said, casting a slightly menacing glance at his friend, the author Brian Teale, "I should use the simplest possible method. The overturned rowing boat, the push over the cliff or, better still, off the edge of a crowded Underground platform—from a murderer's point of view there can be nothing better than those simple recipes. The more fanciful and ingenious ways of committing murder are flattering to the murderer's vanity—how clever I am to have thought of that!—but they are dangerous, because usually once the method has been discovered the murderer's identity is clear."

"Example please." Teale said.

"Why, certainly. Do you remember the case of Professor Roger Magerson?"

"No I must have been out of England. The name rings no bell at all."

Magerson (said Quarles) had just returned from a trip to several of the South American republics, very excited because he'd found some new varieties of snakes, some peculiarly unpleasant scorpions, and so on. He arrived in London, accompanied by his ever-faithful wife Rosalind, who always went on these expeditions with him, and stayed at an eminently respectable hotel.

Magerson had timed his return so that he would be able to address some international congress that was meeting in London on the subject of his discoveries. He particularly looked forward to putting out of joint the nose of a rival named Professor Claypoole, with whom he'd had a great controversy a year or two earlier about the habits of scorpions.

Magerson was found dead in his bath at the hotel about 7.30 in the evening. The times and circumstances are important.

HIS room hadn't a bathroom attached to it. He and his wife shared a bathroom with the room across the passage, which was occupied by an irascible retired colonel named Pickles. Magerson, who was also pretty irritable, had been infuriated, his wife said afterwards, by the fact that Pickles took a bath at exactly seven o'clock every evening, just the time when Magerson himself liked to bath.

46   JULIAN SYMONS

On this particular evening Magerson was intending to steal a march on Pickles by getting into the bathroom just before seven. It was an important evening for him, because he'd invited Claypoole and two other eminent figures attending the congress to dinner. There he was going to reveal his discoveries and crow. Magerson's young secretary Giles Wendle, who had been on the expedition but wasn't staying at the hotel, was also coming to dinner.

Wives, even ever-faithful wives, weren't wanted at such a function. Rosalind Magerson went out at 6.30 to dine with a woman friend. She was seen to leave the hotel; and arrived at her friend's flat just before seven.

At two or three minutes before seven, also a chambermaid in the hotel saw Magerson come out of his room and go into the bathroom.

At seven o'clock precisely Pickles came out of his room, tried the bathroom door, found it locked and returned fuming to his room. He tried the door at intervals of five minutes afterwards, with no success.

At a quarter past seven Giles Wendle, Claypoole, and the two other guests arrived. Wendle telephoned up to Magerson's room, but of course got no reply.

At twenty past seven Pickles was almost apoplectic with rage. He shouted and thumped on the bathroom door, got no answer, and went to call the manager. The manager and Pickles got back to the bathroom at the same time as Giles Wendle, who had come upstairs to investigate. The manager called, and then used his pass key to unlock the door.

They found Magerson in the bath. He'd been using the spray attachment to the bath and it was still on, in the water, so that water was going out through the overflow. Magerson had slipped down under the water and his lungs were full of it. He was quite dead.

QUARLES paused, and looked at Teale with a quizzical eye.

"Well?" Teale said questioningly. And added, "I don't see any puzzle."

"Of course there was no dinner party. Rosalind Magerson was telephoned—Wendle knew where she was—and arrived in a state of collapse. Doctor who lived a couple of doors away was called in. Man was dead, lungs full of water not much doubt about cause of death you'd think. Must have had a heart attack, seizure of some sort, caused him to slip under the water. So sudden couldn't even ring the bell for help. Obvious thing, wouldn't you say?"

"Yes. I should." Teale was bold enough to say further, "I don't see why anyone should think anything else."

"No." Quarles rubbed his big chin reflectively "Bad luck for the murderer in a way I happened to be staying at the hotel. I liked old Magerson. He was a character, although a rough and tough one. So happened I'd seen Magerson a couple of days before and he told me his doctor had just given him a thorough going over, said he was sound as a bell, should be good for another twenty years."

"Even so, doctors can be wrong," Teale objected.

"Doctors can be wrong. But you'll understand why, when I happened to arrive on the scene just after Magerson's body was found. I looked at it with special interest. I found something unusual. I'll show it to you. It was underneath the body. Magerson must have fallen on it when he slipped down in the bath."

From a glass-faced cupboard Quarles took something that reposed on a bed of velvet.

Teale examined the object. It was perhaps half an inch long. The point was as sharp as a gramophone needle, the body was a small, round sac, scaled at the other end. "You mean this little thing killed Magerson?"

"Yes. It contained one of those poisons used by pygmies in Africa and South America, and formerly used by the Red Indians, which don't kill but cause paralysis very quickly. There was a tiny puncture on Magerson's chest—the doctor might have missed it if I hadn't asked him to look. When Magerson became paralysed and slipped down in the bath, this poison dart—that's what it is really—dropped out. If the bath had been flushed it would have run away and the only evidence of murder would have gone."

"You said it was a poison dart. It was fired at Magerson then." Teale's brow was corrugated in puzzlement.

"Yes."

"You said the puncture was on his chest. Was there a window on that side of the room?"

Quarles shook his head. "No window anywhere in the room."

"A glass roof perhaps?"

Quarles shook his head again. "There was no means of exit on entry to the room at all apart from the door."

"Then it must have been fired through the keyhole. Though I really can't see anyone kneeling outside the door with a blowpipe in his hand."

"It wasn't shot through the keyhole."

"I've got it," Teale said excitedly. "Magerson was alive and for some reason didn't answer Pickles. The hotel manager was the first person in the room and—." His voice died away.

"No. Magerson died shortly after entering the bath. Let me give you a clue. The water in the bathrooms came in a quite unorthodox manner, direct off the rising main. The pressure was accordingly very strong."

"The pressure was very strong." Teale thought hard and then almost shouted. "The sprayer."

"The sprayer, I found a very thin smear of sticky material over the sprayer, just enough to check the flow of water without altogether stopping it. The dart had been fixed in one of the jets which hadn't been smeared. When Magerson turned the sprayer on, it popped out as if it had been fired from an air gun. We experimented afterwards."

"Very ingenious," Teale said. "But you said if pointed to a particular person I don't quite see—"

"Why, yes. Magerson's killer was the person who had easiest access to his poisons, who knew he was going to bathe on that particular evening before Colonel Pickles, who knew that in the bath he always used the spray attachment. Only one person could have known those last two things. Magerson's murderess—she'd fallen in love with the young secretary Wendle, and thought that when she was a widow her love might be returned—was his ever-faithful wife, Rosalind."

ANCESTOR WORSHIP

FRANCIS QUARLES saw the advertisement in the "Personal" column, and was amused by it briefly: *Colonel John Jacob Hathermill seeks information about his American ancestors. Such information, if properly documented, will be paid for.*

Hathermill is an unusual name, and Quarles remembered the advertisement a month later, when the name appeared on his appointments pad.

His visitor proved to be Miss Muriel Hathermill, a trim, dapper little woman in her thirties.

"I don't want to see you on my own account, it's about my uncle." Quarles mentioned the advertisement. "That's it. He's suffering from a bad attack of ancestor worship, and I'm afraid he's on the way to being swindled. Trouble is I can't see just how."

"Tell me about it."

"MY uncle isn't a fool, don't think that," she said sharply. "He was a regular soldier, commanded a regiment in the 1914–18 war, Home Guard in the last one. He's shrewd enough, except about one thing. Family. We trace our ancestry back to the 18th century, perfectly respectable wool merchants in the Midlands. That isn't enough for uncle. He believes that there was another branch of the family which went out to America about the time of the Pilgrim Fathers, and settled in Virginia. In family legend this particular Hathermill has the same names as my uncle, John Jacob. That's what has made him so keen on finding out details. That, and the fact that he's tremendously keen on everything American. Would go out there, I think, except that he's got high blood pressure and his doctor says he'd be unwise to travel."

Quarles put his fingertips together. "As I remember, the advertisement mentioned properly documented information. What does your uncle hope to find?"

She shrugged. "Papers, photographs, old books. He doesn't know himself. But he's in the mood to buy anything from anybody. That's what worries me."

"And somebody's turned up with things to sell?"

She said slowly, "I'm not sure that I can say that. It's an American named Jackson and he says he comes from Virginia and has relatives there. He's supposed to be making inquiries. He and uncle seem to spend all day poring over old books and records. I daresay it's all right, but I just don't like the man."

"What do you want to do about it?"

"I wondered if you could come and see uncle one day, and meet Jackson. See what you think of him. I can introduce you as a friend of mine who knows something about genealogy."

Quarles rubbed his chin. "All right." When she had gone he went to the London Library and spent some time looking up appropriate volumes.

FOUR days later he went to Colonel John Hathermill's house in St. John's Wood, and met Jackson. The American was a self-assured man with rimless glasses and a bow tie. He had a bubbling enthusiasm which was infectious.

It had certainly infected Colonel Hathermill, who listened eagerly to everything Jackson said.

Quarles tested out Jackson's knowledge as well as he could from his own casual reading, without finding any flaws in it. In fact, however, up to the present the Colonel's and Jackson's joint researches had discovered nothing.

"What about this relative of yours, Miss Freeman?" the Colonel asked, impatiently cutting short a discussion about the origin of Virginian place names.

"Sarah Lou Freeman." Jackson chuckled. "If anybody can help you, Colonel, it will be Sarah Lou. Although I'm a Southerner by birth I've spent too many years in New York to be much real help. But Sarah Lou now, she just lives for nothing else but antiquities. She collects them, has done since she was a young woman."

"Where does she live?" Muriel Hathermill asked.

"She lives in Richmond, has done all her life. She's a kind of a grand-aunt of mine. But she's paying a visit to New York at the moment, only the third time she's been out of Virginia altogether. As soon as she gets back you can rely on it she'll be doing her level best to find that old John Jacob of yours, Colonel."

"It can't be too soon for me," the Colonel said.

Quarles left with the feeling that Jackson was some sort of confidence man, but without any kind of proof to back it up.

ANCESTOR WORSHIP 51

It was a week later that Muriel Hathermill telephoned and said: "Jackson's got them The proofs. Or so he claims. He's asking three thousand dollars, and uncle's going to pay it."

"What does he want three thousand dollars for?"

"Some kind of book that his grand-aunt's discovered. Oh, Mr. Quarles, do come and see uncle. I made him promise to do nothing before you looked at the things."

In the house at St. John's Wood, Quarles found Jackson and an excited Colonel Hathermill. The American greeted him exuberantly.

"Well, Mr. Quarles, little old Sarah Lou has done it. I told you she would. Just placed that original John Jacob Hathermill right where he lived, in Ceciltown, near Charleston. Seems he was a person of some account, too."

Colonel Hathermill tugged at his moustache. "I'm infinitely grateful to you, Jackson. You don't know what this means to me.

"Might one know exactly what it is that your grand-aunt has discovered?" Quarles asked.

"Sure." Jackson was amiable. "Only she hasn't discovered it, she's had it for years. I told you that woman collected antiquities. Here's her letter and she's sent a photograph of one page from the Commonplace Book she talks about."

The letter covered four closely-written pages. Quarles read fragments of it only.

"My dear Thomas.—We returned ten days ago from New York. What a city! And what lives people live in it scurrying like ants from one place to another, too busy to stand in the street and tell a stranger good day! I thought this especially one day when we journeyed in the lift to the top of the Empire State Building (oh yes, we rubbernecked it like real country cousins) and saw the tiny figures on the pavements below. ...

"Since we returned I have been investigating the affairs of your friend Colonel Hathermill. I am delighted to say that his idea about American ancestors was right. There was a John Jacob Hathermill living in Ceciltown in the 17th century. By the greatest good fortune I have found much information about him in the Commonplace Book kept by Henrietta Freeman. He seems, indeed, to have been rather a flame of hers, although it came to nothing. He was the local doctor, and by way of being a character. I have had one page of the book photographed, and enclose it. ..."

There was much more, to the effect that she would not in ordinary circumstances think of parting with the Commonplace Book, but that the house had been needing repairs for years, and that if there was a prospect of getting them done—well, she left it to her dear Thomas to say what the book was worth.

Quarles looked at the photograph. It showed a page of characteristic 17th century script and told how Doctor Jacob Hathermill had treated the whole Freeman family for mumps for which he had prescribed cooling drinks and warm flannel next the skin.

Quarles read no further, Colonel Hathermill tugged his moustache complacently. "A remarkable fraud." Quarles said. "I don't know what kind of forgery you'll receive for your three thousand dollars, Colonel, but I do know that it won't come from America, any more than this letter did. Or Mr. Jackson here.

"Just look at this letter. The real meat of it is the stuff about the Commonplace Book, the rest is padding. But the padding has been done carelessly. There are two exclusively English words in it, words no American would ever use, unless they'd lived for years in this country, Americans don't talk about lifts, but about elevators, and for them pavements are called sidewalks. That means the letter is a forgery."

"Where's Jackson? The scoundrel!" roared the Colonel.

Below them a door banged. Muriel went to the window. "Mr. Jackson is running very hard down the street."

The Colonel looked sadly at the photograph. "Do you suppose. Mr. Quarles, this means that I never had an American ancestor?"

"I've no idea, Colonel. But I think you would be wise if you rested happy with the English ones."

ICED CHAMPAGNE

PRIVATE detective Francis Quarles looked thoughtfully at his companion in the Sporting Rest. This was natural, for actress Marie Morelli, who had been born Hetty Hodgkiss, was easy to look at.

She was still young enough to appreciate the Sporting Rest, which has some of the best food in London, a reasonably good dance floor and band, and an extraordinarily varied collection of figures connected with the sports of boxing and horse racing. Some of these figures are famous, many of them are rich, and a few of them are shady.

"You see that man with a face like a frog in the corner?" Quarles asked. "Yes, the one sitting alone, drinking coffee. He comes here four nights a week—that's his table. Henry Millikase, one of the biggest gamblers on the turf. You'll never see his name as owner of a horse, but he's got a half share in at least three racing stables, and when his boys start putting on the money, believe me, bookmakers know it's time to hedge. He also has a large part in half a dozen useful fly-weights and light-weights, and it's said he doesn't exactly lose money on their activities."

Marie Morelli stared at Mr. Millikase with wide eyes. "But does he know so much about horses and boxing? Or do you mean that he's dishonest?"

"Nobody's proved that he's crooked—yet. Hallo, what's happening now?"

At the table next to Millikase were seated a silver-haired old gentleman with a thin, rather weakly aristocratic face, and a very pretty girl. They had been doing well, with a waiter in constant attention, and iced champagne in a silver bucket by their side. A young man, swaying slightly on his feet, had crossed the floor and was asking the girl to dance. She shook her head, and a little altercation went on between them.

Finally the young man put out a hand, and grasped the girl's arm. The dignified old man made a feeble protest. Millikase got up, dabbed his mouth with his napkin, walked over and took the young man by the shoulders, swinging him round away from the girl.

The young man aimed a wild blow at Millikase, who coolly ducked it and swung his right arm. The young man sat down heavily with a grunt. He was immediately surrounded by waiters and whisked away out of the restaurant.

"My, my," said Marie Morelli, "We're seeing life."

"Perhaps."

"What do you mean?"

"You might be seeing a cleverly arranged introduction. Look over there." Millikase had brought his coffee over to the old gentleman's table, and was being profusely thanked. "Say that the old gentleman is someone of importance. Millikase thinks he would be a useful man to know, and hasn't been able to manage it—there's as much snobbery in boxing and horse racing as anywhere else. He arranged for this young man to do an insulting act, appears as the heroic rescuer—and there you are. I thought there was something unrealistic about that fight, didn't you? Though I know Millikase keeps himself in condition, and fancies himself as a boxer."

Marie gasped. "Do you mean to tell me that the whole thing was arranged in advance?"

"I don't say it was, I say it may have been. Shall we dance?"

They moved out to the floor, on which half a dozen other couples were shuffling. Soon Millikase and the girl joined them, while the old man watched with an air of benign approval. Millikase and Quarles nodded as they passed each other.

"I WONDER who that elderly man is," said Quarles, when they had returned to their table. "It seems to me I ought to know his face." He beckoned to a cauliflower-eared waiter who had once been a middle-weight boxer named Battling Benton, and whispered to him. Battling Benton went away, returned, and whispered back.

"Mr. Gordon Dalkeith and his daughter. Miss Jennifer Dalkeith," Quarles said. "Been here once before. Unknown to me. I wonder what game Millikase is playing."

Mr. Dalkeith called the waiter on his table, who took away the ice bucket and brought it back five minutes later. A champagne cork popped, wine sparkled, glasses were raised.

"I don't see why he has to have any game. It all seems quite straightforward to me. And anyway why do you want to find out about it?"

"I just like to know things," Quarles said mildly. "What happens now, I wonder? Perhaps you're right, and it's nothing."

AND although Quarles watched closely, nothing did happen. Millikase continued to talk to Mr. and Miss Dalkeith. He danced twice more with Miss Dalkeith. Then, as Quarles and Marie were about to leave the restaurant they heard Millikase exclaim something, his hand searching the inside pocket of his dinner jacket. Mr. Dalkeith was obviously expressing concern. Quarles stopped in the act of putting Marie Morelli's wrap over her shoulders, and went over to their table.

"What's wrong, Millikase?"

"Somebody's pinched my wallet," said Millikase shortly. He continued to feel in his pockets. "I know I had it at the other table, took something out of it for a tip."

"Oh, but really, this is appalling," said Mr. Dalkeith. His voice was like himself, thin and a little worn out, and slightly distinguished.

"It might have been worse," said Millikase. "Though there was pretty nearly four hundred quid in it. I had a very fair day at Hurst Park."

"You're sure you had it when you were at the other table?"

BATTLING Benton said, "I saw it, Mr. Quarles. I was serving that table and it was me Mr. Millikase tipped. There certainly was a pile of money in that wallet."

"Well, then—" Quarles looked at the two Dalkeiths and at Millikase.

Mr. Dalkeith said shrilly. "I see what you're hinting, sir, and I regard it as an insult."

"Now, father, don't be upset," Jennifer Dalkeith said to Quarles. "You mean that my father or I might have taken it?"

"I only meant to state facts. I'm a private detective. I've been watching Mr. Millikase since he came to your table. He's danced with nobody but you. None of you three has left the restaurant. Those are facts."

"That beastly young man," she said suddenly. "The one who tried to make me dance with him. What about him?"

Quarles shook his head. "He never came close enough to touch Mr. Millikase's jacket. I think we should all go upstairs for a word with the manager. There's something odd about this."

THEY went upstairs. Dalkeith and Millikase were searched by Quarles and the manager. Jennifer Dalkeith was searched by the manager's wife in the next room. The search did not reveal the wallet.

"We'd better call this a day," said Millikase. "I appreciate your trying to get back my wallet, Quarles, but what is it after all? It's only money, plenty more to be picked up where it came from."

"Just tell me, Marie," said Quarles, "everything that happened at their table. There's something I've missed."

"First the fight," said Marie. "Mr. Millikase sat down, they talked, he danced with Miss Dalkeith, Mr. Dalkeith ordered more champagne, the waiter brought it—"

"Of course, the waiter." Quarles said to the manager, "He was new, wasn't he, or temporary?"

"New, yes, name of Phipps. Came three days ago from an agency."

"Go and get him—and all his things, bag, spare clothes, everything he's brought."

Five minutes later the manager and Battling Benton escorted the waiter into the room. "You were quite right. Found the wallet at the bottom of the case he brings his stuff in. Got Mr. Millikase's initials on it, and the money inside. Funny thing, though, the wallet's a bit damp."

Millikase looked at it briefly. "That's it. Much obliged to you, Quarles, though how you knew the waiter took it, I don't know."

Mr. Dalkeith beamed benignly. "Most remarkable. I congratulate you, sir, though your methods are somewhat—ahem—rude."

"Just a minute. Phipps couldn't actually have taken the money, though he was concerned in stealing it. There was only one person who could have taken it—you, Miss Dalkeith. You were the only one close enough to Millikase to do it."

"And how did I get rid of it?" snapped Jennifer Dalkeith.

"I'll tell you in a minute. You remember I said there was something unrealistic about that fight?" he said to Marie. "So there was, but I was wrong in thinking that Millikase arranged it. He was the victim."

"I was always a fool for a pretty face," Millikase said, grinning at Jennifer Dalkeith, who was not looking at all pretty at that moment.

"They knew that, they knew you sat at the same table every time you came here, they knew you carried a good deal of money in your wallet. There were four of them in it, the young chap you hit, the waiter and the two Dalkeiths here, who I fancy are known to the police. The fight was designed to get you across to their table, and also to provide a criminal—it was a thousand to one chance that anyone would be watching the whole thing as closely as I was. Then Miss Dalkeith took the wallet while you were dancing, and passed it to the waiter."

"You've so smart, you—," said Miss Dalkeith, using an impolite word. "How did I do that? I was never anywhere near that waiter."

"There was only one way in which you could get the wallet out of the restaurant quickly. That's the reason why it's a little damp. You dropped it in the ice bucket."

NO USE TURNING A DEAF
EAR TO MURDER ...

THE importance of Uncle Giles, Francis Quarles said afterwards in telling the story, lay in the fact that his visit prompted the manner and setting of the crime—although Uncle Giles, he emphasised, had nothing whatever directly to do with it.

For a couple of days before his arrival, his name had been continually on the lips of Quarles's hostess, Deirdre Roberts.

"You'll love Uncle Giles," she said with her brilliant smile. "Lived all his life in Hongkong. Seventy-five now, but still marvellously active. Just done a round the world trip, but do you know this is the first time he's ever been in England?"

"He's your uncle, is that right?"

"Yes. Charles has never even met him, but he's bound to like Uncle Giles. I'm pleased he's coming, it will take Charles's mind off things. He worries, you know. About his health mostly, but I believe there may be something else."

Deirdre, Quarles knew, had been brought up in Hongkong. Her husband Charles was a retired stockbroker, twenty years older than Deirdre, amiable enough but fussy and set in his ways. It was by no means certain that he would like Deirdre's never-seen uncle from Hongkong.

When Uncle Giles arrived however, Charles obviously did like him. He was a neat little mahogany man, who had a habit of always facing directly the person he was speaking to, listening to everything with the most punctillous courtesy, and than answering it point by point.

Quarles put him down as distinctly vain, and intent to be considered twenty years younger than he was, but very agreeable nevertheless. He was surprised when, on the evening of Uncle Giles's arrival, he addressed a remark to the little man about the Malaysia Federation which was completely ignored.

Uncle Giles was talking to Charles Roberts at the time, and Quarles had intervened in the conversation. Perhaps that was the reason. Or perhaps it was simply that he didn't like talking about the Malaysia Federation.

QUARLES'S week-end visit to the modernised priory where the Roberts' lived had begun early, on a Thursday. Uncle Giles came on Friday evening, and on Saturday a dozen guests arrived, in cars ranging from Mini-Minors through Sunbeam Alpines to a Bentley.

Deirdre's smile became more brilliant, her conversation more animated. Charles, by contrast seemed abstracted and progressively gloomier.

On Sunday morning he asked Quarles to come into his study, a big stone room with mullioned windows, one of which had been converted into a french window looking on to the garden. There he paced up and down.

"I'm worried, Quarles."

"So your wife said."

"She did?" Roberts gave him a glance full of suspicion. "Did she tell you why?"

"Something about your health," Quarles said tentatively. "My health." Charles Roberts gave a short bark of laughter. "I've been a fool, Quarles. But I'm not going to be a fool any longer."

Roberts talked a good deal more, but to little purpose. He seemed to Quarles to be a man hesitating on the verge of same vital decision.

LUNCHEON on Sunday was notable both for the sparkling liveliness of Deirdre and the gloom of her husband. She was an excellent hostess, just a little too managing perhaps. After lunch, she organised the party.

Charles went off to work in his study, Uncle Giles was sent to write some letters in the library next door to it, one group was set to playing tennis, another to croquet. Deirdre herself did not play either game but moved about from one group to the other.

Quarles watched her with admiration, while wondering whether there wasn't something feverish about her gaiety, and also whether she wasn't more interested than she should have been in Angus Cobb-Clutton, one of the tennis players.

There could be no doubt, certainly, of her skill as a manager. At four o'clock precisely tennis and croquet players found themselves shepherded into the drawing room, which led into the library.

Uncle Giles joined them, his letters written, neat as ever, rubbing his hands. Deirdre said to him with a slight frown: "You haven't seen Charles?"

He shook his head, and she moved towards the door leading into the library. She opened it, and at that moment they heard the sound of the shot.

Deirdre was first into the library, and ran from there to the study. They heard her scream.

Quarles stopped at the door of the study, and took in the full picture. Charles Roberts lay with his head on his desk. A revolver lay on the desk near to his outstretched right hand. There was a neat puncture in his forehead. A little blue smoke still hung in the air.

THE next minutes were chaotic. Deirdre cried, women comforted her, there was a hubbub of comment about why Charles should have done such a thing. Quarles ignored it, and walked around the room. He found what he was looking for in one of the recesses of the mullioned windows, but only because he was looking for it. There was a dark patch on the stone which, when he bent down, smelled of gunpowder.

"Quiet," he called from the window, in a voice like thunder. "Quiet, all of you."

They were silent—but one person in the room went on talking. Uncle Giles, his back to Quarles, ignored the injunction to be quiet. He did not stop speaking, even when Quarles shouted again, until he realised that nobody was listening. Then he turned to the detective.

"Charles Roberts didn't commit suicide." Quarles told them. "He was shot dead by one of you, ten or fifteen minutes ago."

"But that's impossible. We heard the shot just now," said Angus Cobb-Clutton.

"No. The murderer came in from the garden when you were playing tennis and croquet, shot Charles through the head, put the revolver beside him, and then fixed up a simple little device in the window over there, probably a hollowed-out blank cartridge attached to a piece of slow-burning fuse, and then lit the fuse. A few minutes later we heard the report."

"But where's the cartridge?"

"The murderer picked it up, still has it."

Cobb-Clutton was shaking his head. "You've forgotten one thing. Uncle Giles was next door all the time. If there had been a shot ten minutes ago, he'd have heard it."

"No, he wouldn't. Uncle Giles is a very good lip reader, but he's stone deaf, although he doesn't like to admit it. You saw just now that he didn't hear anything when I shouted behind his back. The murderer used Uncle Giles to provide an alibi, but that was a mistake, because once the trick was understood it meant that only one person could be guilty. The person who said how worried Charles Roberts was—and so he was, but about her, not about his health—the person who was first into this room to collect the spent cartridge, and above all the only person who knew Uncle Giles, and so knew about his deafness, which was used deliberately."

Now Quarles looked directly at the murderer, and named her. "Deirdre Roberts."

THE DUKE OF YORK

IT was a tragic affair and a ludicrous one, too, essentially sordid, but with something strange about it, a simple puzzle complicated by circumstances. At the centre of the puzzle was Mr. Bannerjee, the Indian student, who had nothing to do with the case.

Mr. Bannerjee was not the victim. That part was played by Victor Clayton, a bluff man in his forties who was assistant manager of the Production Department at Murray Pressings, a firm turning out steel pressings mostly for use in armaments. Clayton lived with his wife and daughter in a small villa at Streatham. Although he had quite a good job, they always seemed to be hard up, and Mrs. Clayton let one room to Mr. Bannerjee, a nervous and retiring young Indian.

On a particular Wednesday in December Mr. Bannerjee happened to be the only person at home. Mrs. Clayton had gone with her daughter to the Odeon, leaving her husband's supper in the oven. He always came home at half-past six, and sure enough at that time Mr. Bannerjee heard the front door close.

Clayton, however, was not alone. Two pairs of footsteps could be heard, and a man's voice talking in a complaining tone. Mr. Bannerjee heard Clayton say, "Not so loud," and then the two men went into the sitting-room under Mr. Bannerjee's bedroom.

They talked quietly at first, but then their voices were raised. Mr. Bannerjee heard Clayton say: "Impossible, absolutely impossible. I just haven't got it." Then the other man said something about a rocket.

Inspector Leeds stopped his interrogation and stared. "You're sure he said a rocket?"

Behind his large horn-rimmed spectacles Mr. Bannerjee nodded gravely. "My English is not quick, but I am sure. It was a rocket—a rocket going up to the sky. He said that."

What were the exact words? Mr. Bannerjee could not be sure, but he was sure of the sky and the rocket.

The voices were quiet again. Then Mr. Bannerjee heard Clayton say, "I want that photograph and I'm going to get it if I have to—" Then the other man said something about the Duke of York.

The Inspector stared again. "The Duke of York? You're sure? Just what did he say?"

Mr. Bannerjee shrugged his shoulders helplessly. " 'There is only the Duke of York in here,' something like that."

"That doesn't make sense. Could he have been mentioning the name of a pub?" The Inspector sighed at Mr. Bannerjee's uncomprehending look. "A public-house. Could he have said something like, 'I'll meet you at the Duke of York?' "

"Oh, no," said Mr. Bannerjee sadly. "Nothing like that. He said he had the Duke in here, as if he were in a little box, or in his pocket."

The Inspector muttered something under his breath about people who couldn't get the English language straight.

The voices below were suddenly raised to shouts of anger. Mr. Bannerjee, who was much more timid than he was curious, decided that he did not want to be involved in a vulgar brawl. He skipped quickly down the stairs, out of the front door, and went to the cinema himself. Mrs. Clayton and her daughter returned before him, and found Victor Clayton lying on the hearthrug in the sitting-room. His skull had been fractured by a powerful blow from a poker.

The murderer left plenty of traces. His fingerprints were on the poker and the door handle. In one of Clayton's hands was a brown button, obviously torn from his assailant's coat.

The police reconstruction of the crime was that after Bannerjee left, the quarrel between the two men had become more violent. There had been a struggle, in which Clayton had picked up a heavy brass statuette bearing his prints, which was found on the floor, and the other man had picked up a poker. In the struggle Clayton had been killed.

With all these clues, the Inspector could find no trace of the murderer. Clayton was well-liked at his firm, and had little to do with any secret work, nothing at all to do with rockets. He got on well with his family, and was regular as a good Swiss watch in his habits. He was liked and respected by his neighbours.

The only odd thing that the Inspector turned up was that on the first day of every month for some years Clayton had cashed a cheque for twelve pounds. His wife said that it was not her housekeeping money.

Nobody had been seen to leave Clayton's house near the time of the murder. The fingerprints on poker and door handle did not correspond with those of Clayton's wife or daughter, or with those of any associate at work, or with those of Mr. Bannerjee.

Was he being blackmailed? His wife and daughter could recall nothing in the past that might lend itself to that idea. Then what about the rocket going up into the sky, and the Duke of York?

The Inspector found himself haunted by these phrases. He worked on the supposition that they might be gang passwords, and also put out inquiries about any criminal known as the Duke of York. The inquiries were unsuccessful. A careful reconstruction of Clayton's habits seemed to make it impossible that he could have been in touch with any subversive organisation.

WHEN this apparently simple little case looked like being placed on the temporarily unsolved shelf, Inspector Leeds took it to his friend, Francis Quarles. "It's the bit about the rocket and the Duke of York that gets me," he said. "Sometimes I'm half inclined to think that Bannerjee made it all up."

Quarles shook his head. "He would have invented something more plausible. When did those monthly drawings from the bank start?"

"A little less than five years ago."

"All right. Let's go and see Mrs. Clayton."

The widow was a plump feather-brained little woman in the late thirties, and her daughter Lily was a younger replica of her.

"Mrs. Clayton," Quarles said, "I want you to cast your mind back to five years ago, and to tell me anything you can think of that happened then."

The Inspector said impatiently, "I've already asked that. They can't remember anything that might have been a basis for blackmail."

"Never mind about blackmail. Just tell me anything you can think of that happened five years ago."

It was the year Vic had got his rise to assistant manager, Mrs. Clayton remembered, and so they had bought this house. A lucky year it was, because he had won £300 on the pools at his second try. Never won anything since, though. An unlucky year, too, in some ways, because soon after they moved in Vic had slipped down the stairs and broken his leg, had it in plaster for weeks. Then there had been that other unfortunate accident.

"What accident?" Quarles asked.

Vic had been driving the car, Mrs. Clayton said, really before his leg was quite fit again, and a boy on a motorcycle had turned to go right without making a signal.

His bike had gone right under the car and he had been killed instantly. "We were afraid it might have had something to do with Vic's leg and that he couldn't brake properly, but it turned out there was no doubt about it being the motorcyclist's fault. He didn't signal, you see, and Vic was just pulling out to pass him."

"Were there any witnesses?"

"Luckily there was one, a man who saw the whole thing," Mrs. Clayton said happily. "I can't remember his name, but I know he gave evidence."

The drawings from the bank had begun two months after the accident.

"Why didn't you tell me this before?" the Inspector said.

Mrs. Clayton looked at him round-eyed. "You didn't ask me."

THE record of the inquest showed that the witness's name was Joseph Burman, and that he had confirmed Clayton's story in every detail, saying that the motorcyclist had turned right into the path of the car without making a signal. It was not the story that made Quarles and the Inspector look at each other when they read the report, but the nature of Burman's occupation. This was given as "street photographer."

"He must have managed to take a photograph at the time of the accident, and blackmailed Clayton till the poor devil was at his wit's end," said Quarles. "Then he stepped up his demands, Clayton went for him and Burman killed him in a panic."

On the following day the Inspector telephoned Quarles. The police had traced Burman. He was at present engaged as a marker at the Wun-O-Wun Billiards Saloon at Brixton.

"A billiards saloon," Quarles repeated, and burst out laughing. "What fools we've been. Let's go down to Brixton."

The Wun-O-Wun Billiards Saloon was dingy and, at that time of the afternoon, empty. The marker was a jaunty little Cockney with bad teeth.

"I've seen you before somewhere," Quarles said as he was selecting a cue. "But I've never been in here before. Where could it be now?"

"At the boozer across the old frog and toad, very like," said the marker cheerfully. "I often nips over for a drop of pig's ear in the evening."

Quarles unobtrusively dropped the billiards chalk on the side of the table down to the floor. "Have you got a piece of chalk?"

Burman's hand went to his trouser pocket, and he drew out a piece of chalk. "Always keep the grand old Duke of York in my skyrocket, never without it."

"Thank you, Burman." With no change of tone Quarles said: "You're too fond of rhyming slang. You used it when you were talking to Clayton, didn't you? I expect first you told him he would have to dip deep into his skyrocket to find the money you wanted, and then when he threatened to attack you to get the photograph you said you had nothing there but the old Duke of York That's about right, isn't it? Then when he went for you, you got panicky and killed him."

Burman backed away, "Self-defence," he whispered.

"You can tell that to a jury."

"He'd 'ave killed me."

"I don't know that I'd have blamed him much. No, you don't." He thrust out a foot as Burman turned and ran. Two constables stood in the doorway.

IN Burman's lodgings they found the photograph which had earned him a tidy income before he became too greedy. He must have taken it a moment before the accident, perhaps with the idea of selling it to a news agency before he found a better use for it. It showed a motorcyclist turning to the right, arm clearly extended. The car was almost on top of him, and the camera had caught perfectly the look of wild horror and despair on Clayton's face.

DOUBLE DOUBLE CROSS

THE last of the preliminary bouts was over. Francis Quarles settled himself more comfortably in his ringside seat and said to his companion, sporting journalist Jack Lint: "Who's going to win, Smith or the champion?"

"Shouldn't like to say. Billy Bradstreet should be out of Smith's class, but there are too many rumours flying about. Brad was a three-to-one favourite a fortnight ago, now it's even money. They say he's going to take a dive."

"Why should he do that?"

"Cashola. Brad and his manager Lynx Lenehan are both on the rocks. Fancy themselves at picking outsiders at race meetings, would you believe it? They're cleaned out, from what I hear. And Billy's had a good run at this game, he's no chicken, due to retire pretty soon." Lint stopped a sharp-featured little man who was hurrying past with his hat on the back of his head. "Who's going to win it, Ike?"

"The champ's got my money, Jack. Only I'm strictly against gambling, see."

"What's this tale about him taking a dive?"

"Tale's the word." The little man closed one eye. "That's on the best authority," he added, and passed on.

"THAT'S Ike Pazeki. Some of the big boys use him when they want to put money on quietly. Now there's a man who knows whether Brad's going to lie down, if anyone does." Lint pointed to a fleshy man in a bottle-green dinner jacket who had come in with two thickset companions. They sat down to the left of Lint, and Quarles and one of the men leaned over and asked a question of the man in the green dinner jacket, who held up four fingers. "Sammy Tarrant, the night club owner," Lint said. "Got an interest in half a dozen boxers, quite unofficially, you understand, and I happen to know that Kid Smith's one of them. When he wants his fighters to win they win, or so they say. Here they come now."

The fight was for the European light heavy-weight championship.

Kid Smith, the challenger, was seven years younger than Bradstreet, but the champion looked bigger and tougher. Both men got a good hand from the crowd, although in Bradstreet's case it was mingled with some booing. In Bradstreet's corner his manager, Lynx Lenehan, a man with a wrinkled humorous face and a mop of grey hair, talked to him earnestly. Kid Smith's manager, a bulky former boxer named Cruiser Harrigan, patted his boy on the shoulder and looked round complacently. The bell went.

AFTER three rounds Quarles said, "What do you think, Jack?"

"Hard to say. Brad's not punching his weight, but he's right ahead on points. He's way out of Smith's class, and I don't think the Kid's got the punch to take him for a knock-out."

Quarles looked about him. Sammy Tarrant, detached and a little bored, was smoking a big cigar. Ike Pazeki, four seats away from them, sat with his hands picking at the knees of his trousers. Bradstreet looked as fresh as paint. He nodded while Lynx Lenehan talked to him and made gestures with his right hand. The champion had opened a cut over Kid Smith's eye and Smith's seconds were sponging it carefully.

The end came in the next round. Bradstreet pushed a couple of lefts into Smith's face and then brought over a right arm like a sledgehammer. Smith swayed and ducked so that the blow went harmlessly over his shoulder and at the same time brought up a vicious uppercut that jerked back the champion's head. Bradstreet was shaken. Smith gave him a left to the body and a right cross to the jaw. Bradstreet went down for a count of five. When he got up Smith drove him round the ring for nearly a minute. A left-right-left went to the champion's body and head, and another right uppercut sent him down. This time he stayed down.

The crowd went wild. The referee raised Kid Smith's hand. Sammy Tarrant knocked the ash off his cigar. Ike Pazeki stood up with his mouth open, goggling at the ring. Smith helped Bradstreet up, and over to his corner. The champion was shaking his head dazedly.

Jack Lint was shaking his head too. "I just don't know whether it was straight or not. Brad made it look good, but I shouldn't have thought Smith could hurt him that much. And he certainly left himself wide open to that uppercut. Still, the crowd loved it. Give him the benefit of the doubt."

But somebody was not prepared to give Billy Bradstreet the benefit of the doubt. Somebody stood in a dark corner outside the stadium and shot the ex-champion twice through the chest, killing him instantly.

The killer stood close to Bradstreet, for there were powder burns on the front of the dead man's raincoat.

"It's plain now that somebody thought the fight was crooked." Quarles said to Jack Lint. "But there are two or three things I don't understand about it. Can you take me to see Sammy Tarrant?"

They found Sammy Tarrant in the back room of his Zero Club. He was wearing a lilac-coloured double-breasted suit and a pearl-grey shirt. "I know your name," he said, and smiled pleasantly at Quarles.

"What were you paying Bradstreet to throw the fight last night?" Quarles asked.

Tarrant touched his big nose. "Mr. Quarles, do you know why my nose is such a beautiful shape? Because I keep it out of other people's business."

"Come now, you'd even fixed the round. I saw you hold up four fingers."

"You see too much."

"And you don't see enough. The police are looking for a murderer. If you told Bradstreet to throw the fight and he did what you told him, why should you kill him? That's your alibi, Tarrant. There's only one odd thing about it. If you were betting on Smith, you'd want the odds to be as long as possible against him, but in fact they'd dropped to evens. That's because of the rumour that Bradstreet was throwing the fight. Who started the rumour?"

Tarrant clenched a pudgy fist. There was no doubt of his sincerity as he said, "I wish I knew the fool who opened his mouth. I'll swear it wasn't one of my boys."

"Perhaps it wasn't so foolish. There could have been a purpose behind it."

Tarrant looked merely puzzled.

"I'm not admitting anything," said Lynx Lenehan. "But what if Brad did throw the fight? It's been done before, it will be done again, especially by a fighter who knows he hasn't long to go. Not that I would ever be a party to such a thing," he added virtuously.

"You didn't clean up on the fight, then?"

Lenehan waved a hand round his shabby office. "I'm giving this up, can't run to it any more. Brad and I had been buddies for a long time. Now I shall have to find another boy to manage, and I'll be lucky if it's one like Brad."

Cruiser Harrigan was indignant. "The Kid won the fight fair and square. He could have beaten Bradstreet with one hand tied behind his

DOUBLE DOUBLE CROSS

back." Kid Smith modestly agreed with him. "The Kid didn't need no favours."

"Still, it's nice to know you're betting on a certainty."

"I don't know what you mean." Cruiser Harrigan said. "I may 'ave 'ad a small flutter on the Kid, but betting on a certainty ain't sporting, and if there's one thing the Kid is, it's a real sportsman."

"You didn't spring a leak about Bradstreet throwing the fight, then?" Quarles asked innocently.

"Now you get out," said Cruiser Harrigan. "And if you dare to repeat such an insinuation I'll have the law of you."

THEY found Ike Pazeki in the canteen of Billy's National Sporting Club, drinking coffee. He did not look pleased to see them.

"Ike," said Jack Lint. "You remember the night of the fight? You thought Bradstreet was going to win when nobody else thought so. Where did you get your information?" The little man did not answer.

Quarles leaned forward. "You said it was all a tale about Bradstreet taking a dive. You said, 'That's on the best authority.' What did you mean?" There was still no reply. "I'll tell you. Somebody had given you a lot of money to put on Bradstreet to win. That somebody spread the rumour about Bradstreet throwing the fight to get a better price, right? You know that, and so you said what you did. You needn't answer. Is this the name of the man who backed Bradstreet?" He wrote a name on a piece of paper and Pazeki nodded. He was looking past Quarles, and his eyes were frightened.

The detective turned to see the humorous face of Lynx Lenehan. "Just the man I was looking for," he said cheerfully. "Sit down and have a cup of coffee. Ike's been telling us a story about a neat little double cross that turned into a double double cross. It seems there was once a fighter and his manager who were very hard up. So it was a blessing for them when they were approached by a big-time gambler who asked them to throw the fight. At least that's what the fighter thought. But the manager was smarter. Do you know how smart the manager was?"

"I'm listening," said Lynx Lenehan. His right hand was in his pocket.

"Let's call things by their names, then. The manager—that's you—spread a rumour that the fighter—that's Bradstreet—was throwing the fight. When the price had come down to evens you put all the money you could raise on Bradstreet to win, through Ike here. But Bradstreet got cold feet, or perhaps he decided that he'd sooner be in with Tarrant than with you. He played a double double cross on you, and threw the fight after all, instead of fighting to win as you had arranged he would. It was a dirty trick, and it ruined you, but you shouldn't have shot him. And you shouldn't do that, either." His hand shot out and caught Lenehan's wrist. The revolver in it fell to the ground.

"I made Brad," Lynx Lenehan said. "Without me he would have been nothing. When I knew he'd crossed me I went mad. But I don't see how you picked on me."

"Very simple. Whoever spread that rumour must have done it because he wanted to force down the price and back Brad to win. Now who could that have been, and who could Ike mean when he said that he had it on the best authority that Brad wasn't taking a dive? There was only one person who fitted the picture, and that was you."

TATTOO

THE girl who sat in Francis Quarles's office was young, blonde and pretty. She would have been prettier but for two vertical lines of worry that marked her forehead. "My name's Jean Gladwin," she said. "You won't know me, but I expect you've heard of my stepfather. He is Joseph Kitson."

Quarles nodded. He was a big man with a deceptive air of sleepy laziness. His eyes were almost closed as he murmured. "Company promoter. Getting on in years now and thoroughly respectable, but was considered a bad security risk and a pretty shady operator not so long ago. Early background unknown. Married his secretary—or was it his housekeeper?—about ten years ago."

She coloured. "I see you do know about him. My mother was his secretary. My father was killed in a car accident when I was a child. I know people say bad things about my stepfather, but he's always been good to me, especially since mother died three years ago. I've never seen him really worried or frightened, Mr. Quarles, but he's frightened now."

"Tell me about it."

Jean Gladwin told her story. After her mother's death her stepfather had taken a suite of rooms in a South Kensington hotel, the Royal Warrant. She had a room in this suite, and acted as his secretary. Two weeks ago a letter had come, addressed to Alfred Rains, care of Joseph Kitson. She had spoken to her stepfather and had been about to open it when he took the letter from her and put it in his pocket. She noticed that he was pale and upset.

He asked her to give him any other letters that came similarly addressed. In the past week there had been two more of them.

She had given them to her stepfather, and had been alarmed by their effect upon him. He had become noticeably jittery and irritable in his behaviour, and had begun to drink heavily.

"You haven't got any of those letters?"

"I've something else to tell you, but—" She opened her bag. "One came this morning. I kept it from him."

The envelope was addressed in clumsy printing to Alfred Rains, care of Joseph Kitson. It was post-marked the previous day, from London, W.1. Inside there was one sheet of cheap paper. On it, in red ink was a crudely executed scroll with inside it the words DEATH TO COPPERS. Underneath, in the same clumsy printing as the envelope, was written, YOUR TIME IS NEAR.

"Death to coppers," Jean Gladwin said. "Do you think he could have been a policeman when he was young? He never talked about the past, not even to mother. And why is there a scroll round it?"

Quarles was looking thoughtfully at the paper. "That scroll, and the wording, reminds me of something, but I can't think what it is. You said you had something else to tell me."

"It's what happened this morning. Stepfather had been downstairs in the bar, and I went down to fetch him. We came out of the bar to the reception hall and he seemed all right. We couldn't take our usual lift because apparently a child had been sick in it, and the liftman was cleaning it out with pail, scrubbing brush and disinfectant. So we had to go along to the other lift, which drops us farther from our suite.

"There weren't many people in the reception hall—it's a rather gloomy and draughty place, with old copies of illustrated magazines scattered about. People don't usually sit in it unless they're waiting for somebody.

"The desk clerk was there, and the hotel manager, Mr. Munnings, was standing talking to a man called Major Waite, who's only recently come to the Royal Warrant. And an elderly woman called Miss Silver, who's been there for years, was sitting reading *The Tatler*. And the two liftmen, Maitland, who was on his knees with sleeves rolled up scrubbing away inside the lift, and Lake, the other one, in his uniform.

"I was holding stepfather by the arm—he's got sciatica and can't walk very well—we'd passed the first lift and had almost reached the second when he fainted. Simply dropped to the floor. The manager, Lake and I got him up to the suite and he recovered. But, Mr. Quarles, he was terrified. Something had shocked him. I've never really seen a frightened man before. He wouldn't speak, just kept staring from one to the other of us. The doctor came round and gave him a sedative. I stayed with him until he was asleep, and then came round to you."

Quarles took his hat from the wall. "Come along then. From what you tell me there's no time to lose."

THEY found the Royal Warrant transformed from its usual placidity to a state of confusion, with anxious-looking men scurrying about everywhere in a purposeful manner. The desk clerk hurried over. "Miss Gladwin, I'm afraid there's some bad news about your stepfather."

He accompanied them to the lift. Both lifts were working now. Quarles noticed, and they went straight up to the Kitson suite. The liftman, Maitland, white-faced and grim, muttered a few words of sympathy. Jean Gladwin said nothing. Her hands were clasped tightly together.

Inside the room the manager, Munnings, was almost effusively sorrowful. "My dear Miss Gladwin—such a tragedy—"

She said, dry-eyed, "Is he dead? I should like to see him, please."

Joseph Kitson lay on the bed, a doctor bending over him. The doctor told them that he had been stabbed three times with a long thin stiletto-like dagger which still protruded from the body. There had been little external bleeding.

He had not wakened from the sedative, and had never known what happened to him. Death might have occurred at almost any time during the half-hour before discovery of the body by the manager, who had come up to present his monthly account.

QUARLES put through a telephone call to his old friend Inspector Leeds at Scotland Yard, told him what had happened, and asked him to find the answer to a particular question. Then he set about discovering who had had access to the suite in the past half-hour. There was no staircase to this floor, and the doors to the suite stretched along a corridor with Maitland's lift opposite to them. Round an angle of the corridor was the second lift run by Lake, who said that he had brought nobody up to nor down from this floor in the past half-hour.

Three people had come up in Maitland's lift, according to the white-faced liftman.

The first was a business associate of Kitson's, named Whatley. He stayed five minutes and went down again in the lift, saying that he had found Kitson asleep, and had written a note. The note was there, propped on the mantelpiece.

The second, a few minutes later, was Major Waite, who told Maitland that he had called to return a lighter of Kitson's, which he had borrowed and retained by mistake. He rang for the lift again after a couple of minutes—plenty of time, Quarles reflected, to walk in, stab an unconscious man, and walk out again.

The third visitor, some twenty minutes later, was the manager.

QUARLES walked over and looked again at the body, placid now with all its terrors washed away. The sleeve of Kitson's jacket had ridden up and on the man's left wrist Quarles saw faint indications of tattoo marks. They were almost indistinguishable, but by holding a magnifying shaving mirror close to the wrist the detective could see the faint outline of a scroll and one or two of the letters inside it. In sudden excitement Quarles stood up. He had remembered what the anonymous message should have told him.

As he straightened up. Inspector Leeds arrived, in a slightly irritable mood. "Got the answer to that question of yours, but I don't know what it's got to do with anything. Alfred Rains was a member of a big forgery gang. Turned King's evidence at their trial, and I don't know that we'd have got a conviction without him. One of them called Monroe wounded a police officer, and got life. Rains identified him for us. Monroe swore he'd get Rains one day, but he left prison a good while back and may be dead himself now for all I know What's it got to do with this case?"

"Just this. Rains transformed himself into Joseph Kitson." The Inspector whistled. "And here's an anonymous letter he received." The Inspector looked at it, and whistled again.

They walked out into the corridor, and Quarles put his hand on the liftman's shoulder. "It's all up, Monroe."

"My name's Maitland," said the white-faced liftman hoarsely.

"I don't think so." Quarles said to Jean Gladwin: "I said that the message reminded me of something. I should have known at the time that it was a tattoo mark. Tattoo marks are interesting. Men in various occupations often have a mark that denotes what they do—crossed hammers for mechanics, razors for a barber, and so on. Criminals use them a lot. It's quite common for members of a gang to be tattooed with the same mark or motto, a badge of fellowship as it were. On your stepfather's wrist you can just see with a magnifying glass the scroll and a letter inside it, although most of the mark has been removed."

"The message." She put her hand to her mouth. "You mean he was a member of a gang."

"In his youth, yes, and that was their sign. Later he broke free of them and became a well-known business man. When he began to get the messages he knew his identity in the past had been discovered, and that he was in danger. But it wasn't until today that he knew how close the danger was. How long have you been here, Monroe?"

"A month," the man growled.

"A month to gloat over your victim, who had no idea of your identity until this morning. When he found out who you were, you knew that you must act at once."

"But I don't understand," said Jean Gladwin. "How did my stepfather know that this man had been a member of his gang?"

"In the only possible way—by seeing the tattoo mark. That was what made him faint. And in the reception hall downstairs there was only one man on whose wrist he could have seen any kind of mark—the man who was working with his sleeves rolled up, scrubbing a floor."

Quarles snatched the lift-man's unresisting arm, pushed up the uniform and the wrist watch underneath it. They saw the tattoo marks hidden by the thick strap of the watch: a bold message in red within a delicately executed scroll: DEATH TO COPPERS.

JACK AND JILL

THE sun was a hot yellow. Grains of sand ran warmly between the fingers. Francis Quarles congratulated himself on having picked out what must surely be the best fortnight in the year.

He decided that his back was sufficiently browned, and turned over. Lazily he watched the five other occupants of this quiet Devon beach. To his right an elderly couple were eating their picnic lunch.

He rolled over to his left and looked at the young man and two girls who were bouncing a coloured ball near the sea's edge. The three of them were staying at his hotel. The magnificently bronzed fair-haired young man was Jack Innis. The girl in a white bathing cap was his wife Jill, the girl in a black bathing cap his sister Lena. Both looked attractive in bikinis.

What was it they said up at the hotel, about Jack marrying Jill for her money? As a private detective Quarles was prepared to believe that Jack might have married Jill because she was rich. As a man on holiday he saw that they looked happy, and reflected that it was good to be young.

They tired of the game and came up the beach to sit down a few yards away. The girls took off their bathing caps. Jill revealing a neat dark head and Lena a mass of crisp golden curls.

Idly Quarles watched the three of them unpacking a picnic case, drinking orange squash out of paper caps, eating sandwiches. Then he turned over again and concentrated on his sun tan.

IT was almost half an hour later that he waked out of a doze to hear the three of them arguing about whether they should swim to the raft which was moored rather more than a quarter of a mile out to sea.

He caught fragments of conversation. It was Jack who wanted to swim to the raft. Jill who was tired, Lena who thought they had done enough swimming. Jack got his way. The girls put on their bathing caps and ran down to the water.

When they reached the raft Jack merely touched it as he went by and went on swimming out to sea. The girls clambered aboard the raft and lay there for perhaps ten minutes while Jack swam steadily out to sea. Then they stood up and dived together off the raft.

They stayed submerged for what seemed a long time. Then Jill's white cap came up. She was waving her arms and calling something. For a moment Quarles thought that she was simply signalling to Jack. Then he suddenly realised that these were distress signals, and that Lena had not yet reappeared. He jumped up ran over the hot sand to the water, and began to swim out. He saw that Jack had noticed Jill's signals, and was swimming back.

Quarles was first to near the raft. He saw a cap bobbing up and down, and arms desperately waving. But the cap was black, not white, and the girl was Lena not Jill. She clutched at him and babbled words. "Cramp—left leg—Jill trying to help—"

Now Jack was up to them. "Get her back," he shouted. "I'll—." Then he dived. With Lena's arms round his neck Quarles swam back to shore and put her down on the beach. Then he went back to meet Jack, and the limp burden he was carrying.

Jill's white bathing cap was bobbing on the water. Quarles retrieved it and noted that the clip which held it had been pulled violently away. He came back to find Jack and a coast-guard desperately giving Jill artificial respiration. A number of people had appeared as if from nowhere, two hikers, a woman with her dog, and the local policeman Lumley who was well known to Quarles. Lena was telling them what had happened.

"As we dived from the raft I felt my left leg go, just couldn't move it—I've had cramp like it before. I called to Jill and she came under to help me, got me to the surface. Then I don't know just what happened—she must have got cramp herself or something. Her arms round me just seemed to lose strength. I got to the surface but it was all I could do to keep afloat. I'll never forgive myself." She began to cry, then pulled off her close-fitting black cap and wound a towel quickly round her head.

Quarles watched her, then strolled over and stood looking down at the picnic luncheon of the three. He examined the paper cups, and picked one up carefully by the edge.

A voice above him said, "What do you think you're doing?" Jack Innis was glaring down at him. "That's my picnic case."

"Is your wife dead, Mr. Innis?"

"They're still trying, but I'm afraid there's no hope. What are you doing with that cup?"

QUARLES called to the constable, "You can arrest this man and his sister, Lumley."

The policeman looked astonished. "Arrest them. Mr. Quarles? What for?"

"The murder of Mrs. Innis. They doped her at lunch time by putting a powerful sedative in her orange squash. You'll find the dregs of it in this paper cup. Then her husband persuaded her to swim out to the raft, and went well out of range while his sister drowned her."

"But we saw her trying to save Miss Innis," protested Lumley. "We all saw the white cap."

"That's just what you did see," said Quarles. "The white cap. When the two girls made their dive from the raft Lena Innis held Jill under water and drowned her. Then she pulled off the white cap—you can see that it has been dragged off—put it on and surfaced as Jill, waving her arms for help. She dived again, took off the cap and reappeared as Lena. At that distance the woman was only recognisable by the cap."

Jack Innis said with a sneer: "A fine tale, but where's your evidence?" His sister was rubbing her head with the towel.

"This cap is part of the evidence, the broken chinstrap on the white cap is another part. But as it happens, there's something more. I said Jill didn't put up much resistance, but she did manage to drag Lena's cap off so that she couldn't put the white cap over her own black one as she intended. Instead she was bareheaded while she was changing caps."

"What then?" said P.C. Lumley.

"I saw Lena bare-headed before she went in, and her head was a mass of golden curls. I also caught a glimpse of it when she took off her black cap and wound a towel round her head. Remember that by her own story the black cap was on her head all the time, keeping it dry."

Quarles yanked at the towel. It came off to reveal the wetness of Lena's straight lank golden hair.

THE CONJURING TRICK

FRANCIS QUARLES was walking up the pier at Brightsand, sniffing the sharp sea air, when he saw his old friend Inspector Leeds looking in a brooding manner out over the railing.

"I have never known you take a holiday," Quarles said. "So you must be here on business."

The Inspector's voice sounded more than usual like a file being rubbed on emery paper. "Heard of Flash Miller? He's a front man for the Grimes gang, and he's down here to pick up some dope. Heroin."

"Well?"

The Inspector continued, almost as though talking to himself. "The stuff comes into Brightsand and the Grimes gang gets it out somehow. We've had a man planted in the gang for some time now, and he rang a couple of days ago to say that Flash Miller was coming down today to collect a packet. He's going to pick it up somehow at the concert party show on the pier, the Merry Mirthsome Minstrels. Our chap couldn't find out more than that."

The Inspector continued to brood, and then said suddenly: "Like to come along to-night and keep an eye open? I'll be in the background myself, but I've got three men down here keeping tapes on Miller."

"What's Miller like?"

"Good looking chap, pretty almost, with a nasty squint. Flash dresser, that's how he gets his name. Great family man though, very fond of his wife and two boys, one ten years old and the other six. Takes them about with him everywhere, but he's alone this time. That's a sure sign he's on business."

Quarles took his seat that evening in the third row of the stalls at the Pier Pavilion. Reynolds, one of the Inspector's men, sat next to him. Five minutes before the performance was due to start, Reynolds said, "Coming in now."

Flash Miller wore a tightly waisted camel-coloured jacket, brown trousers, and fawn coloured shoes. His hair was like a shiny black mat, and his face was delicate and darkly handsome. Quarles noticed, one could not help noticing, the squint in the dark brown eyes.

Miller took his seat just across the aisle from them. He looked bored.

There was nothing unusual about the Merry Mirthsome Minstrels. They were a depressingly average kind of pier concert party. There were half a dozen dancing girls who were approaching middle age; there was a fat funny man with a red nose, who sang out-of-date sentimental songs and told immensely old jokes with an air of false enthusiasm, and a thin funny man, who kept being pushed about by the fat man and falling over things, and seemed only too genuinely depressed.

The fat man, the thin man and two of the girls played a comic sketch as two pairs of newly wed couples.

Quarles could feel the tenseness of the man at his side. Reynolds was not watching the show, but watching Miller.

JUST before the interval a man who had not previously appeared came on and did conjuring tricks. He was listed on the programme, Quarles saw, as "Monty the Mysterious in a Medley of Magic."

Monty the Mysterious briskly tore handkerchiefs into pieces and made them whole again, produced eggs out of his head and turned them into white mice with the wave of a wand, and ate a mass of coloured streamers. A number of children among the audience applauded enthusiastically.

The conjurer appealed for child volunteers to help with a trick. Three went up, and Monty found sausages coming out of their necks and large alarm clocks hidden in their pockets. Finally he showed the children the white mice, waved his wand and transformed them into boxes of chocolates, and gave one box to each child. The children trotted back down the aisle, past Quarles. Idly he watched them go by.

Suddenly he felt a pressure on his arm. Monty the Mysterious had asked for three gentlemen volunteers. Flash Miller, stubbing out the cigarette he had been smoking in defiance of regulations, rose as if at a signal and strolled up to the stage.

"This is it," said Reynolds.

Monty prepared a dinner for the three men who came up. He lifted lids to show a squawking chicken, unpeeled potatoes and carrots and a rectangular block of jelly. The lids were replaced and the wand waved. Then they were lifted again to reveal a cooked and steaming hot mass of chicken and vegetables, and the jelly wobbling delicately in a moulded shape. The men tasted the food and said it was excellent.

"Drinks," said Monty. He poured water into a small barrel and drew off gin, whisky and beer to taste. Good average concert party stuff, thought Quarles. Miller had gone through the process of eating and drinking with a kind of bored condescension. Even from the stalls, his squint was visible. Something tugged at Quarles's mind.

Now the turn was finished, Monty gave to each of the men a squarish packet. "Finest quality shaving cream and most delicate talcum powder," he said. "Boys, your wives won't know you after you've used it."

Reynolds rose as Miller came back to his seat, and tapped the man on the shoulder. "I'm a detective, Mr. Miller. Can I have a word with you outside?"

Miller looked at Reynolds, then at Quarles, and shrugged his shoulders. He followed them outside. The package was still in his hands.

INSPECTOR LEEDS was outside with another man in the entrance hall. "You know me, Miller," the Inspector said. "Just hand over that parcel."

"What, *this*? That geezer on the stage told you what was in it, shaving stuff. What do you think it is, gold dust? Here, catch." Miller threw the parcel at the Inspector, who caught it awkwardly and unwrapped it. Inside was a jar of shaving cream and a tin of talcum.

They looked at each other. The Inspector screwed the top off the shaving cream. "More likely the talcum," said Reynolds. He ripped the top off the tin, shook out powder, sniffed and tasted. "No, that's talcum all right."

"And this is shaving cream," the Inspector said.

Miller burst out laughing, and fixed them with his squinting stare. Quarles remembered what he had seen. "Has anyone come out of here in the last five minutes?" he asked the Inspector.

"Yes. A woman and a boy. She said he wasn't well. They went down the pier towards the exit. But what—"

"Come on," said Quarles. He ran into the darkness, followed by Reynolds. Behind them Miller, in the Inspector's grasp, gave a cry of anguish and despair.

QUARLES and Reynolds caught the woman and the boy just before they went through the turnstiles leading off the pier. "You'll have to come along," Quarles said. "And I want that box."

"Don't be so silly," said the woman. "It's the kid's box of chocolates. The man gave them to him for going on the stage." The boy said nothing.

"I want that box, Mrs. Miller. Stop her, Reynolds." The woman made a wild attempt to throw the box over the side of the pier, but Reynolds caught her arm. He opened the box, tasted the powder inside and nodded. "Heroin."

They met the Inspector coming down the pier with a dejected Miller. "Very neat," he said admiringly. "They passed out the stuff through the conjurer—I've sent a man back to pick him up. They must have found out that we were on their track, and tried a little conjuring trick of their own, using Miller as a decoy. Your boy picked up the stuff. Miller, and then you went up so that we could make fools of ourselves. That right?"

Miller's head jerked up. "Dickie knew nothing about it, only did what he was told. I wouldn't have brought him in, but the boys made me do it."

"I'll bear that in mind," said the Inspector. "What I don't see, Quarles, is how you tumbled to it that the boy had been given the stuff."

"He passed me on his way out, and I had a good look at him."

"What of it. He's not much like his father." Then the boy looked up and the Inspector said "Oh."

For Dickie, though fair where Flash Miller was dark and quite unlike him in feature, had an exact replica of his father's squint.

HAPPY HEXING

WHEN Happy Hexing put down the telephone he said to his secretary, Miss Venables: "I think that settles Porley's hash."

"Does it?" asked tall, elegant Miss Venables coolly.

Hexing was a big, effusively handsome man of forty. He had at all times an air of good-humoured self-confidence, which had earned him the name of Happy at school and had attracted the favourable attention of a great many women.

Happy Hexing had first met John Porley at the Placksteed Engineering Works in Birmingham. Porley had been at that time, a brilliant engineer; and an inventor, too. The two young men lodged in the same house, and became friendly. It was a coincidence, no doubt about it, that both young men should fall in love with the same girl. Sybil Morton, who also worked at Placksteed. Perhaps it was a blow to Happy Hexing when she decided to change her name to Porley. But it was generally agreed that he took his disappointment very well.

NOT long after his marriage Porley made the invention that brought him fortune. He formed his own firm, Porley Adjustable Screws, and made a lot of money.

When Happy Hexing heard about this he laughed loudly and was full of words about good old Jack's thinkpiece. But Happy Hexing, who was then still an engineer working for six pounds a week, must have studied the patenting details of the Porley Screw very carefully, for he found a flaw in them.

This flaw permitted him to found a rival firm named Hexing's Fixings which manufactured a screw almost identical to Porley's, with just enough variation to evade any question of patent infringement.

When Happy Hexing met Porley at a trade conference and Porley refused to shake hands, Happy was hurt.

And he was more hurt at the treatment given to his letter suggesting that he and Jack should join forces.

This letter came back to him torn into many little pieces, enclosed in an unstamped envelope.

FIVE years had passed since that day.

And now? Smiling happily, Happy Hexing said to his secretary: "You heard that telephone conversation. That was Walter Strick, and he owns twenty per cent of the shares in Porley's company. He's hard up. He's just sold them to me for £45,000. That's about twice what they're worth. Silly of me to buy them, wasn't it?"

"You're never silly."

Happy Hexing had been sitting with his chair tilted back. Now the chair legs struck the floor with a bang. "You're right there." Hexing laid his finger to his nose. "And shall I tell you why? Because, though Porley doesn't know it. I own thirty-five per cent of the shares in his company already. And what does twenty and thirty-five add up to, Milly?"

"Fifty-five."

"Full marks, my dear. And fifty-five out of a hundred is a majority holding. Shall I laugh when I see Jack Porley's face at his next general meeting when he sees the majority stock-holder—*me*. I can hardly wait."

Happy Hexing looked at his watch. "Quarter past five. My word, I'm late. I've got a conference with Mutilateral Steel in a quarter of an hour. Now look, you write me a letter to Strick confirming what I've told you, and leave it on my desk. I'll come back to sign it and send him a cheque. Now get me a cab. And ring up Louise and tell her I may be a few minutes late calling for her."

Happy Hexing, who had sworn that he would stay a bachelor, was now engaged to be married to Louise Babbacombe, daughter of Babbacombe Mouldings.

So Happy Hexing went off in his cab and was driven straight to his conference, where he overflowed with high spirits.

He took a cab back to his office, where he was dropped at about ten minutes to seven. And there he was found at 8.15 by the night watchman, who saw a light in his room. He had signed the letter to Strick left by Miss Venables, and he had also signed the otherwise blank cheque gripped in his hand. On his face was an expression of absolute astonishment.

He had been shot twice through the chest from fairly close range—slight powder burns were visible. Hexing had died at about seven o'clock. Nobody had been noticed entering or leaving the building at that time.

THE case of Happy Hexing resolved itself for the police into the breaking of an alibi.

Porley had been at his London office until just after a quarter past five that day. He had then, by his own account, taken the 5.45 train from Charing Cross to his home at Bexleyheath.

The train was always a crowded one, and there was no confirmation that he had boarded it. The ticket collector at his home station remembered him, however, because Porley had called attention to the fact that his season ticket expired that day. He had then added, the ticket collector remembered: "My word, they ought to put some more trains on this line. It's a crowded train, that 5.45."

Porley had then walked home, and at seven o'clock, when Happy Hexing was shot in London. Porley's wife was prepared to swear that he was sitting in front of the fire reading the evening paper several miles away in Bexleyheath.

INSPECTOR LEEDS was not at all satisfied with this alibi, and when he was dissatisfied he often consulted that bulky private investigator Francis Quarles.

On this occasion Quarles listened to the Inspector in silence, and at the end of the story murmured: "The most important element in the case would seem to be time."

"Just so," Inspector Leeds brought his fist down with a thump on Quarles's table. "How did Porley manage to trick that ticket collector into believing that he travelled on the 5.45?"

"That's not what I meant. How did Porley know about Hexing's arrangement to buy his stock? Hexing spoke to Strick just before 5.15. Porley left his office just after that time. The only way he could have learned about the deal was by telephone. Did Porley receive a telephone call just before he left his office?"

The Inspector snapped his fingers. "He did at that. But what he said about it doesn't make sense. He says somebody telephoned, asked for him, and said: 'What time are you leaving, Mr. Porley?' Porley said he was leaving now and the voice said: 'That's very wise.' Couldn't say whether it was a man's or woman's voice. Call was made from a Central London call-box."

"And then there is the curious point about the blank cheque."

"What's curious about that?"

"The fact that it was blank," Quarles said.

LOUISE BABBACOMBE was a dry-eyed buck-toothed woman in her early thirties, who had already divorced two husbands. She did not pretend to great grief for Hexing.

Quarles asked her: "Do you know of anyone who might have wanted to kill him?" She opened her mouth. "Besides Porley, I mean."

Her stare was hard and intelligent. "You mean you don't think Porley did it? Well, Happy would make a pass at any good-looking woman who got within a few yards of him, and some of them were very keen about him. He was always keen on looks, although in my case," she said with no perceptible bitterness, "of course, it was money."

"Just one more thing," Quarles said. "Where were you when he was killed?"

She looked angry for a moment and then burst out laughing. "I was at home in this flat. Waiting for Happy."

"Alone?"

"Quite alone." With her direct gaze she said: "Make what you can of that, Mr. Quarles. You won't find anyone who saw me leave the house."

WALTER STRICK, the small grey-haired man who had agreed to sell his shares to Happy Hexing, said: "He'd been pestering me for I don't know how long to sell, and he was offering a lot more than they'd have fetched in the market. I could have done with the money. That's all there is to it."

JOHN PORLEY received Quarles in his office. The head of Porley Adjustable Screws was a slight, dark, shy man with a diffident smile. "Are you another of the gentlemen who has come to break my alibi?"

Quarles shifted his large body a little in the chair. "Let me give you a little reconstruction, Mr. Porley, of how this crime *could* have been committed. That mysterious telephone call *could* have been from a friend of yours in Hexing's office, who *could* have told you of Hexing's arrangement to buy Strick's shares, giving him a majority holding in your company.

"You are a fast thinker. You went home and neatly established an alibi—but *your wife came up to town*. The ticket collector remembered your coming off the train, but nobody has thought to inquire whether your wife was at home with you at seven o'clock."

The smile had left Porley's face. He said coldly: "I'll thank you to leave my wife out of it. And now, if you'll excuse me, I have some cheques to sign."

Quarles stood up and, like a man in a dream, watched Porley writing his neat signature. "Of course," he said. "Of course."

HAPPY HEXING   87

WITH apparent bewilderment Inspector Leeds, Miss Venables and Hexing's accountant stood watching Quarles as he laboriously looked through a great pile of Hexing's old cheques returned from the bank.

On the desk, at one side, lay the blank cheque, with Hexing's name on it, which had been found in his hand.

There were perhaps two hundred cheques in the pile, and it took Quarles some minutes to look through them. At last he put them aside.

"Every one of them typed, I'm afraid." He sighed and said to Miss Venables: "Why did you do it? Because he was going to marry that woman? Believe me, he wasn't worth it."

A dainty revolver had appeared, as though by magic, in Miss Venables's hand. "He was to me. I knew all about Happy, but I wasn't going to let another woman have him. God knows how you knew about it, but you're right. Out of my way," she snapped to the startled accountant, who skipped hurriedly to one side. Holding her dainty little revolver trained firmly on them, Miss Venables opened the door. "Goodbye," she said, and stepped into the waiting arms of the sergeant outside.

"WHEN I saw Porley signing cheques I knew it must be Miss Venables," said Quaries.

"I don't see why," the Inspector grated.

"When you write a cheque you don't sign it first. You write in the amount and add the signature at the end. There are two exceptions to that rule. One is when you don't know the amount of the cheque—but even then you usually write in the name before the signature. The other is if *somebody else is writing the remainder of the cheque for you.* In Hexing's office all cheques were typed. And so the fact that he was holding a blank, but signed cheque in his hand, was the most damning possible evidence against Miss Venables. He must have been holding it out for her to type in the name and amount when she shot him. No wonder he looked surprised."

"And the telephone call to Porley?"

"Miss Venables made it, of course. She didn't want to see Porley in trouble—having taken advantage of a heaven-sent opportunity for murder that would leave her motive unsuspected—so she warned him to go home. She was a kind-hearted girl," Quarles said. "But I'd lay odds, Inspector, that she'll hang."

NO DECEPTION

FRANCIS QUARLES happened to be in Mr. Rafferty's antique shop when the American came in. The shop was small, poky, and filled with junk.

Mr. Rafferty was a little more than five feet tall, had a bad squint, and wore a toupee which was always going slightly astray on his head. He was a true eccentric, who shut up his shop from one to three o'clock every day while he sat by a first-floor window and watched what went on in the street outside. He often sold the few good things he had at absurdly low prices, while he tried to obtain exorbitant sums for pieces of complete rubbish.

For years Mr. Rafferty had been expecting to bring off by these methods some really profitable sale. When he had done so he intended to travel to Morocco, a country where he was convinced immensely valuable articles could be bought for a few shillings. Such was Mr. Rafferty's dream. Quarles was in his shop on the day when dream became reality.

He was poking about among unstoppered decanters and incomplete Mah Jongg sets. A fresh-faced young assistant, a recent importation named Parker, hovered helpfully round. Mr. Rafferty was up above, no doubt looking out of his window at people going in and out of the back entrance of the Minorca Restaurant opposite. The shop bell jangled, and there was the American.

A large American he was, with rimless glasses, an extravagantly coloured tie and a great beaming smile. He began to poke about as Quarles had done, whistling tunelessly as he did so. then the whistling stopped. Quarles, who had his back to the man, could feel a certain tension in the air.

"Hey, son, just help me out with this thing." The American was obviously excited.

Young Parker pushed and tugged until the thing was out in the middle of the shop. It was so thickly covered with dust that little could be seen beyond the fact that it was heavy and rectangular. As Parker dusted, however, it became plain that the object was an iron fireback, possibly Georgian.

"I believe we've got something." the American said. He took the duster himself, and went down on hands and knees. The outline of a peacock could be discerned, with lettering above it in a semi-circle. As the American rubbed, this lettering became clear. Quarles read: *Jno, Blunt. 1774.*

"I've got it" said the American. "I've found it. Will momma get a kick out of this. Are you Mr. Rafferty?" he asked Parker.

The assistant went to the stairs and called. The antique dealer came down fumbling at his toupee. In a moment the American had darted forward and taken Rafferty's gnarled fist in his great paw.

"Congratulate me, Mr. Rafferty. Here's something my momma asked me to look for when I came to England, and I've found it."

The American pulled a letter out of his pocket. "I'm John Blunt of Chicago," he said. "I'm here on holiday, and I got this letter from momma a week ago." He genially waved Quarles over to the little group, and the detective read with the others:

Went to the theatre last night, and saw Somerset Maugham's Lady Frederick. Such an English play, and so nice. Put me in mind of the old country and how I've always wanted another of those firebacks great-great-grandfather John made before he came out to the land of the free. You remember I have one in my lounge, with a peacock in the centre of the panel, and old John's name above it in a semi-circle. If you can find one, do get it.

"There's the story in a nutshell," the American laughed. "Old John was a fine metal-worker who emigrated to the States, and the family's been there since. Momma is American as they make 'em, but I guess a bit of her heart's still over here."

"Has she spent much time in England?" Quarles asked.

Mr. Blunt looked at him. "Came over for a couple of months when she was a girl, that's all. Now, Mr. Rafferty, just name your price and I'll pay it."

The little antique dealer rubbed his nose with one finger. Quarles, who would have put the value of the fireback at three or four pounds, wondered what he would say.

John Blunt slapped his thigh. "Tell you what, Mr. Rafferty, we'll have a bit of sport. Momma would want me to pay you value for this article. You write down your figure for it and I'll write mine."

"We'll hand 'em to this gentleman." He indicated Quarles. "Then whichever is the higher—get that, the higher, not the lower—I'll pay. How about that?"

Mr. Rafferty tugged at his toupee until it was sliding down over one ear. "All right."

They both wrote on slips of paper, and handed them to Quarles. He opened Rafferty's first, and read £20. Then he looked at the figure on the other slip. It was £100.

"The price is a hundred pounds," said Quarles.

Mr. Rafferty gasped. The American roared with laughter, patted the antique dealer on the shoulder, and counted out a hundred pound notes from a wallet which seemed to contain as many more. Then he shook hands with everybody, called a taxi, and Parker carried out the fireback to it. A hand waving goodbye out of the taxi was the last they saw of Mr. John Blunt.

Mr. Rafferty sat on a battered oak chest and stared at the notes in his hand. "I can go to Morocco," he said. "I shall go to Morocco. No deception about these." He went upstairs in a dazed way and stared out of the window. Quarles followed him.

"Who will look after the shop?"

"Parker. He came to me to learn the business. I took him on as an apprentice, don't pay him any money—can't afford to."

"He has private means, then?"

"I suppose so. Never inquired. This will be his chance." Mr. Rafferty squinted up at Quarles and said confidentially; "He can't go far wrong. Don't believe there's a thing in the shop worth more than five pounds just now."

They looked out into the street. Three waiters came out of the Minorca Restaurant back entrance. "Do you know what I shall miss most?" Mr. Rafferty asked dreamily, "Watching the street here in the afternoon. Every day for years I've done it, seen the people who go in and out of the restaurant, watched the routine. Good as a play it is, sometimes. Don't think anything would have made me miss it, except the chance of going to Morocco. I could tell you everything that happens in this street, every day, one to three o'clock."

"Tell me a few things," Quarles said. He walked over to a back window and looked out thoughtfully on to a quiet side street at the back that led to the main road, while Mr. Rafferty talked, still dreamily, for five minutes.

Then the antique dealer put his toupee straight. "I'm talking a lot of nonsense. How long shall I be away, after all—three or four weeks."

A WEEK later Mr. Rafferty passed over the keys of his shop to Parker, and set off with bags packed for his trip. On the following Friday, punctually as always at two o'clock in the afternoon, the manager of the

Minorca Restaurant came out of the back entrance, accompanied by the cashier, who was carrying a big leather bag.

The manager was about to open the door of his car when two men with silk handkerchiefs pulled over their faces jumped out of Mr. Rafferty's shop, ran across the road, held up manager and cashier at revolver point, and snatched the cashier's bag. The job was quick and neat. In less than a minute the men were back in the shop and had slammed the door.

They had left their car with engine running in the quiet side street at the back, but when they came out of Mr. Rafferty's back entrance half a dozen policemen were waiting for them. Quarles and Mr. Rafferty, standing at the end of the street, saw the handkerchiefs pulled off the two men. One of them was young Parker. The other was that friendly American, Mr. John Blunt.

"I'M fascinated," Mr. Rafferty said, tugging his toupee over one ear. "Quite fascinated, and very pleased that I put off my holiday for a couple of weeks at your suggestion. They were—ah—professionals, I suppose?"

"Very much so. Blunt's name is really Jackson, and he's no more American than I am. They found out that the restaurant banked its weekly takings, generally a couple of thousand pounds or more, on Fridays, and saw that your shop would give them a perfect getaway through the back entrance. But they had to get you out of the way, which wasn't easy, since you said nothing would have made you miss your daily view across the street except a trip to Morocco. So they arranged the chance of a trip for you, with that preposterous story about the fireback. I realised what they were up to, when you told me from your observation of the street about the restaurant manager banking his money every Friday. Then I simply notified the police and the restaurant. That brown bag contained nothing but paper."

"Simple when you explain it," said Mr. Rafferty. "But what makes you say Blunt's story was preposterous? His money was real enough, no deception about that."

"That was the only genuine thing in the whole story. Blunt made two mistakes. He showed excitement too soon about the fireback, while it was still covered with dust. He had no reason to be excited then, because he couldn't see the peacock or the name. The other mistake was worse. In the letter supposed to be written by his mother, who had lived all her life in America, the words "theatre" and "centre" occurred. Now, in America they spell those words *theater* and *center*, and no American would ever spell them in any other way. I knew when I read the letter that Mr. Blunt's momma was a fabrication, like the rest of his story. Though he has got a mother, that's true enough. She's doing a term in Holloway for receiving stolen goods."

THE SECOND BULLET

FRANCIS QUARLES heard the sharp crack from behind him, and heard the bullet also. It buzzed so close to where he was sitting, in one of the deckchairs on the lawn of the Hotel Beau Rivage, that he clapped his hand to his ear.

His companion, the French detective Jean Dupont, said sympathetically: "What is the matter, my friend? You are stung by the wasp, yes?"

Quarles took away his hand. "No. Unless I'm much mistaken somebody was trying to shoot me. Or you," he added as an afterthought.

He turned and looked at the hotel, which revealed only innocent-looking windows. At the same moment a small feminine scream came from the other side of the bright flowering shrubs some 10 yards away, that separated them from the sea.

Dupont got to his feet and ran to the bushes. Quarles followed him in a more leisurely manner. They found a pretty girl, whom he recognised as one of the hotel guests, Marjorie Brown. She had also been sitting in a deck chair, but now she was leaning on Dupont's arm and her face was frightened.

"Look," Dupont said. He held out the straw hat Marjorie Brown had been wearing. In it there were two neat punctures. "It was not you or I, but this young lady at whom the shot was aimed," he said solemnly.

"It knocked my hat off," Marjorie Brown said, and shivered.

"Then the bullet should be about here." Quarles looked for it while Dupont patted Majorie Brown's shoulder avuncularly. After a couple of minutes' search he came back to them with the bullet in his large palm. He had found it a few yards farther on, by the stone steps that led down to the beach.

"Now, my little one—the question is who fired this bullet at you?" Dupont said, while Quarles turned the bullet over in his hand, looking up occasionally at the hotel's windows as if they held some secret. "In a phrase, who wishes your death?"

"Nobody," the girl said, and burst into tears.

"Papa Dupont has noticed you. You have the great charm, you have the handsome husband, Monsieur Johnny, you are young. And yet you are not happy. You cannot deceive Papa Dupont. Now tell me."

"Johnny—Johnny doesn't love me any more."

"But how is that possible?"

"I tell you it's true. He loves my cousin Eileen. You must have seen them together. He never looks at me now. And I've done everything for that girl, taken her into our home, given her clothes, jewellery, everything. Only yesterday I gave her my blue dress so that she could wear it to the masked ball. And behind my back she plays up to Johnny. But I can't believe that he—" She broke off. Her voice was high. "Where's Mr. Quarles going?"

Francis Quarles, still holding the bullet in his hand was walking back to the hotel.

Dupont patted her shoulder again. "Leave yourself in the hands of Papa Dupont. He will see that no harm comes to you."

AN HOUR later Dupont found Quarles standing beside the flowering shrubs and told him all that Marjorie Brown had said "But what are you doing?" the Frenchman said. "Why did you go into the hotel? And what are you holding in your hand? You are surely not still interested in that bullet."

"Shall I tell you the most interesting thing about this affair? The second shot."

"What do you mean? There was no second shot."

"As our friend Sherlock Holmes would say, that was the interesting thing. For here is a second bullet. I have just found it among these shrubs." Quarles opened his hand to reveal two little leaden pellets.

During the afternoon Quarles made some discreet inquiries about the Browns by means of a telephone call to a friend of his on the Evening Standard. He learned that Johnny Brown was the rich playboy son of an oil millionaire. Two years ago he had married a model named Marjorie Mellors, who had a certain reputation around town.

Eileen Gray, Majorie's poor relation cousin, had come to live with them six months back, because Johnny Brown had begun to take an active interest in business, and was away from home a good deal. Brown's name had been linked with several women, but nobody knew of any affair between him and Eileen Gray.

Quarles also made some inquiries in the hotel. He learned that Brown was said to be interested in Lola Montigny, the leading lady of a company performing at the local theatre.

THE SECOND BU[...]

THE masked ball had just begun when Quarles, standing at [...] was nudged by a short man with a sizeable paunch.

From behind the man's black mask came Dupont's voice. "Mo[...] Brown has had a telephone call and is suddenly called away before [...] ball begins. Is that not interesting?"

"Very."

"And something more interesting still. He has gone no farther tha[n] the place where we sat this morning. Out there is darkness. It is an assignation he attends, would you not say that?"

"Come along," Quarles said sharply. "There's no time to lose."

They left the bar and looked in the ballroom. There some two hundred men and women moved, masked, in each other's arms. Quarles looked among them for an ice-blue dress, but did not find it. He walked quickly along to the door that opened on to the terrace and stepped out there Dupont followed him.

OUT on the terrace, and in the garden beyond, there was stillness except for the murmur of the sea. The scent of flowers was strong. But Quarles did not notice the stillness or the flowers. He was watching a girl walking away from the hotel towards the shrubbery. The girl was slim and upright, and in the moonlight her dress showed ice blue.

"Miss Gray," Dupont whispered. "She goes to the assignation."

Quarles moved quietly along the terrace. At the other end of it, past the ballroom, moonlight again glinted on something blue, the barrel of a revolver pointed at the back of the walking girl.

Quarles raised his voice. "It's no use. Mrs. Brown. I took the bullets out of that revolver this morning."

A woman in a dark red dress with white mask turned towards him. She said something unprintable and squeezed the trigger. There was a click, nothing more.

By now Quarles was up with her, and had pulled off the mask. Marjorie Brown's face, distorted with fury, stared at him.

Dupont looked at her in amazement. "Mrs. Brown—but why—?"

Quarles spoke briskly. "She got her husband out here with a fake telephone call—no doubt it told him that Lola Montigny would meet him out in the garden. Then she sent Eileen Gray in the same direction on some pretext probably to get something she had left there. She meant to shoot Eileen, throw the gun out by the body and go back into the ballroom. Her husband would come out and be found with the body. It was his gun. No doubt his prints are on it."

he t
sieur
the

d he kill Eileen Gray?" Dupont asked.

ng a frock that Marjorie Brown had just given her, . It would be assumed that he had killed her in mistake u and I, my dear Dupont, were meant to testify that d been shot at this morning. Johnny Brown was tired of she knew it. She did it for the money."

know then, this morning, that she was playing a trick?"

it immediately. The bullet that was fired flew past my ear. It possibly have made a hole in Mrs. Brown's hat several yards on the other side of some shrubbery. When she showed us the ., and I found the bullet which she had dropped on the steps. I knew that she was up to something. I left you, made an illicit entry into her hotel room, and found the revolver there, connected to an automatic time switch. I took out the bullets, replaced the revolver, and waited for Mrs. Brown to stage the climax."

PRESERVING THE EVIDENCE

"THE plain fact is my wife's trying to kill me." Herbert Watling, managing director of the Watling Tool Company, put his hands on his knees and looked almost angrily at Francis Quarles. He was a long-nosed, self-important, carroty man of about fifty. "Poison," he added.

The detective stared thoughtfully across his big desk. "How do you know?"

Watling patted his stomach. "Haven't been feeling myself lately, stomach cramps, sickness after meals. She's putting stuff in my food."

"Have you seen a doctor? You may have a stomach ulcer."

"Don't believe in doctors, they're all quacks. But this is no stomach ulcer, she's trying to poison me I tell you."

"Allowing that what you say is true, and that there is poison involved, why should you think it's your wife? You've told me there are other people living in the house, your sister Edith, your son Edward, the cook Mary. Why shouldn't it be one of them?"

Watling's gaze shifted uneasily. "It's Bella all right. She'd be the one to profit by it. Besides, she's hated me for years."

"Why?"

Watling embarked on a rambling recital of petty disagreements. Obviously he was not telling the whole truth, yet it seemed to Quarles that the man was genuinely worried.

Finally the detective agreed to come down on the following day to investigate the situation, posing as a business associate of Watling's. "In the meantime, you'd better be careful what you eat and drink."

Watling smiled grimly. "Believe me. I watch what she eats at meals before I touch anything myself."

An hour after Watling had gone, Quarles's secretary came in and said that Mrs. Watling was outside. Quarles raised his eyebrows. "Show her in."

Bella Watling was a small, blonde determined woman who had once been pretty. She came to the point at once. "Mr. Quarles, I've been having my husband followed and I know he's been to see you. What has he been saying? That I'm trying to poison him. I expect."

"If he said that, would it be true?" Quarles asked politely.

She snorted. "He's always had bad indigestion and it's been worse than usual these last few weeks, that's all. He doesn't believe a word of it himself. He simply wants to get rid of me."

"To poison you, do you mean?"

"No. He's covering up his own guilty conscience. Oh, Mr. Quarles, if you knew the life I've lived with that man." She poured into Quarles's ear a long tale of her husband's constant and very varied infidelities. "Now he's after somebody fresh. I can always tell. But this time I'm going to get a divorce when they've found out who it is. I'm having a watch kept on him from the time he leaves home in the morning till he comes back at night."

"And what have you found out?"

"Nothing yet. My husband's a clever devil. He knows I mean business this time and he doesn't want his home broken up. He's fond of Edward. I will say that for him. All this nonsense about being poisoned just means that he's going to make things as awkward as he can for me."

Quarles considered. "I was supposed to come down tomorrow as a business associate of your husband's but—"

"Oh, come down by all means," she said with rather dreadful gaiety. "Come and watch the poisoner at work."

BUT Quarles did not get down to the Watlings' house at Porlow in Buckinghamshire in time for that At ten o'clock on the following morning he heard the gritty voice of his friend Inspector Leeds on the telephone. "Quarles? Did a man named Watling come to see you yesterday—and his wife, too? Man claimed she was poisoning him? Well, looks as if he might not have been far wrong. At any rate, he's dead. Nearly two grains of arsenic in the organs. He died of acute arsenical poisoning." The Inspector paused.

"The wife bought an arsenical insecticide a couple of weeks ago. Got a widower named Jenkins who lives in a cottage in the ground, with his daughter and looks after the garden. She says Jenkins told her it was needed, he can't be sure, but thinks she mentioned it to him. Anyway we found it in the dustbin, empty. The puzzle is, how the poison was given to Watling."

AND that remained a puzzle. Quarles talked to Bella Watling, to her son Edward, who was a boy of fifteen, to the dead man's sister Edith, a gaunt spinster who made no secret of the fact that she believed Bella had poisoned her husband, and to the cook, Mary Squires. It was Mary

PRESERVING THE EVIDENCE 99

who had prepared the evening meal of roast lamb with mint sauce, baked potatoes and runner beans, followed by plum pie, that had been eaten by everybody. The food had been served in the dining-room by Bella.

Watling had drunk with the meal the best part of a bottle of wine which he opened himself, and this had made him rather excited and quarrelsome. Bella Watling and her mother had drunk one small glass each of the wine.

Watling was extremely fond of fruit, both cooked and raw, and he had had two large helpings of plum pie, but then other people had eaten the pie in smaller quantities with no bad effects. He was a non-smoker and had not taken any medicine. There was no glass or bottle by his bedside.

At about eleven o'clock the household had gone to bed, Watling and his wife in separate rooms. Half an hour later Edith Watling had heard somebody go downstairs and come up again almost immediately. Presumably this was Watling, since nobody else admitted to going downstairs. At about half past twelve Bella Watling was awakened by groans coming from her husband's room. Five hours later he was dead.

How, then had the poison been administered? Inspector Leeds scratched his grey head and admitted himself baffled. He was certain that it had been given to Watling at some point during the meal, and impressed this on the men who were searching every room in the house.

QUARLES roamed about, poking in corners and opening cupboards without quite knowing what he was looking for, or where he expected to find it.

He unscrewed the jars and bottles on Bella Watling's dressing-table, and investigated the patent medicine bottles lining the cupboard in the bathroom. He examined Watling's toothpaste and shaving-cream and searched the dead man's bedroom carefully. In the waste-paper basket of the bedroom he found a small object which he picked up carefully and put into an envelope, putting the envelope into his pocket.

Downstairs again Quarles discovered that the wastepaper baskets were cleared every day before lunchtime. Then he wandered about the dining room, watched apprehensively by Bella Watling. He stood looking out of the French window. "A beautiful garden," he said appreciatively. "You grow all your own fruit, I suppose. These, for instance." He touched a bowl on the dining table containing apples and pears.

"Yes. Jenkins picks them fresh every day and brings them in."

"Don't I see peaches, too, sheltering under that red brick wall?"

"Yes. Not very many, though. They were all kept for Herbert because he was so fond of them."

"Very proper. Come and look at the garden. Inspector, I know you love flowers." The Inspector stared incredulously, but allowed himself to be led out on to the terrace. Quarles showed him what he had found in the wastepaper basket. "Your man must have missed it, or didn't attach any importance to it."

"I'll speak to him," the Inspector said grimly.

"Oh, come now, it's hardly what you told them to expect. Let's go and find Jenkins."

They did not find him, but in the vegetable garden a girl was bending over a row of runner beans. Quarles stopped. "Ah, you'll be Jenkins's daughter."

She straightened up, a dark handsome girl with eyes red-rimmed from recent weeping. "Yes."

"A sad thing, isn't it, about Mr. Watling's death? Or don't you agree? Would you say he was a harsh employer or a kind one? Were you happy here?"

She put a hand to her throat and said in a choked voice; "He was—I don't know what you mean."

"I think you do. He told you he was in love with you, didn't he?"

Her face went pink. She dropped the basket in her hand and ran. A voice at Quarles's elbow said, "Let the girl alone." He turned to face a grizzled man with a spade.

"You're her father. She was in love with Watling." The gardener said nothing. "It had to be someone round here, because Mrs. Watling had a watch kept on him at other times, and found out nothing."

"She is a good girl," Jenkins said fiercely.

"But she wouldn't have stayed good for long with Watling making a set at her. That's why you killed him."

The grizzled man stared hard at Quarles. "I don't know what you mean."

"I think you do. Watling thought he was being poisoned, and he assumed his wife was doing the poisoning. Inspector Leeds thought so too, until I found a small piece of evidence that made him change his mind. But in fact it was you who suggested to Mrs. Watling that she should buy some insecticide. Then you experimented with small doses that made Watling feel ill. Yesterday you increased the dose to a fatal one."

"Prove it," said Jenkins.

"Watling died of something he ate or drank last night. What was it? At dinner everything he ate and drank was taken by other people, too. But after he went to bed he came downstairs took from the dish of fruit one of the peaches that were always kept for him, and ate it. You knew that you were safe enough in poisoning the peaches, because nobody else ate them. Watling didn't suspect them because he was convinced that his wife was poisoning his cooked food."

"Prove it," the gardener said again. "Prove that he ate a peach."

"Unfortunately for you we can." Quarles said. "You see, Watling preserved the evidence." And he held up the peach stone that Watling had thrown into the waste-paper basket.

DEATH FOR MR. GOLIGHTLY

DEATH came for Mr. Golightly one dark winter evening, for little Mr. Golightly who was so tender-hearted that he could not read about the deaths of animals without tears coming to his eyes. Somebody strangled him with a scarf and left his body, limp and purple-faced, on Blackheath ten minutes' walk away from his home.

Who could have wanted to kill harmless little Mr. Golightly? The 40 years of his working life had been spent in the engineering firm of Bardin's, where the force of time rather than native ability had brought him to the post of chief assistant to a junior director, Peter Arbuthnot.

HE lived quietly at home with his widowed sister Mrs. Stoner. He was a vegetarian, did not smoke or drink, was fond of gardening and enjoyed a good play on the radio. His neighbours regarded Mr. Golightly's butterfly collar, spats and rolled umbrella with a certain amount of amusement, but they liked and even respected him in an odd way.

Who killed Mr. Golightly? His sister Mrs. Stoner had no doubt about the answer to that question. Sitting in the office of private detective Francis Quarles she demanded: "Why haven't the police arrested that man Horden?"

She was a big, bony, horse-faced woman dressed in black. Quarles considered her carefully before he replied. "Hadn't he got an alibi? Golightly was killed about half-past six and Horden was in a cinema until eight o'clock. Isn't that it?"

She snorted in a formidable manner. "Alibi, indeed. I know what alibis are worth. I've read detective stories. Criminals always have alibis. Who else could it have been? Eustace hadn't an enemy in the world."

Quarles sighed. "Just what do you want me to do, Mrs. Stoner?"

"Put Horden in prison where he belongs. Break his alibi."

"You want me to find your brother's murderer?"

"That's what I said."

QUARLES'S old friend, Inspector Leeds, was not very helpful. "The old girl's a bit batty, if you ask me, though it's true enough that Horden's the only one we've found with any motive. He lost his job through friend Eustace, but he'd have lost it anyway in a few weeks.

"The firm employed him as a traveller on Golightly's recommendation—Horden was a friend of a neighbour of his in Blackheath—and he tried the old traveller's trick of turning—in orders for a lot of stuff he hadn't sold to get the commission. You can't last long at that game, but as it happens it was Golightly who caught him a couple of days ago, through getting in touch with one of the firms Horden was supposed to have visited. The old chap was very cut up about it apparently, thought it was his responsibility. Of course Horden was sacked straight away, and he doesn't seem to have taken it too well. He was in the cafe where Golightly had lunch, and there were some pretty strong words. The old chap doesn't seem to have been upset at the time, but he went and talked to his boss, Arbuthnot, about it later on."

"What about Horden's alibi?"

"He went in the cinema about five, came out just after eight. Sat on the end seat of a back row kept chatting with an usherette he knew. Could be a phoney, but I doubt it. The cinema was in Woolwich twenty minutes walk away from where Golightly was killed. He was strangled between six-thirty and seven-thirty, may have been dropped out of a car."

"How about the office? That seems to have been the chief interest of his life."

The Inspector shrugged. "Right enough. May have been a bit worried there—Bardin's haven't been doing too well lately. Don't see that can have anything to do with it, but go and talk to them by all means. Break Horden's alibi for me while you're about it, too."

QUARLES tried to break Horden's alibi, and failed. The usherette, who knew Horden well, insisted that she would have known if he had left the cinema for more than a few minutes. Quarles believed that she was telling the truth.

Then he went to Golightly's office and talked to crusty old Bardin and slick young business man Sayers, who had been brought in a year or two before over the head of burly Peter Arbuthnot to pep up the firm.

Quarles found that Bardin regarded Eustace Golightly as a pillar of the firm. Sayers thought him an old fusspot, and Arbuthnot complained of his painful concentration on detail. All three paid tribute to his irreproachable honesty and fanatical devotion to the firm's interests.

Quarles retraced the events of Golightly's last day. He had worked all the morning with Arbuthnot on a tender for United Schools and they had finally worked out the price ten minutes before lunch. Then Golightly had gone to lunch just round the corner at the Tuck Inn with Burke a junior from his own section.

BURKE, a bright young man in his twenties, described the incident at lunch when Horden had come up to them. "He really went for old Golly, called him a dirty sneak, said Golly had always had it in for him, swore he'd only borrowed the money and would have paid it back in a couple of weeks. Golly was splendid, didn't turn a hair, offered to lend Horden money if he was hard up."

"How did it end?"

"Horden went off swearing he's get his own back one day. Didn't seem to mean much by it, though."

"And Golightly wasn't upset?"

"Not at the time. Must have had a kind of delayed action effect. I left Golly at the Tuck Inn drinking his coffee—I had to get back early to take a phone call. He came in about a quarter of an hour later, face like a sheet, went in to see Arbuthnot."

QUARLES talked to Arbuthnot again. The burly man looked at him curiously. "Yes, he was in rather a state after lunch. I couldn't make it out. Said he thought he ought to retire, he was no good any more, always making mistakes, he'd let this chap Horden put one over on us and so on.

Arbuthnot hesitated. "Matter of fact, he was in such a state I fixed an appointment for us to see old Bardin the next morning. Only did it to soothe him down; of course, we had no idea of accepting his resignation."

Bardin confirmed that Arbuthnot had rung through on the house telephone shortly after lunch to ask for an interview for himself and Golightly. Bardin had been engaged in a conference, and had fixed the appointment for the following morning.

"What's that got to do with anything, Mr. Quarles? Arbuthnot's told you that Golightly had some bee in his bonnet about retiring."

"Yes," Quarles said thoughtfully. "But all the same—"

THE manageress and waitresses of the Tuck Inn stared at Quarles as he asked: "Did any of you see Golightly talking to anybody after he was left alone at the table?"

There was silence. The manageress said helplessly, "There are so many here at lunchtime."

"Perhaps somebody took their coffee to his table. Perhaps they stood and talked for a moment—"

One of the waitresses exclaimed sharply. "That Miss Holdsworth, she stopped at his table a minute. Don't know what she said though."

"Who is Miss Holdsworth?"

"She's a secretary in some engineering firm. What's the name now? Oh yes, Babbitt and Broune, down the street."

QUARLES'S card with the words "about Mr. Golightly" written on it, took him into Miss Holdsworth's office. She was a tall, slim girl who seemed frankly puzzled. "I didn't know Mr. Golightly at all well, never did more than have a little chat with him about business. Our firms are more or less rivals, you know."

"And you had a little chat at lunchtime on the day he died." She nodded. "What did you say to him?"

"Why, nothing important." She was bewildered. "Though it was rather indiscreet. I just said we were a thousand below his firm's figure on the United Schools contract. We were in competition for it. Mr. Broune had told me just a few minutes before, and it was fresh in my mind. He really didn't seem to take it in at first. He asked me to repeat it to him, and then just said 'Oh.'"

"I see," said Quarles. "You'd better take me in to see Mr. Broune."

LATER that day Bardin, Sayers and Arbuthnot sat with Inspector Leeds in Bardin's office. Quarles stood with his back to the fire and talked to them.

"The first thing that struck me about the case was the feebleness of Horden's motive. In the ordinary way nobody would have dreamed of suspecting him. He only became a suspect in this case because Golightly was such a harmless little man that nobody could imagine him being murdered. There was only one thing he felt strongly about and that was the firm. So it was in his relations with the firm that I looked for the cause of his murder. I hadn't to look far. On the day of the murder he had come back from lunch with a face like a sheet. Everyone assumed this was because of his argument with Horden at the lunch table. But in fact as Burke said, Golightly didn't turn a hair during the argument. Something else had upset him, something that happened after Burke left, and made him go straight to Arbuthnot on his return.

"What was it? Arbuthnot said Golightly was upset over the Horden business and wanted to retire. In a man as devoted to his work as Golightly, and in view of the coolness with which he had treated Horden at lunch, that seemed to me frankly incredible."

Somebody stirred. Quarles went on. "I found out what had shocked Golightly. The secretary of a rival firm, Babbitt and Broune, had indiscreetly told him that Babbitt's were a thousand pounds below Bardin's on a contract for United Schools. When Golightly took it in, he realised the implications of what she had said. He had worked out Bardin's price for that contract ten minutes before lunch. At lunchtime a rival firm knew it, and was able to undercut their price accordingly. Somebody had deliberately passed on Bardin's price, and Golightly knew it could be only one person. To a man like him it was an unforgivable betrayal. He went back and taxed the guilty person, the man who had worked out the price with him. It was agreed that they would see Bardin the next morning. But by that time the guilty person had caught Golightly as he was going home across Blackheath, and Golightly was dead."

There was silence. Charles said, "It's no good, Arbuthnot. I've talked to Broune and to half a dozen others. You've been systematically wrecking Bardin's business for more than a year, and you must have made a pretty little packet out of commission."

Arbuthnot pointed at Sayers. His voice was full of bitterness. "It wasn't the money. Why did Bardin bring in that nincompoop over my head?"

A MAN WITH BLUE HAIR

"THAT man's across the road again, Mrs. Kazakis. The man with blue hair." Bella Kazakis ran out of her bedroom when her maid called, and they looked at the man together from the drawing-room window. He was of medium height and olive complexion, with a large straight nose and a little pointed beard. But the remarkable thing about him was the fact that his hair was a metallic shade of blue.

Bella Kazakis ran to the front door and called out: "You there." The man began to walk away rapidly. By the time Mrs. Kazakis reached her front gate he had vanished round the corner into the main road. She walked, frowning, back into her house, put on a coat and got out her car. Half an hour later she was telling her story to private detective Francis Quarles.

"WE'VE seen him half a dozen times now," Mrs. Kazakis told Quarles. "Sometimes I see him, and sometimes my maid Laura. He doesn't do anything—just stands looking at the house, or walks up and down. If anyone comes out he goes away."

"Has your husband seen him?" Quarles had learned already that her husband was a wealthy fur trader.

She shook her head. "He always comes in the daytime. It seems so foolish to go to the police, and my husband would never forgive me if I made him look ridiculous."

She hesitated. "I'm worried, Mr. Quarles. I'm English, but my husband is a Greek. I married him in 1945 when he came over here. He spent the war in Greece, and I'm afraid he may have been in some kind of trouble there. I mentioned this man to him, and I believe he knew who it was, though he wouldn't say so."

"Is the blue hair a wig or a blue rinse?"

"I've never been near enough to see. That blue hair gives me the shivers, Mr. Quarles. What can be the meaning?"

"I can think of two obvious reasons for his wearing a blue wig, and no doubt there are twenty others."

"Can you send somebody down to follow this man and find out where he lives? If we can find out what's behind this, perhaps we can deal with it."

Quarles looked at her steadily. She was a dark handsome woman, with good features and a firm jaw. He nodded.

JACKSON, the man Quarles had put to watch the house, did not see the man with blue hair that afternoon. About five o'clock Mr. Kazakis, a short tubby man much older than his wife, came home.

An hour later in gathering dusk, a man walked briskly round the corner on the other side of the road from Jackson, and opened the front gate of the Kazakis house. He walked up the steps and rang the bell.

As the man passed under a street lamp just before he reached the gate, Jackson noticed with a thrill the metallic blue of his hair. He noticed also that the man wore lemon yellow gloves.

The door opened. A light in the hall showed Bella Kazakis standing there. Her hand went to her mouth at sight of the man. They said something to each other and she went away while the man waited. Then she came back and the door closed behind the man.

Jackson fidgeted. This was not quite what he had been told to expect. But he stayed where he was for ten minutes. Then the door opened again. It was not the man with blue hair, but Bella Kazakis who appeared. She screamed...

THE police and Quarles arrived almost together. They found Mrs. Kazakis lying on a sofa. A fresh-faced young man named Colin Ellis, who proved to be her cousin was giving her sips of brandy. Kazakis was in his study with a revolver by his side and a bullet through his heart. Powder burns marked his coat jacket. There was no sign of a struggle.

Bella Kazakis told her story. "This is Laura's afternoon off, so I answered the door bell. That man was standing there. His blue hair and the yellow gloves he wore and the look in his eyes—I should know him again anywhere. He said that he had come to see my husband. His English was good, but he spoke it with a strong accent. I asked his name and he said that he came from the Black Band. I went and told my husband. He took a revolver from his desk drawer—it is the one that is by his side now—and said 'Very well. Bella, show him in.' I took the man in and my husband told me to leave them. I went upstairs to my own room. A few minutes later I heard a shot. I ran down and found my husband dead. There was no sign of the man."

Colin Ellis patted her hand. "I live near and I often come in for a drink before dinner. I got here just in time to give Bella some brandy."

A MAN WITH BLUE HAIR 109

"There's nothing else you remember?" Quarles asked Bella Kazakis.

"No—yes, there is. Just as I was going upstairs I heard the man ask for a telephone number. I noted it down." She gave him a clip of paper with a Paddington number on it.

A French window led from the study to the back lawn. The man with blue hair had presumably walked out there and through the garden gate, which opened on to a narrow lane.

In Kazakis's desk Inspector Gregory found letters and papers which confirmed Bella's story, and made clear the nature of the Black Band. The documents showed that Kazakis had been a leading member of a black marketeering gang of that name in Greece during the war. Afterwards several of the gang had been imprisoned and it was clear that Kazakis had informed against them.

While Inspector Gregory was making these discoveries Quarles had been giving instructions to his man Jackson, who disappeared for several minutes. He returned with a large envelope which he handed to the detective.

The Paddington telephone number proved to be that of J. Varangopoulos, 115, Chesney Street W.2. "A Greek," said the Inspector, and rubbed his hands "Shall we go and have a look at him?"

J. VARANGOPOULOS occupied a room and kitchenette on the second floor of a dingy house. The room contained only the barest necessities of living, a table a chair, a few pieces of cutlery. The Inspector gave an exclamation of triumph as he opened a cupboard at one end of the room. The cupboard was bare of clothes, but at the bottom of it was a wig of metallic blue hair and a neat dark beard. Quarles examined them with interest.

"Now to trace Varangopoulos," said the Inspector. But that did not prove easy. He had stayed at Chesney Street only one or two nights a week, arriving at night and leaving early in the morning. The landlord of the house gave the most coherent picture.

"Quiet kind of chap he was, couldn't speak English very well. Had his right arm in a sling, broken his wrist or something. Signed our agreement left-handed and made a fair scrawl of it."

"Have you got the agreement?" Quarles's eyes were gleaming. The landlord produced it.

"Don't see what you're getting at," the Inspector said. "It's a clear enough case of a gang killing. Mr. Varangopoulos, alias the man with blue hair, went to see Kazakis to try and get some money out of him. He failed, grabbed the gun and shot him, came back here and left the disguise which was no use to him any more, and then skipped out."

Quarles held up the wig and beard. "If you'd looked more carefully at these. Inspector, you'd have seen that they're the type attached with spirit gum and that there are no marks on them. In fact, they have never been worn."

"AN interesting case," Quarles said when they were back at the Kazakis house. "And dependent on the man with blue hair.

"I told Mrs. Kazakis that I could think of two obvious reasons for such a bizarre disguise. One was to draw attention away from some other striking physical characteristic like a squint, another that the hair colour might be in some way a signal or a warning to Kazakis. Neither of those ideas seemed borne out by the facts. It wasn't until Kazakis had been shot that the true explanation occurred to me. It was simple enough. *The man wore a blue wig because he wanted to be noticed.*

"That was the key to the case. The maid couldn't fail to notice such a conspicuous figure; she told Mrs. Kazakis and Mrs. Kazakis came to see me. I was asked to place someone outside, and sure enough he saw the man entering the house. The man was designed to lead us on to another figure named Varangopoulos, who had killed Kazakis for revenge. It was a clever plan, but the attention to detail wasn't very good. We were asked to believe that the man with blue hair had come without a weapon, so that he had to snatch up Kazakis's own revolver and also that he had for some curious reason telephoned himself. Then the wig that he was supposed to have left in flight had never been used. That was very careless."

Bella Kazakis said with a frown: "Do you mean the man with blue hair wasn't Varangopoulos?"

"I mean that the man with blue hair didn't exist, and Varangopoulos didn't exist either. He came to his flat only once or twice a week and then at night when he wouldn't be seen; he signed an agreement with his left hand under the mistaken impression that handwriting tests can't be applied to left-handed writing.

"This whole Black Band story was hatched by Mrs. Kazakis when she wanted to get rid of her elderly husband, and use his money to live happily with her youthful lover. She'd seen at one time or another those papers in her husband's desk, and she cooked up the whole thing out of that. It was ingenious, but you shouldn't have let her persuade you into helping her, Ellis."

"What do you mean?" Colin Ellis said hoarsely.

"Shall I tell you what really happened? When you rang the bell this evening wearing your blue wig, Mrs. Kazakis opened it. She went straight in and shot her husband, standing so close to him that there were powder burns on his jacket. It's not likely that he would have let anybody else get that close without a struggle and there was no sign of a struggle. Then you simply walked in, took off your wig, beard and gloves and went out through the back gate, returning shortly afterwards in your own character to console the stricken widow. She burned the things in the kitchen fire, from which my man Jackson was able to salvage some useful fragments of wig and gloves. Then she opened the front door and screamed."

"I didn't shoot him," Colin Ellis said: "I did what she told me. I never wanted to do it."

Bella Kazakis stood up. "Shut up, you fool" Her hand cracked across his face.

"I can sympathise with you in a way, Ellis," Quarles said pleasantly. "As her husband discovered, she's a very formidable woman."

THE TWO SUITORS

ANNE FORESTER was a widow in her thirties, neat, fair and intelligent. Her husband, who had died on an African lion shoot, left her a tidy little house in Richmond, and a microscopic income on which she just managed to maintain it and herself.

She was therefore no particular catch in the matrimonial market, yet she was the kind of woman about whom people say with absolute certainty, "Of course, she'll marry again." Apart from her physical attractions, which were notable without being overpowering, she was awfully good company.

She was enthusiastic about racing and lawn tennis, and she could say something intelligent at a symphony concert or an art show. If somebody suggested a visit to the latest film it always turned out that she had been dying to see it; if the suggestion was a tour through dockland ending up at the Prospect of Whitby she thought that would be terrific fun.

She had her own fascination, Anne Forester, and she had a number of suitors.

Gradually they narrowed down to two, and it was generally understood that she would marry one of them—Denis Goldman or Charles Morley. But which? She went with Denis, who was a hard-up younger son with good future prospects, to race meetings, dog tracks, boxing matches and dances. She went with Charles Morley, who was the rather uninterested senior partner in a struggling firm of stockbrokers, to operas, concerts, and lectures about the influence of cubism on Picasso.

Denis was blond and handsome, Charles dark and saturnine. Denis was twenty-five and Charles a little over forty. Denis was gay and dashing, Charles romantic and reflective.

But different though they were in temperament, and much though they disliked each other, the two men had in common the fact that they were both deeply and passionately in love with Anne Forester.

Perhaps both of them were fascinated chiefly by her bewildering changes of mood, so that neither was ever quite certain just what kind of woman she was. She could move in a moment from gaiety to seriousness, from apparently calculating flirtatiousness to disconcertingly prim solemnity. She could seem quite thoughtless of money in one moment, and well aware of the main chance in the next.

Did she love either Denis Goldman or Charles Morley, or was she chiefly aware of Denis's good future prospects and Charles's apparently comfortable income? And which of them would she marry?

Through a summer in which her friends pondered these problems she kept them, and the two suitors, on tenterhooks. In fact she married nobody.

One Wednesday afternoon Anne Forester's friend Miss Dewsbury came hurrying in to tell her that Charles Morley's lack of interest in his business had found him out. A junior partner had perpetrated an ingenious swindle, and Charles Morley was ruined. Watching Anne Forester closely. Miss Dewsbury said that she had a brother on the Stock Exchange who had told her all about it at lunchtime, and she had thought that dear Anne would be interested to know the terrible news.

Dear Anne disappointed her friend Miss Dewsbury. She listened to the news without apparent emotion, thanked Miss Dewsbury sweetly for telling her so promptly, and showed her the door. The time was then four o'clock.

Just after six o'clock Anne Forester was found dead in the sitting room of her house. She had been struck on the head three times by a heavy brass candlestick which had fractured her skull. There were no finger-prints on the candlestick. There had been no incoming or outgoing telephone calls during the afternoon. Death had probably taken place at about five.

On the table, in very plain view, was a letter in Anne Forester's writing. It began without prefix:

Today I heard some news that has made up my mind for me. I hope you will understand when I say that I cannot marry you. We should never be happy together. I'm an awfully unsatisfactory person in lots of ways, and I'm sure you'd have found me so if we'd got married. My dear, I hope you won't take this too hard. There are lots of women in the world who would be much better wives for you than I should.

Anne.

"FASCINATING little problem," Inspector Leeds said to his friend Francis Quarles as they sat in Leeds's office. "She wrote it to one of them, and from the tone of it and what had happened it was almost certainly to Morley. But between knowing she wrote it to Morley, and proving that he came there, got turned down and murdered her in a fit of passion, there's a good deal of difference."

"But surely—" Quarles began, and stopped.

"I've got Morley outside now, and the other man too—Goldman. In separate rooms, of course."

"What do they say?"

"Both swear they never went near Richmond that afternoon, and we haven't found anyone to disprove them yet. Neither of them has a cast-iron alibi. Both crying their eyes out for her. They don't know about this note—after all, it's the only piece of evidence we've got."

"Perhaps we could have them in together. There are one or two questions I'd like to ask."

THE two men certainly presented a striking contrast. Denis Goldman's tie was carelessly knotted, his clothes were creased, he was unshaven and pale, but there was still a bursting vitality in his movements and in the stare of his bright blue eye.

Charles Morley, taller and thinner, looked merely crushed by the weight of misfortune that had fallen on him. Goldman made a quick movement towards the other man, but was checked by a police sergeant.

"You both say that you neither spoke to nor saw Mrs. Forester on the day of her death." Quarles said.

Morley nodded. Goldman said, "That's right."

"Did you think that she was on the point of making up her mind about marriage?"

"She hadn't made it up," Morley murmured.

Goldman said defiantly, "She would have married me. I'd asked her often, and she always put me off with a joke or a laugh, but I never had any doubt that she meant to marry me."

Morley seemed stirred a little by this. "I don't remember her joking and laughing. She was a serious-minded woman. I never had any doubt of that. It was what attracted me to her."

"That's what you thought, Morley. She often told me that she was bored to tears with all the arty affairs you dragged her to, though she was too kind-hearted to show it."

Morley winced perceptibly.

"The only advantage you had over me was that you had cash in the bank, while I was waiting to step into somebody else's shoes," Goldman went on. "Anne was a girl who wanted a good time, and I don't blame her. When you learned yesterday that you'd lost your money you knew it would mean the finish with Anne. You couldn't stand that, could you, Morley?"

Morley made a feeble gesture with his hand. "Anne wasn't like that."

Quarles murmured, "She left a note for one of you."

"Saying good-bye to you, Morley," Goldman mocked. "It's been nice to know you, but I've heard the news and I've made up my mind that I can't marry you. Very sorry and all that but we shouldn't be happy."

"What made you think the note was written to Morley?" Quarles asked.

Goldman looked startled. "Well—wasn't it?"

"It wasn't addressed to anybody. But some of the phrases you've used come almost directly from it."

"Do they? Accident," said Goldman tersely.

"In any case, how did you know Mrs. Forester had heard the news about Morley?"

Goldman was pale. "I telephoned myself and told her."

"No. She had no telephone calls. She did know—she learned the news at four o'clock. But there's no way you could have found that out unless you called on her. When you called you learned that Anne Forester had a streak of self-sacrifice and generosity in her. She had learned the news and she had made up her mind to marry Morley. That was too great a shock for your self-esteem to stand. You killed her in a fit of fury."

Goldman said nothing.

"Then you saw the note that she had written to you. You read it, saw that it wasn't addressed to anybody by name, and decided that it would be clever to leave the note where it was. That was a big mistake, and because of it I knew you were the murderer before you came into this room. For on the face of it the letter pointed directly to Morley. The fact that it hadn't been destroyed was the strongest possible proof of his innocence. For if Morley had been the murderer he would certainly have destroyed such an incriminating document. If you were the murderer on the other hand, you would have a strong and obvious motive for leaving the letter exactly where it was."

AIRBORNE WITH A BORGIA

THE flight to Rome began badly for Francis Quarles. Fog held up the airplane, so that, although the flight was scheduled for six o'clock, it was more than an hour later when he walked up the gangway. Then there was the matter of seating.

Quarles liked to sit at the back of airplanes, believing that this was safer in case of accidents. One of the back seats was occupied, however, and a polite and smiling stewardess, with the name "Della Harris" printed on her blue and white cap, foiled his attempt to sit in the other.

"That's reserved for Mr. Cogan." she said, and led Quarles a little further up the aisle. Muttering under his breath, the detective took the seat allotted to him, and watched for Mr. Cogan's arrival. He came a little after the other passengers, a balding, plump, white-faced little man carrying a bulging briefcase.

"Good evening, Mr. Cogan," said the smiling stewardess.

"Evening, Della. Made up my mind at the last minute as usual. Glad you could fit me in. Favourite seat, too." He sat down heavily in the back seat, opened the briefcase and took out some papers.

A bearded man sitting beside Quarles jerked his head round at the mention of the name "Cogan," and got up to speak to him. In a mirror just ahead of him. Quarles saw Cogan look up with no very pleased expression. The bearded man bent over, they talked for a moment or two, and then Cogan nodded dismissal and returned to his papers.

Not for long, however. A woman sitting further up the airplane had also turned her head at mention of Cogan's name. Now she swayed down the airplane, putting one foot before the other with studied grace. Light in the airplane struck glints from her red hair.

"Billy, you didn't tell me you were taking this trip. What a nice coincidence." Her voice was husky, with something foreign about it.

Cogan's voice had an undertone of irritation. "Tamara, my dear. Lovely to see you. Didn't know myself until a couple of hours ago."

"You will be staying some time in Rome?" Cogan's reply was inaudible. "We shall meet, however. You are free tomorrow?"

This time there could be no doubt of the irritation, as Cogan said: "I'm going to be very busy in Rome, Tamara."

The woman swayed up the aisle again. The stewardess said: "Fasten your belts, please." Quarles fastened his belt, which had a new-fangled clip device. The airplane taxied round and rose from the ground in the evening twilight, Quarles looked at his watch. The time was 7.16. Behind him Cogan gave a sharp exclamation of annoyance. In the mirror the detective saw the little man looking angrily at his hand.

DELLA HARRIS came round to ask for dinner orders. Was it an effect of the light, Quarles wondered, or was it true that her face was slightly green? The bearded man sitting next to Quarles shifted and spoke.

"Recognise that woman with red hair? Tamara Delaney, the film actress. Old Cogan's got pretty good taste. You know old Cogan?"

Quarles said that he didn't know old Cogan.

"He's a director of this airline, that's why they always find room for him. Wouldn't think it to look at him, but old Cogan's worth half a million, so they say. Gets the girls too, you saw Tamara after him. Always moving on to the next one, though."

Della Harris was walking down the aisle with a tray in her hand when she was suddenly and quite violently sick. Quarles noted admiringly the lack of fuss with which her departure was managed by two more attendants who emerged from what Quarles took to be the galley. Or was it called the kitchen on an airplane?

"OLD COGAN'S as mean as they make 'em." the bearded man said. "My name's Foskiss. Used to be a pilot on this line. Coogan sacked me—just like that—because I was a bit late for a flight once. Claimed I'd had a few too many." The bearded man leaned over. His breath smelled of whisky. "I've just had the pleasure of telling Mr. Cogan I've got a much better job in Italy. He took it well. I must say."

Mr. Foskiss, no doubt about it, was a bore. Quarles resolutely opened his book and read until dinner was served. "Hallo, Jimmy. How's Della?" Foskiss asked the little man who brought it.

"She is upset." The little man patted his stomach. "Lying down. She will be better soon, I think."

In the mirror Quarles saw Cogan merely pecking at his food. He passed his hand over his eyes rapidly once or twice, like a tired man, then returned to studying the papers from his briefcase.

They were in the middle of the sweet course when a sudden crash came from behind them. In the mirror Quarles saw Cogan with his head on the table. The sauce from his peach melba stained the cloth like blood.

Della Harris, looking white and ill, swayed down the aisle towards him, but Tamara was in front of her. She bent over him and looked up, distraught. "He is ill," she said. "He needs a doctor."

"Excuse me," Quarles said. He pushed past Della, down to where Cogan lay. He lifted the lax head, felt for the heart and the pulse, put a glass to the blue lips. "This man does not need a doctor," he said. "This man is dead."

IT seemed natural to everybody that Quarles should take charge, especially when Tamara screamed that Cogan had been poisoned. "Look at his lips," she said. "They are blue. And his face."

Certainly Cogan's face was uncommonly red and bloated.

"Had a fit," Foskiss said. "No need to make a mystery of it."

"Fits don't usually kill quite like that," Quarles said thoughtfully. "What did he have to eat?"

WELLS, the man who had served the meal, confirmed that Cogan had eaten very little. He had had a mouthful of soup, hardly more than a mouthful of chicken, and none of the sweet. The food had been the same that everybody else ate. "I prepared it myself and then I served it, too, when Della was taken sick."

"And nobody else touched it?"

"Nobody else touched it, sir." said Wells.

It seemed all right. But Quarles had developed over the years a sixth sense which told him that it was not all right. There was something else also, something significant that he was trying to remember.

"Mr. Cogan looked funny when I came to serve dinner," Wells said. "I don't think he was feeling well then."

And suddenly Quarles remembered. He remembered Cogan's exclamation of annoyance, and the angry look at his hand, just before the airplane took off. Now he looked himself at Cogan's hand and saw the tiny punctures on it. Then he inspected the new patent clip belt which Cogan, like the rest of them, had unfastened. Glued behind it he found what he was expecting, a tiny metal container. Quarles detached the container carefully from the belt and fumbled with the back of it. Two tiny needles, like a forked tongue, shot out.

"What's that?" asked Foskiss.

"Unless I am much mistaken, it is a kind of modern version of a poison ring. Murder by the Borgia method, you might call it. It tells us not only how Cogan was killed, but also who killed him."

"And the motive, I suppose?" said Della Harris, who stood now at the back of the little group.

"I don't know the motive, though I should guess it was jealousy, based on the fact that Cogan moved on rapidly from woman to woman. But in this case knowledge of motive is not necessary. Cogan was poisoned when he fastened his safety belt. You have to push the belt quite hard with your hand to fasten it. When Cogan pushed he ran his hand into these two needles, which injected poison—we shall have to wait to discover just what poison—into his veins. The needles are retractable, so that when they are pushed hard they discharge their poison and go back into the little case which had been fixed at the back of the belt. When Cogan looked to see what had run into his hand he found nothing."

"But how does that tell us the murderer's name?" Tamara asked.

"There was only one person who could possibly have used such a method. The person who knew that Cogan was coming on this flight, and so had time to fix this device who knew the seat he liked and kept other people out of it, who was conveniently taken sick so that she should have no connection with the serving of food—but who had recovered sufficiently to be on the spot to retrieve her little poison box, except that Miss Delaney was too quick for her."

Quarles waved a hand at the stewardess who stood, pale and defiant, watching him. "In fact, Miss Della Harris."

ART-LOVING MR. LISTER LANDS A FAKE ...

THE painting on the wall of the sitting room in the flat, a blend of blues and greens with the sun shimmering through the colours, showed a girl on a swing, her head thrown back, laughing.

Three men stood watching in silence while a fourth examined it. Then the fourth, little Mr. Delauney, said: "It's a fake. Quite a good fake. But it is not the Renoir."

"You hear that, Grott?" one of the other men said. He was an American named John Lister. "What have you got to say?"

Mr. Grott, the proprietor of Grott's Gallery, tall, thin and nervous, said: "The picture I sold you was a Renoir."

"Seems I've been cheated," Lister said. "I don't like that. You can take back your picture. I'm stopping the cheque."

Mr. Grott was pale with anger. "Do that and I shall sue you."

Lister pushed his face near to the art dealer's. He said softly: "If you think it's a Renoir, why should you worry? You know yourself it's a fake."

The fourth man in the room was private investigator Francis Quarles. "Gentlemen," he said, and there was authority in his voice, "let us bring a little logic into this. Mr. Lister is a steel manufacturer, here on vacation. He is making a collection of Impressionist paintings—"

"Just beginning to, you mean," the American said. "And if this is a sample of the treatment I'm going to get, I'll give up right now."

"Two days ago he came into your gallery, Mr. Grott, saw the Renoir picture, liked it, and arranged to buy it. I suppose you told him where it came from?"

"It's provenance was unimpeachable," Grott said stiffly. "I bought it six months ago from a descendant of the Duc de Malherbes."

"Very well. Still, Mr. Lister wanted to check on that unimpeachable provenance. He asked Mr. Delauney to look at the picture. Mr. Delauney said it was genuine. Right?"

Little Mr. Delauney nodded.

"That was on Tuesday morning. On Tuesday afternoon, Mr. Grott, you brought this picture personally to this flat, where Mr. Lister's staying in London. How did you bring it?"

"My secretary, Miss Handly, hired a car from the Speedfast Company. I have used them before occasionally."

"This was rather unusual, surely?"

"Yes. But Mr. Lister was returning to America within a few days, and he particularly wanted to have the picture to hang in his flat while he was here."

Quarles turned to the American. "You were here yourself when the picture arrived. What happened?"

"I don't know what you mean. Nothing happened. He brought it in, we unpacked it. I gave him a cheque. Then I hung it up over there."

"Did you look at the picture when it was unpacked?" Quarles asked Grott.

"Only for a moment. Miss Handly had arranged another appointment for me. And why should I look at it carefully? I'd seen it half an hour earlier."

Lister took up the story. "I was proud of having it, see? So on Tuesday evening I had some people in for drinks, really to show them the picture. One of them, fellow named Saunders, some sort of artist, said he thought it was a fake. And he was the one who introduced me to Delauney here, mind you. I felt like giving him a good punch on the nose. But he was so sure about it. I—well. I asked Delauney to come along today and take another look. He said it was a copy."

Quarles was looking speculatively at the picture. "It looks rather big to go inside a car."

"It was put in the boot," Grott said. "I've done it before."

"Are you prepared to swear that the picture you delivered was the Renoir from your Gallery?"

"Of course. It was never out of my sight." He glared at Lister. "My Renoir's been stolen. That's why I called you in."

The detective asked Delauney: "You think this picture is not the one you examined in the Grott Gallery?"

"I do not think, I know. I am the consulting Professor of Art at—" and he named a London college of art. "I will stake my reputation on it."

"It comes to this, then," Quarles said. "The copy was substituted for the Renoir at your gallery, Mr. Grott ..."

"Impossible. Delauney saw it on Tuesday morning. I was in the gallery myself from that time until I brought the picture here."

"Or at this flat, Mr. Lister."

"That won't wash," the American said. "Tuesday afternoon Grott brought the picture here, and I was in the flat alone until people came in the evening."

"Thank you, gentlemen." Quarles moved towards the door. They stared at him. "Aren't you going to do anything?" Grott asked.

"Certainly. I am going to think."

"Think!"

"Either you are lying, Mr. Grott, and I should be sorry to think that my client was lying to me. Or Mr. Lister is lying." Before the American could speak, he said: "Or there is a third explanation."

"I KNOW the answer," said Molly Player, Quarles's secretary, when he told her the story. "It's a Renoir all the time. Delauney's not really a professor, and Lister's not a business man. They're a couple of con men—"

"Won't do. I've checked on Delauney, he's tremendously respectable. And there are people who'll vouch for Lister."

"Oh. Well, then, Grott's working some sort of fiddle on Lister."

"Grott's respectable, too. There are shady art dealers, but he's not one of them."

"I don't see what has happened then."

Quarles told her. When he had finished he said: "This is what I want you to do."

THE girl Molly Player followed that evening was trim, pretty and self-assured. She took an Underground train from Bond Street to Charing Cross, looked around when she came out of the station and then got on a bus to Pimlico.

She walked down the basement steps of a street off Belgrave Road, opened the door and went in. There was a telephone box almost opposite and Molly rang up Francis Quarles.

Half an hour later he arrived in a car with a bewildered Mr. Grott. They went down the steps and Quarles rang the bell. The girl opened it.

"Why, Miss Handly," Grott said in surprise. "I thought you lived in Kensington."

The girl's face was white. She screamed as Quarles pushed past her. In the sitting room a young man sat eating dinner. On the wall opposite to him was the painting of a girl on a swing, a blend of blues and greens with the sun shimmering through the colours. The young man half got up, then sat down again as Mr. Grott followed Quarles in.

Grott saw the picture, went over to it, said: "My Renoir." Then he looked at the young man. "Why, it's the chauffeur from the car people."

"Not from the car people," Quarles said. "When you asked Miss Handly here to get a car she saw her chance and told her friend. They must have planned this quite a while ago. They had the copy of the Renoir all ready."

"It was her idea," the man said. "We were going to stage a robbery of the Gallery, but she thought it was clever to do it this way."

Mr. Grott was baffled. "I still don't see how it was done."

"One of the oldest tricks in the world is the one where you steal a briefcase by having a duplicate which you substitute as soon as your victim puts down the one he's carrying. I knew this was just a variation on it as soon as you said the picture was 'put in' the car boot. If you'd put it in yourself you'd have said so. The chauffeur put it in for you. He had the copy in the boot similarly packed, and he simply handed you that when you arrived. They're a pair of villains, but you must say one thing for them. They haven't hidden the beautiful thing they stole, but put it on the wall where they could look at it. At least they have a taste for art."

THE COLLECTOR

FRANCIS QUARLES stopped by the entrance drive and looked at the gate which bore the name Fair Haven in letters, once gilt, now almost eradicated by wind and weather. The gate, almost off its hinges, was in keeping with the weed-grown drive and the unkept hedges.

The house itself stood forty yards from its nearest neighbour in this small Kentish village of Mulhead. Its early Victorian grey stucco facade had once perhaps been attractive. Now the stucco had peeled, the front door was scratched and blistered, the windows were bleared with dirt. Obviously, the residence of an eccentric, and Quarles had gathered that Greville Armstrong was a truly eccentric man.

The day was mildly autumnal, the ground dry underfoot, though there was moisture in the air. Quarles walked up the six worn steps and pulled vigorously at a bell. No sound came from within the house, and he saw a card above the bell with the words in a spidery crawl: "*Out of order, please knock, tradesmen, hawkers and busybodies not wanted*. He lifted the discoloured lion's head on the door and knocked, three times. The sound thundered away into silence.

The detective knocked again. Somewhere above him a window went up with a scream, a voice commanded: "Show yourself."

He stepped out on to the drive and looked up. A thin man in collarless shirt stood staring down at him from a first floor window. His face was leathery, deep furrows running from nose to mouth. The heavy old rifle in his hand pointed casually downwards. The detective had an uncomfortable feeling that it might just as casually be fired.

He said quickly, "I'm Francis Quarles. You wrote a letter, asked me to come down from London. I'm a little early."

The man continued to stare down. He said, as though debating with himself. "You don't *look* like John Magruder."

"If I were Magruder how would I know about your letter?"

The rifle was slowly lifted.

"That's right, how would you." He continued to peer, then said suddenly, "Coming down."

Five minutes later the door was opened nine inches, but still kept on its chain. The thin face peered through the gap. "Have you got the letter you say I sent?"

"Why, yes. But——"

"Taking no chances. Give it me." A calloused work-worn hand and skinny forearm came through the gap.

Quarles passed over a letter in the spidery scrawl. It was a rambling screed which told him that Greville Armstrong's life was being threatened by his half-brother John Magruder, a devil incarnate who had sworn to kill him. It asked Quarles to come down and see him at three o'clock on a certain Thursday afternoon. "If you can catch this madman you can name your own fee," the letter ended.

ARMSTRONG was not on the telephone, as Quarles discovered when he tried to get further details. He found that the man had a reputation as a dilettante bibliographer and as an eccentric but wealthy collector of first editions. Then he caught a train to Mulhead. On the way down he read the morning papers and noted the tragic and ironic conclusion of another case on which he had been working. Abel Ferrar, the financier, had been killed with eleven other passengers in an air crash on a flight to Buenos Aires. Ferrar would have been arrested and held for extradition on fraud charges as soon as he reached the airport of Buenos Aires.

The letter was thrust back at Quarles. The chain rattled, the door opened. "Come in. Forgive my suspicions. It is many years since I have seen Magruder. He might have changed. I had to be sure."

They went down a dark narrow passage. The thin man flicked a light switch and exclaimed with annoyance when it did not work. He opened a chocolate-painted door on the right. Quarles found himself in a library, small and high. Books were stacked from door to ceiling, narrow passage-ways led through books piled six deep on the floor.

The collector, still collarless but wearing now a dressing-gown that was too large for him above his dirty trousers and muddy shoes, moved muttering among his treasures. From a cupboard he produced a bottle of whisky and poured drinks into two dirty glasses that stood among the books. Seen thus close he was painfully gaunt and thin, with cheeks on which the bones showed like knuckles in a clenched fist. Dark brown eyes of passionate intensity blazed in an anguished face.

"You think I'm mad, I expect." It was a statement rather than a question. "It's what they think in the village. No servants, they say, no radio, no telephone, no papers. Never comes out except to get his food, just lives there with ten thousand books—that passes for madness nowadays. Not so long ago it would have been called a wise man's life, a life of meditation. Do you know that I haven't left the house for three days?"

Quarles's eyes were almost closed "Are you sure that is not fear, rather than desire for meditation?"

"I'm not afraid. I take necessary precautions, that is all."

"Including chaining the door and threatening strangers with a rifle?"

"Magruder is a dangerous man. A devil, he's a devil. He was that even when we were boys together."

"Why should he want to kill you?"

"Because he's mad. He's a mad one if you like. Claims I cheated him out of his inheritance, burned father's will. All lies, I don't need to tell you, all damned lies. Can you prove it, John, I asked him, can you prove a word of what you're saying? If not you'd better keep quiet or I'll have you in prison. Gave him £500 in the end, and he went off to Australia. The money belonged to me, I tell you, it belonged to me."

Quarles said, "That must have been a long time ago."

"Twenty years or more. Heard of him occasionally, he never did any good out there. Farmed for some time, a bit of acting, odd jobs."

"And why should Magruder suddenly begin writing threatening letters—they were letters. I suppose?" A nod for answer. "Why should he do that after years of silence?"

"Some old woman—father's companion—met him out in Australia—told him ridiculous tales. Claimed she'd been bribed by me to keep her mouth shut about the will. It was wicked to tell such a story, don't you agree?"

"Very wicked. If it was not true."

"And if it were true? Does that give him a right to kill me?" The man's artificial composure collapsed, his face twitched with terror. "He's coming for me, I can tell you I can feel it. He's near the house. You've got to help me keep him away, catch him. Whatever I did we were young then and I didn't mean to harm him. I've used the money well." His arm waved at the books. "Don't let him kill me, Mr. Quarles, don't let him kill me."

He clung to Quarles's knees, actually weeping. It was a painful and humiliating scene.

FROM the back of the house they heard a crash. In the kitchen a window was broken, glass lay on the floor. A water jug was also in fragments.

"He's in the house," the thin man whispered. He shrieked and pointed to the kitchen door. "There."

Quarles wheeled in that direction and threw himself to one side, knocking up the other man's hand as he did so. A long thin knife clattered to the floor. "It's no good, Magruder," he said. "You may have had some justification for killing Greville Armstrong but you have none at all for trying to knife me."

The thin man was trembling uncontrollably. "I am not John Magruder."

"Oh yes you are. You came here, broke in through the kitchen window, killed Armstrong, and would have been away in half an hour's time. Armstrong's body, suitably concealed, might not have been found for weeks. When I arrived you were probably changing your clothes. You made the best of a bad job by tilting a water jug so that in a few minutes it would fall to the floor, and in the meantime trying to convince me that you were Armstrong.

"But I knew you weren't from the moment you put your hand through the door for that letter he wrote to me. Your hand is hard and calloused, the hand of a man who has done manual work for years—farming in Australia, as you said. Not the hand of a book collector.

"Then it was plain you didn't know much about the house from the way in which you used a switch that didn't work, and had to search for a drink."

The blaze had gone out of Magruder's eyes. They looked now like dull brown pebbles "All right. But it was true, that tale I told you—except that Armstrong would never have told it."

Quarles nodded pleasantly. "I daresay. Hardly sufficient reason in the eyes of the law for killing the man and burying him in his back garden."

Magruder gaped. "How do you know where I—"

"I didn't. I guessed it from the large quantity of mud on your shoes on a perfectly dry day."

GHOST FROM THE PAST

"SOMEBODY'S trying to kill my wife." Harold Morgan, a baldish man in his late forties, put his hands on his knees and looked earnestly at Francis Quarles across the detective's desk. The detective shifted his bulk more comfortably in a revolving chair.

"It's a ghost from the past." Quarles raised his thick eyebrows, and Morgan explained. Ten years ago he had married his secretary, Lavinia Baxter. She had broken her engagement to a young man named Christopher Rogerson, who had left Britain for New Zealand and from there had written to Lavinia several reproachful and abusive letters. The letters came for three years after the marriage. Then they stopped.

"They accused her of marrying me for my money." Morgan hesitated. "That may have been true—she's twelve years younger than I am, and Rogerson was her own age—but I put it to her fairly. I told Lavinia she could choose between poverty with Rogerson and a comfortable position as my wife. She chose with her eyes open."

"And after three years the letters stopped?"

"Until a few months ago. Since then we've had half a dozen, and we've kept them all."

QUARLES looked at the letters that Morgan gave him. They were all typewritten, and all posted in London. In vaguely Biblical and unmistakably threatening language they accused Lavinia Morgan of having broken her plighted troth and said that she should suffer for it. "Your life has been an abomination in the sight of the Lord ... He who suffers an evil-doer to remain upon this earth is evil also ... Pray to your Maker for forgiveness, for your days upon this earth are numbered." The letters were signed in a shaky hand, "Pug." Morgan explained that this had been Lavinia's name for Rogerson, a name known to the two of them alone.

"I checked on Rogerson through an enquiry agent," Morgan said. "He left New Zealand six years ago after his farm failed, went to Canada and up to Alaska. There were rumours that he died there."

Quarles tapped the letters. "These are vague. You spoke of actual attempts to kill your wife."

"There have been three. A month ago we went on a cliff walk near Eastbourne. She was a few yards behind me and a boulder dropped near her. Fortunately it was at a moment when she was screened by a jutting lip of rock. Two weeks later our chauffeur Meeker got Lavinia's car out because she wanted to do some shopping. She realised outside the gate that she'd forgotten her shopping list, so they turned back. Meeker ran slap into the house—simply couldn't stop. The brakes had been loosened so that they were useless. Fortunately he wasn't doing more than five miles an hour. The point is that there's a steep hill outside the house leading down to Debfield, where Lavinia goes to shop."

"Is the car kept locked in a garage?"

"Most of the time. But it's a double garage. I keep a Rover for my own use. Lavinia has a Singer—and when I leave for the office I usually leave the garage open."

"What about the chauffeur?"

"Meeker? He's been with me just over a year, chauffeur and general handyman. He'd hardly tamper with the brakes of the car he was driving himself.

"The last attempt was made two days ago. Lavinia received a box of chocolates through the post. She thought a friend had sent them as a surprise, and ate three or four. She was very ill. Half a dozen of the chocolates in the top layer had been filled with cocaine."

"Cocaine?" Quarles's eyebrows went up. "Why haven't you called in the police?"

"Lavinia has heard about you. She wanted me to come and see you. We're giving a birthday party tonight—my birthday. Will you be one of the guests?"

Quarles said: "If somebody really wants to kill your wife, Mr. Morgan, and is prepared to take enough chances, there's not much I or anyone else can do to stop it. Do you still want me to come?" Morgan nodded. "Then you had better get out your cheque book."

LAVINIA MORGAN was in bed when Quarles arrived. Her complexion was bad, and there were bags under her eyes. Quarles gathered an impression of a spoilt and petulant woman. He met also Bessie Martin, the pretty maid whose gaze followed Morgan with obvious adoration, the cook Ellie, a swarthy Italian manservant named Lorenzo, and the chauffeur and handyman, Meeker, who was washing down the Rover car with a hose.

"I reckon those brakes must have got themselves loose, though I don't know how I could have missed seeing it," Meeker said. He was a well-set-up and handsome young man, with something odd about his eyes. There was a bandage round the upper part of his right arm, and the chauffeur flushed a little as he saw Quarles's speculative stare. "Took the skin off it this morning getting too near to a blowlamp," he said.

The guests for the birthday party included neighbours, the local doctor, and some business friends of Morgan's. Nobody seemed very festive. Lavinia Morgan, white, listless and uneasy, complained of the heat. She sat in an angle seat by an open window gently waving a red silk scarf.

Morgan opened the French windows so that light streamed out on to the lawn. He seemed to sense the uneasiness of the guests, and to dispel it they played one party game after another. At last Morgan clapped his hands and said briskly, "Charades."

A young woman next to Quarles leaned over to him. "Harold's marvellous at impersonations. He does a perfectly killing one every year in some of Lavinia's clothes."

Morgan went outside with another man and a woman. Five minutes later they came back. The woman was wearing a shirt, slacks and a cummerbund, the other man an old morning coat and a top hat, and Morgan had put on a woman's dress, high heeled shoes and a curly wig, and was wearing a large picture hat. "Lavinia's new hat," whispered Quarles's companion.

Morgan swung round precariously on his high heels. He cast a long shadow out on to the lawn as he stood with his back to the French window.

Suddenly Lavinia Morgan stood up and screamed. The scarf dropped from her hand. At the same instant they heard a crack Morgan put his hand to his head, spun round and fell to the carpet.

Quarles dropped to his knees by the body and saw that the bullet had only grazed Morgan's head. He said to the doctor: "Stay with him. Don't let anyone else touch him." Then he asked Lavinia: "Which way did he go?"

She pointed to a dark clump of trees on the right. "Rogerson—over there."

"He was in the trees?"

"Yes, I saw him. Quick, for God's sake."

Quarles took a torch from his pocket and ran round to the left. His torch probed through blackness to find a shadowy figure running by the garage. The figure turned, and in the torchlight a knife flashed.

Quarles closed with the figure, caught the wrist holding the knife, and twisted. The knife dropped to the ground with a clatter. Torchlight shone on the face of the chauffeur Meeker. In the man's pocket was a pair of gloves, the smell of cordite still strong upon them. "The game's up, Meeker."

"All right. It was that she-devil drove me to it."

"INGENIOUS plot, clumsy execution," Quarles said afterwards to his friend Inspector Leeds. "Lavinia Morgan had fallen in love with her chauffeur. To get rid of her husband without suspicion falling on herself she thought of this ghost from the past who made attempts on her own life. First Meeker typed the anonymous letters on a friend's machine. Then the attempts were faked. He dropped the boulder, taking care that Lavinia was safely hidden. Then he tampered with the brakes—of course with no intention of going down the hill. Finally he provided the cocaine in the chocolates, and she ate just enough to make her ill. Nobody who really wanted to murder anybody with poisoned chocolates would use cocaine—the victim would have to eat too many. I was looking for a dope addict in the household, and when I saw the dilated pupils of Meeker's eyes and noticed the bandage put round his arm to hide the puncture marks of injections, I knew I'd found him. With the stage set and a detective called in, Morgan was supposed to be killed in mistake for her, by the mysterious Rogerson, who would then of course have vanished for ever. She knew her husband would do the charade wearing a few of her clothes—it was a regular yearly feature. Her scream and the dropped scarf was a signal to Meeker, but fortunately he lost his nerve and shot a few inches to the right. Then she tried to send me the wrong way by saying that she'd seen Rogerson—as though she could have seen anything in a clump of trees on a dark night. I knew if she told me to go right Meeker must have gone round to the left and when I caught him he told the whole story.

"She was really the moving spirit—he was only the tool, and a poor tool at that."

THE SWEDISH NIGHTINGALE

GRAVEL on the drive crunched under Francis Quarles's feet. He looked up admiringly at the perfectly symmetrical Regency front of Mallaby House, and so did not notice the disconsolate figure in the white frock who came round from the garden at the back until she spoke. "Hullo. You're Francis Quarles, aren't you?"

"That's right." He looked down on a small heart-shaped face. A hand hardly bigger than a child's rested in his. "And you're Mr. Fisher's ward, Susan Shelby, who telephoned when I was in the middle of lunch." She blushed. "You sounded awfully urgent."

"So did Uncle Cyrus, but I don't know what it's all about."

"How is he? It's years since I saw him."

"Rather crotchety, but very well really for his age." She hesitated and then said vehemently, "It's the others I can't stand his beastly relations."

"I met his brother Oscar once, and was not favourably impressed. But you speak with passion."

"They're all out now, thank goodness: went to the races at Market Standing this morning." She shuddered. "Oscar's like a vulture, but I think the niece and nephew, Mary and William, are the worst. They're just waiting for Cyrus to die: they show it in the way they look at him. Not that I think they'll be lucky. Doctor Smolett's just left and he says Cyrus is remarkably fit."

"And they make your life unpleasant, too, I expect."

"They treat me as if I were after Uncle Cyrus's money like themselves, just because I live here and keep house for him. But I'm not. I can't help it if Cyrus told my father he'd look after me, can I? The way they act and talk when they come down at week-ends—" She rubbed her eyes like a child.

Quarles patted her shoulder. He was a big man, and it was a hot day. He felt himself beginning to sweat.

"But I shouldn't keep you standing out here. Uncle Cyrus wants to see you in his study. That's an honour—I'm never allowed in there though the doctor's been in today."

CYRUS FISHER had inherited from his father a flourishing tea merchant's business in Assam. He had spent thirty years of his own life in India, during which the business had expanded enormously. Then he had retired into the country to live on his considerable fortune, and indulge a passion for playing with mechanical toys and contrivances.

He had been doing this now for some twenty-five years and must, Quarles reckoned, be at least eighty years old. Quarles had met him some years back in connection with a complicated fraud that was being carried out on his firm. He had gathered the impression then of a highly puritanical autocrat, benevolent when he was obeyed, but a savage and self-righteous enemy.

Susan Shelby led him down a passage, knocked at a door and said, "Here is Mr. Quarles, Uncle Cyrus," and left him. Quarles went into the room, which central heating and a gas fire made overpoweringly hot. Condensation obscured the French windows to the garden. Cyrus Fisher, his blood thinned by years of life in India, found the hottest days of English summer uncommonly cool.

"Ah Quarles, delighted to see you." Cyrus Fisher was a small man with a lean yellow malarial face, and a booming voice. "You're just in time. See that bust up there."

He pointed up to a marble head of a woman on top of a bookcase. "Know who it is? Jenny Lind, the Swedish Nightingale. Listen to this." He pressed a small switch on the table in front of him and a voice was raised in a distorted fragment of song.

"It really sounds as if it comes from up there." Quarles said.

Cyrus chuckled. "It does. Had a little bit of the head hollowed out and the mechanism put inside. Like it? And look at the tortoise over there—see him moving along. Know what makes him work? Connected to the electric clock; moves across the table there as the clock goes round. Rigged that up after lunch. Like it?"

"Most ingenious," Quarles said politely, and wiped his forehead. The room was full of gadgets. Cyrus showed him animals operated by various mechanisms, a rhinoceros that lowered his head and charged, an elephant that picked up a tin bun, a cat that said "Miaow," washed itself and curled up in a basket. Cyrus limped round among his treasures with a stick, and explained that he now suffered badly from arthritis.

After twenty minutes among the gadgets Quarles said, "Your ward rang up at lunchtime, asked me to come down urgently."

"So she did." Cyrus Fisher looked at him from under thick grey eyebrows. "False alarm. A certain party had—um—threatened me over a certain little matter, but it's settled now. Man in my position, squire of the village and all that, has to be a kind of custodian of local morality, y'know."

His tone was unctuously self-satisfied. He was really, Quarles thought, a rather odious little man. "Don't go, stay to dinner. We don't dress. Meet my precious family, they'll interest you. They all hate Susan, but Susan's a good girl, never had any trouble with her."

When he had left Cyrus. Quarles asked Susan Shelby whether there had been any telephone calls since lunch. None, she said—and Uncle Cyrus hated talking on the telephone, always asked her to speak for him, so she would have known. And no letters? No, the afternoon post had brought only a circular.

He asked Susan another question which surprised her a good deal, but which she answered. He thanked her thoughtfully, and stayed to dinner.

DINNER was not a pleasant meal. Before it he met William the nephew, a podgy and sulky looking man of forty, who was something dubious in the City, hatchet-faced and acid-voiced Mary and her meek husband Philip Mayhew, and Oscar who was like a bald version of Cyrus, with a great wart-like mole in the middle of his forehead. The party was made up by plump and rubicund Doctor Smolett, who attempted unsuccessfully to pour oil on the troubled waters.

"Shouldn't eat roast beef at your age, Uncle Cyrus," Mary snapped "I'm surprised at Susan serving it to you."

"Your solicitude does you credit my dear Mary," Oscar said. The great purplish mole stood out on his forehead. "No doubt you have prepared a weekly diet sheet for Cyrus."

"He could do worse than follow one." Mary turned to the doctor. "Isn't that so?"

Caught between the open malevolence of Mary's gaze and the more subterranean balefulness of Oscar, the doctor coughed and mumbled. "A good digestion ... a little roast beef ... remarkable for his age ... no harm in it ..."

CYRUS, who had remained alone in his study until dinner time, calmly cut up and ate his meat with apparent enjoyment. After dinner he drank brandy, which was the signal for more upbraidings from Mary, in which William joined. Susan looked at them scornfully. Cyrus placidly drank the brandy, and then went back to his room.

He had been gone some half hour, and Quarles was thinking that it was time for him to leave when there was a loud crash.

"Uncle Cyrus," cried Susan. As they ran along the corridor Smolett appeared from the washroom ahead of them. Mary and her husband came out of their bedroom. Oscar and William came in from the garden. When Quarles reached the study the doctor was bending over Cyrus's body just by the window. Near the door lay the marble bust of Jenny Lind in fragments. The fall of this bust had obviously caused the crash.

"He's dead," the doctor said. His rubicund face was pale for once. "He's had a blow on the back of the head."

The rest of the family were standing in the doorway. "And he named his murderer," Mary said dramatically. She pointed to the condensation on the window. Written there, as a child writes on a steamy bathroom mirror, was the word MOLE. It was enclosed in a crudely drawn and uneven circle which was thicker on the right side than the left.

There was a babel of accusation and denial. Oscar's face was ashen. Quarles, ignoring the noise, was on his knees examining the broken bust and the tiny mechanism inside it. He looked cursorily at the body, then moved over the carpet on hands and knees until he came to the mechanical tortoise, to which a length of thin rope was now attached.

They were suddenly quiet, watching him a little fearfully as he measured the rope in relation to the bookcase where the bust had been standing.

"How long has he been dead?" he asked the doctor.

Smolett shook his head doubtfully. "Wouldn't like to say exactly. A few minutes certainly, but less than half an hour."

"All right. This is what happened. The murderer came in here after dinner, struck Cyrus, on the head with some heavy object, possibly *this*"— Quarles touched a black ebony ruler on the desk in front of him—"and then set the scene for an accident.

"He tied a piece of rope round the base of that marble bust of Jenny Lind and tied the other end round the mechanical tortoise which Cyrus had set to inch forward with the movement of an electric clock. The tortoise would slowly pull the bust off the bookcase, the bust would fall on Cyrus's head and crush his skull completely, and the whole thing would have the appearance of an accident. The murderer intended to make sure of being first in the room to remove the only piece of evidence, the rope which would still be attached to the tortoise. But things went wrong. Cyrus wasn't quite dead. He was just able to move from the point at which he had been placed, crawl over to the window and write something there. So he wasn't beneath the bust when it fell. And the murderer didn't remove the rope. He had something else to do."

THERE was a taut and terrible silence in the hot room. "Now, who was the murderer? All of you were away long enough after dinner to kill the old man, all of you had a motive. But one of you had a special motive. Cyrus telephoned through Miss Shelby at lunchtime, and asked me to come down here. When I arrived he told me that the matter was settled. During that time he had received no telephone calls or letters, and had spoken to only one person."

The doctor coughed. "I visited Cyrus professionally after lunch."

"Precisely. You were the person. Cyrus mentioned mysteriously that he had to be a custodian of morality down here, and when I asked Susan if any scandal was linked with your name, she told me that it had been joined in a very unprofessional way with that of a married woman. Cyrus must have ordered you to give up the relationship, and you agreed. Or rather you pretended to agree."

The doctor's face was white, but he said. "That's not evidence."

"Evidence, yes. You were the only person besides myself who knew about the tortoise—Cyrus told me he had fixed it up since lunch. And you took care to be the first person in the room."

"But he didn't take the rope off the tortoise," Susan cried. "And what about Cyrus writing MOLE?"

"I told you the murderer had something else to do. Cyrus didn't write MOLE—why should he, when he could have written OSCAR? And he certainly didn't enclose what he wrote inside that crude circle. He wrote his murderer's name, SMOLETT, and that was what Smolett saw on the window when he came in.

"His mind worked quickly, and he saw that he could make the word point to somebody else if he rubbed out the S and two Ts. Then he drew the circle round to conceal what he had done, thicker on one side than the other because he had two letters to rub out after MOLE and only one before it. But he hadn't time to take away the rope as well. He was quite clever with that rope trick, just clever enough to hang himself."

THE BARTON HALL DWARF

AN elderly man with a thick grey beard, rather shabbily dressed, met Francis Quarles at Barton Halt, and drove him five miles through narrow Essex lanes to Barton Hall.

The man evidently sensed Quarles's surprise at being driven in a van with covered back and sides rather than in a car, and commented on it.

"You'll be wondering about the van, sir. Mr. Ryder's instructions. Never use the car except for himself or Miss Julia. It's a Daimler, sir. Wouldn't be at all economical, Mr. Ryder says. We use this little van for everything from selling kitchen garden produce to taking the cook to Marltree on her half day."

The man's voice was educated, and his tone ironical. Quarles learned that his name was Franklin, and that he had been employed at Barton Hall for the last six months, as handyman around the place. He learned also that Quentin Ryder, at whose request he had come down, was an eccentric woollen manufacturer, a hypochondriac who had retired to the country in search of rest and quiet for his nerves.

They turned in through great rusting iron gates and drove the best part of a mile along a winding weed-grown carriageway.

Barton Hall, as Quarles saw it in the fading light of a winter afternoon, was a large, decaying Georgian house, which might have been used to maintain a thesis that not all old houses are beautiful. Inside there was a square hall, a reasonably elegant staircase, and a very odd smell. A large, pale-faced woman dressed in grey sacking hobbled across the hall, with the aid of a stick, to meet him.

"I am Julia Ryder. And you are Mr. Walls."

"Quarles."

She went on as though he had not spoken. "My brother will be pleased to see you. He is disturbed about the dwarf, although I have told him that such manifestations are part of the spiritual aura of the place." Miss Ryder gave him a sudden, surprisingly shrewd glance. "I see you're sniffing. It's dry rot. And damp, of course. The whole place is falling down. That was why Quentin got it so cheap—that and the forgers."

"The forgers?"

"Seven years ago this place was occupied by a gang of forgers. Their plant was never found, but the men themselves were caught and imprisoned. It is all part of the aura. The dwarf, of course, was little Sir George Hammersley, no more than three feet tall, who hanged himself with his braces in 1787 for love of the beautiful Lady Ann Pitt."

An old man in rusty black tottered across the hall. "Williams, tell Mr. Ryder that Mr. Wales is here."

The old man turned and began very slowly to climb the stairs. Miss Ryder gave Quarles a vague but charming smile. "I must go and cultivate my garden. A herb garden, you know."

QUENTIN RYDER had a long, thin face in which the creases were so deep that they might have been marked with an iron. His arms were white and hairless.

He sat up in a great four-poster bed, propped by pillows, in a large room with painted panels in the walls showing various scenes from the Odyssey. Quarles noticed Penelope and the suitors, Circe, and the great one-eyed Cyclops with Odysseus in his cave. On the table by Ryder's side stood more than a dozen half-empty medicine bottles and jars of ointment. The man in bed spoke in a harsh, rasping voice.

"You're supposed to be clever. I want you to find out who's trying to kill me, and why. First they drug me, then they send this dwarf. I tell you, Quarles, if I can't clear this up I shall have to leave the place. My nerves won't stand it."

"Tell me about it." Quarles settled himself in an armchair which creaked under his weight. "How long have you been here?"

"Four years, I came for peace and quiet—and rest. I don't get up more than half an hour a day, the rest of the time I keep to my room. Do you know what the local doctor had the insolence to say to me when I called him in last? Said that exercise would shake up my liver. I told him that he had evidently no idea of what real nervous prostration meant. What's the time?"

Quarles looked at his watch. "Just after four o'clock."

Ryder uncorked a bottle of sickly green medicine and took a swig from it. "You've met my sister Julia, I expect. She lives with me here. Crazy but harmless—keen on table rapping, voices in the air, all that sort of stuff. But she doesn't disturb me. I must say that it was peaceful here until things began to happen, a few weeks ago."

"What sort of things?"

"Two pictures fell down. A mirror dropped and broke. That upset

Julia, you can imagine. Then I found a lot of sand in my lunch one day when Williams brought it up here. The old man's blind as a bat, swore he had nothing to do with it. But then, who had? The cook swore it was all right when she served it out in the kitchen.

"And a week ago I was drugged. The stuff must have been put in the glass of hot milk I take at night. Tried to find out who could have done it, but it might have been anyone—old Williams, Mrs. Wilson the cook, Rose, the girl who comes in to do scrubbing, or that odd job man Franklin. Or Julia. She brought it up to me."

"What makes you think you were drugged?"

"I slept until ten o'clock the next morning, and I always wake at seven. And somebody had tried to get into the room that night. There were scratches round the lock."

Quarles looked, and saw the slight scorings on the outside of door. "What about the dwarf?"

Quentin Ryder shuddered. He seemed genuinely frightened. "The night before last I went along the passage to the bathroom, as I always do. Then I saw it coming at me, a little hunchbacked man with such a look on his face as I have never seen. I ran back to my room, locked the door and rang the bell for help. Franklin and Williams came up almost together."

"Did either of them see the dwarf?"

"No. But I didn't imagine it." Ryder thumped his thin hand on the bedside table, shaking the bottles. "It leered as it came at me, so close I could almost have touched it. It was the most evil thing I have ever seen."

Quarles picked up the magnifying glass that lay among the medicine bottles "You use this for reading?"

Ryder's voice rose to a shout. "I'm short-sighted, yes. But I'm not imagining things. *There was a dwarf in that passage.*"

THE passage that led from Quentin Ryder's bedroom to the bathroom was dark, and was feebly illuminated by the glow of a 15-watt blue night lamp. The bathroom was on the half landing below Ryder's room.

Quarles thoughtfully considered the blank wall at the end of the passage, and the narrow ledge for ornaments at the top of it. He went down the two steps into the bathroom, and was trying the handle of a door next to it when Julia's voice made him start a little.

"That old cupboard is never used, really nothing is kept there but odds and ends. I am afraid you will find it extremely dusty. I have no time—" Her voice faded away.

Quarles opened the cupboard door and shone his pocket torch inside. There were some old chairs and pictures, and there was dust. But the dust was not undisturbed. Quarles pointed out a deep narrow ridge where something had stood, and beside it the marks of feet.

Julia Ryder giggled. "The footprints of the dwarf."

"Perhaps." Quarles closed the door. "Is there a fun fair at Marltree?"

"You think the dwarf might have come from there? How clever. But I really could not tell you. Shall I ask Rose? She is a young girl, and frivolous."

"Don't do that. I will borrow your van and find out for myself."

Quarles visited the public library, as well as the fun fair, at Marltree. When he came back he went in again to see Quentin Ryder. As a result of what he said a protesting Ryder moved into the spare bedroom that evening. The whole household was kept in turmoil by the job of settling the invalid and his full cargo of medicines into the new room.

IT was one o'clock in the morning when Quarles, concealed by the curtains of a hanging cupboard in Ryder's now disused bedroom, heard the click of the door opening.

A pencil of light played over the room and settled on one of the panels, a dark figure moved over to it. The panel was that showing Odysseus and the Cyclops, and the light picked out the Cyclops's one staring eye. The eye was obliterated by a finger, the panel swung inwards. It was at this point that Quarles spoke.

"It's no good, you know. You're never going to get that plant back." There was a gasp. The pencil of light moved about the room, found the hanging cupboard. "Don't try any tricks. They'd be of no use to you now. I'll give you half an hour to get away, before I tell Ryder."

A voice said, "Thanks. You're a sport. But I wish you hadn't come down. I'd lay a dud fiver to a bob that the dwarf would have scared him off."

QUARLES smoked three cigarettes, mussed up his hair and collar, and went along to the spare bedroom, where Quentin and Julia Ryder were waiting for him.

"Well?" said Quentin. "Did you catch him? Was it Franklin, as you said?"

"It was Franklin all right. We had a fight, but he got away. However, you won't be troubled by him again. His real name was Robert Morrow, and he was head of that gang of forgers Miss Ryder told me about. I got the details of the case this afternoon in the Marltree public library. When Morrow came out of prison a few months ago he decided to try to get hold of his old plant—you remember the police didn't find it. It was hidden behind the Cyclops panel in your bedroom, but he couldn't get at it because you were always in the room. He drugged you and tried to get in to look at the plant, but couldn't manage to pick the lock, and then, he tried to frighten you away. I must say he did it in a rather gentlemanly way."

"The the dwarf was not a spiritual manifestation," said Julia Ryder.

"I'm afraid not. Franklin or Morrow managed to borrow one of those distorting mirrors they have in fun fairs from Marltree, brought it back in the van, and hung it from the ornament ledge at the end of the passage. He went and stood in that cupboard by the bathroom, and waited. After Mr. Ryder had seen the dwarf and run back into his room, Franklin took the mirror down again, put it in the cupboard, and returned it to the fun fair next day."

Julia Ryder began to laugh. Quarles coughed, and looked down at the floor. "The light was poor, and Mr. Ryder's sight is not good, and it was a distorting mirror."

Quentin Ryder was red and furious as a gobbling turkey. His sister was almost helpless with laughter. "The most evil thing I have ever seen," she said. "Oh, Quentin. You saw yourself."

THE PEPOLI CASE

"WE are going this evening to see the Pepolis," Agatha Wilding said to her week-end guest Francis Quarles. "You remember them?"

"Of course." Clarissa Pepoli was a nervously beautiful woman in her late thirties, who had married a man of English birth but Italian descent named Robert Pepoli. Agatha Wilding, who was a short-sighted spinster in her seventies with a kind heart hidden by a formidable manner, made no secret of her dislike of the man. Yet nothing very definite was known against him. He had dabbled in half a dozen dubious financial enterprises, been a second-rate actor, and written two unsuccessful plays. He had been vaguely mixed up in a currency scandal.

It was a perpetual annoyance to Agatha Wilding that Clarissa seemed to be perfectly happy with him. "How are they getting on?" Quarles asked.

"Very badly from what I can see." Wrinkling her nose, Agatha Wilding said: "His cousin's come to live with them."

Quarles raised his eyebrows in surprise. Whatever one might think about Robert Pepoli, there was no doubt about his young cousin Edward being what Agatha Wilding called a bad lot. At the age of thirty he had served two prison sentences, both for smuggling drugs. "Has he been staying long?"

"Three months. And it's three months too long, if you ask me. I don't like Robert, but now that this snake in the grass has come—well you'll see."

THAT evening Quarles did see. Robert was away in London, and at dinner Edward acted as host and treated Clarissa as though she were his personal property.

Edward Pepoli was a younger, smaller, rather coarser, version of his cousin, and Quarles guessed that it amused him to show his power over Clarissa in Agatha Wilding's presence. "Give me a light, Clare," Edward said after dinner and placed his hand on her bare arm while he lighted his cigarette from hers.

Agatha Wilding raised her lorgnette and asked abruptly: "What are your plans for the future. Mr. Pepoli?"

Edward Pepoli smiled lazily. "I think I'll stay here until Clarissa turns me out."

"And what will Robert have to say to that?"

Robert, who came in while they were drinking a liqueur, had nothing to say to it. He greeted his wife but did not kiss her and almost ignored his cousin. His face was pale, he seemed unsure of himself, and Quarles noticed that he had developed a nervous trick of pulling at his upper lip.

After a little desultory conversation, Robert said: "I've got a headache. I'm going to bed Good-night." On Edward Pepoli's face, when Robert left the room, there moved what could only be called a smile of triumph.

"I HAVE known them for five years," Agatha Wilding said the next day. "I feel it my duty to do something."

On the following morning she mysteriously disappeared, and returned obviously pleased with herself. "I think that's settled master Edward's hash. Clarissa and Robert are going off on a three weeks' cruise. Edward is leaving when they go, and he will not return."

The old lady coughed. "I'm going with them—at Clarissa's request. She said I was such a successful diplomat."

A FEW weeks later when the *Southern Queen* docked at Southampton Quarles heard Agatha Wilding's story. He had read the headlines that said *Actor Playwright's Death at Sea*.

"It was on the eighth night out," she said. "They had seemed so happy. Robert and Clarissa. It was a cold night, but fine, and I went for a walk on the promenade deck about half-past ten as I had done each evening before going to bed. The deck was deserted and then suddenly I saw two struggling figures near the end of it, about thirty yards from me. I couldn't recognise them—you know I can't see much without these things." She tapped her lorgnette. "I could see the figures, though, and I ran towards them While I was still several yards away one of the figures lifted the other above his head and flung him down over the rail."

"You're sure of that?" Quarles repeated her last words.

"Yes of course. What's odd about it?"

"Go on."

"I heard the body strike the water. I saw the figure who had thrown it run into the darkness of a passage. Then I screamed."

"LET me tell you the rest, as I've gathered it from the reports" said Quarles. "The ship's officers could find no sign of a struggle, and they were inclined to dismiss what you'd seen as a trick of light. The ship circled, but could find nothing. It wasn't until a couple of hours later that it was discovered that Robert Pepoli was missing.

"What you had seen was presumably Robert and his murderer. Who was it? Clarissa had a perfect alibi. She had not moved from the bridge table for two hours. You decided that the murderer must be Edward Pepoli and that he was on board. You and Clarissa saw all the passengers and satisfied yourselves that Edward Pepoli was not among them. Right?"

She nodded.

"And you still think that Edward somehow murdered Robert?"

"I'm sure of it. If he's not the murderer, where has he got to? He vanished on the day the boat sailed and hasn't been seen since." The lorgnette tapped insistently on Quarles's arm. "Find him for me."

QUARLES went down to Southampton. He saw the place on the promenade deck where Agatha Wilding had seen the struggle, and also inspected the Pepolis's cabin.

"Did you have any seasick passengers on this trip, who kept to their cabins?" he asked.

Inquiries showed that there had been two—Miss Marilyn Hunter who was in her late seventies, and a middle-aged man from Brighton named Richard Paget.

Quarles looked at Mr. Paget's cabin, and noticed some fresh and deep, scratches round the porthole, for which the steward had no explanation. He made a note of the Brighton address Paget had given, and within a short time a street directory, backed by a telephone call to the Brighton municipal authorities told him that no such address existed.

QUARLES then paid a call on his friend, the theatrical costumier Theodore Holtz.

Holtz scratched his bald head at Quarles's inquiry, and gave him a list containing some thirty names. Quarles set out to call on all of them.

At the twelfth visit he found what he wanted. Then he went to see Inspector Leeds at Scotland Yard.

Four days later Clarissa Pepoli paid a visit to London. She did a little shopping at two or three places in Oxford Street, stopped for a moment to look at a street vendor's nylons, and then turned down one of the streets that lead to Wigmore Street.

Here she came to a man who stood selling matches, with head bent and a placard round his neck. She took a box of matches and dropped something into his box. The man touched his shabby hat and then his fingers moved automatically to his big, drooping moustache.

A police car pulled up. Quarles and two plain-clothes policemen jumped out. The man turned to run, but one of the policemen tackled him and brought him down.

The man began to cry: "She made me do it; I never meant to do it, she made me." Quarles pulled at the moustache. It came away to show the face of Robert Pepoli.

"IT was simple enough," Quarles said to Agatha Wilding. "Robert and Clarissa loved each other, but had no money. They had, however, an insurance policy on Robert's life for thirty thousand pounds and they proposed to realise it by his apparent death. In a few months they would have joined up together abroad. They used Edward as an unconscious accomplice, and you, too, I'm afraid. Clarissa persuaded Edward that she was in love with him and planned with him to get rid of Robert on the cruise. Edward booked a cabin in the name of Paget, and stayed in it out of sight. Clarissa was to doctor Robert's drink one night. They would then push him through the porthole, and Clarissa would swear that he had fallen overboard.

"That was the plan as Edward knew it. In fact, it worked the other way. Clarissa went to Edward's cabin and doped his drink. Robert came along and they pushed him out of the port-hole, scratching the paintwork in doing so. Then Robert put on that comedy of a struggle on deck to show himself being murdered. The point of it was to make sure there was no possible suggestion of suicide—in which case, of course, the insurance claim would be void."

"But I distinctly saw *two* people."

"You saw Robert holding a theatrical dummy with weights on, which he threw into the sea. He'd been over-confident enough to have the dummy made at a theatrical costumiers, and I traced it. Then he became Richard Paget for the rest of the journey—easy enough when Edward had stayed in bed all the time, and they resembled each other anyway. With a bit of make-up he had no difficulty in deceiving you when you came round with Clarissa. Once we realised what had happened it was just a matter of following Clarissa around until she got in touch with him. She slipped a note in his box arranging a meeting in a fortnight's time, but that little nervous trick of pulling at his lip gave him away. Then he collapsed completely and admitted everything."

"I don't understand what made you think of the trick in the first place."

"*You* did, when you told me how the man you saw had lifted the other figure *above his head*, before he threw it in the sea.

"To lift a man who's struggling with you over your head is difficult enough for a professional wrestler, impossible for an ordinary man. And certainly nobody would do it when struggling to push somebody else over a rail. And then it occurred to me that what had gone overboard might not be a man but a dummy."

NOTHING UP HIS SLEEVE

MICHAEL FRANKLIN, well known as the worst-tempered character actor of screen and stage, smiled sourly at his audience and took a sip of water.

"If there's one thing I dislike more than another it's making speeches," he said. His audience laughed appreciatively. "And if there's one part of England I detest it's this village of Dembry where I had the misfortune to spend my childhood, and where I'm sorry to see as I look round me that a lot of the people I most abominate are still living."

He blew his nose. This time there was less laughter. Of course Michael Franklin had a reputation as almost a professional insulter, but this was a bit strong. Franklin's young secretary, Desmond Carr, looked round uneasily. Above him on the stand the great man rocked backwards and forwards, leering at the matrons and retired civil servants of Dembry who had gathered round to listen to him.

Colonel Hawkley, Chief Constable of the county, who owned the field in which this charity bazaar was being held, murmured to private detective Francis Quarles "Do you know, I believe the man's been drinking." But now Franklin's grating voice was heard again.

"And if there's one kind of function that seems to me more a waste of time than another it's this sort of so-called charity bazaar where people go round looking for things to pick up cheap, and try to pretend they're doing good to other people. The sooner it's over the better, and then we can all go home. I therefore have much pleasure in declaring this bazaar open."

THIS time there was no laughter at all. Mrs. Meaker, president of the Women's Institute, said a few vague words about how happy they were to welcome Mr. Franklin. There was a little clapping. Then, slowly and carefully, Michael Franklin got down from the stand, blew his nose with a loud honking sound, and stared about him.

Desmond Carr hurried up to Franklin and said something to him, and Franklin began to make the round of the stalls with Mrs. Meaker, while Carr hovered anxiously in the background. Quarles and

Colonel Hawkley were drinking orange squash, and Franklin stopped by them.

"My old friend the Colonel," he said. "Still chasing poachers off your land, eh? Chased me off once, remember? Funny thing is he's so bad a shot he couldn't hit a battleship at ten yards. Is that why they put you on the retired list, eh, Colonel?" The thickness in Franklin's voice was very noticeable. The Colonel turned puce.

The woman at the stall offered Franklin some orange squash. He drank it and shuddered. "Filthy stuff, not that I can taste it. And who's this at the stall?"

The woman simpered. She was about forty, and rather plain. "Miss Parkes. You remember me, don't you, Mr. Franklin?"

"Remember you? I'd know that moustache anywhere." He turned to Carr. "The ugliest girl in Dembry, and she's turned into the ugliest woman, isn't that bad luck?" He moved on slowly, stumbling as he did so. Mrs. Meaker went with him.

QUARLES looked after them thoughtfully. "You know, I can't help thinking it was a mistake to ask him to open the bazaar. Whose idea was it?"

The Colonel muttered. "Think Mrs. Meaker suggested it, but we run these things through a committee and everyone approved. Couldn't tell he'd come down in that state. What's up now?"

There was a clamour of voices from a few yards further on. Quarles and Colonel Hawkley found that Franklin had suddenly collapsed. His face was flushed and his breathing heavy. Doctor Lacey, a well-known pathologist who lived in Dembry, was bending over him. Carr was standing anxiously by.

Lacey's face was puzzled. "Clear a way there, we must get him to a tent. I want to have a closer look at him."

HALF-AN-HOUR later Michael Franklin died without emerging from the coma into which he had sunk after his collapse. A grim-faced Doctor Lacey talked to a small group which included Quarles, Mrs. Meaker, Colonel Hawkley, some of the other committee members, Carr, and the local police Sergeant Wilcox.

"This man has been poisoned. There is a smell of oil of bitter almonds about his nose and mouth, and I have noticed it also round his left sleeve."

"Prussic acid," said Colonel Hawkley knowingly, but Lacey shook his head.

"No. The action of prussic acid is much quicker than seems to have been the case here. It's impossible to be sure without further examination, but the symptoms of apparent drunkenness and unsteadiness in walking are consistent with nitro-benzene poisoning. Nitro-benzene has exactly the smell of prussic acid."

"How quickly does it act?" Quarles asked.

"Hard to say." Lacey stroked his chin. "Anything from a quarter of an hour to three hours if it has been drunk. Longer than that if it has been inhaled. But that isn't likely, because, of course, the smell is very noticeable."

"Somebody gave it to the chap in his drink," said Colonel Hawkley. "Can't say I blame 'em much. He hadn't got many friends here."

Mrs. Meaker screamed and put her hand to her mouth. "That glass of orange squash. Do you remember he said it was filthy stuff?"

Quarles walked over to where the body lay, covered by a sheet. All of Franklin's clothes had been laid out on a table beside him, and the contents of his pockets—watch, money, papers, keys, wallet—had been put by the clothes. Quarles sniffed at the left sleeve of Franklin's jacket and looked again, this time more carefully, at the clothes and other things. Then he had a word with Sergeant Wilcox. "Are you sure that you put everything he had with him on that table?"

The sergeant looked surprised. "Of course, Mr. Quarles."

"I didn't see—" Quarles said, and he named something.

The sergeant looked more surprised. "That's right, sir. He hadn't got one on him."

"But he had, Sergeant. I saw it. Come on." Quarles left the tent and the sergeant followed him. They retraced the path Franklin had taken, from the stand to the soft drinks stall, without result. "Someone picked it up," the sergeant suggested.

"I don't think so. Well, let's try the most likely place. Which was Franklin's car, Sergeant?"

"The Wolseley over there. I've got the keys. But we've had a look inside it already."

"Yes, but then you didn't know anything was missing. Now that we're looking for something, I think we shall find it."

They found the missing article underneath the back seat cushions, wrapped in paper.

WHEN they got back to the tent Quarles took Lacey and Colonel Hawkley aside, and talked to them for a minute or two. The Colonel said,

"Mr. Quarles has made an important discovery. I'll leave him to tell you about it."

Quarles stepped forward. "It is an important discovery, although it doesn't tell us everything. It doesn't tell us the motive, for instance. Franklin wasn't much loved here or anywhere else, and the murderer was one of many people who hated him. It doesn't tell us, either, how the murderer got hold of nitro-benzene, though it isn't difficult for anyone with some chemical knowledge to produce it."

"Your discovery doesn't seen to tell us much," Carr said.

"It tells us the murderer's name." There was silence. "It has been suggested that the nitro-benzene was given to Franklin in a drink, such as the orange squash. But that was very improbable. How could the murderer be sure that Franklin would drink it, or wouldn't notice the smell?"

"Why didn't he notice the smell anyway, however it was given him?" asked Mrs. Meaker.

"Because he had a cold. Don't you remember that he kept blowing his nose? And when he drank the orange squash he said he couldn't taste it. Now this was a premeditated crime. The murderer was somebody who knew that Franklin's sense of taste and smell was deficient on this particular day. And that lets out everybody at Dembry, because they couldn't possibly have known that in advance. In fact, there is only one person here who could have known it in advance—the man who travelled down with Franklin from London. His secretary, Desmond Carr."

Carr said with a sneer: "And I suppose you know how I did it."

"Certainly. You damped the handkerchief Franklin was using with nitro-benzene, probably telling him that it was something like oil of eucalyptus that would do his cold good. Every time Franklin blew his nose he inhaled the stuff with results just as fatal as if he had drunk it. The fact that he was at Dembry was an additional piece of luck for you, because it offered several ready-made suspects. When he collapsed you were standing by him, and managed to get hold of the handkerchief, which you hid in the car. Here it is now." Quarles picked out the handkerchief from its paper wrapping, and held it up. "Hold him, Wilcox," he cried as Carr dived for the door.

"I DON'T see why you were so sure it was the handkerchief," Colonel Hawkley said afterwards. "After all, it might simply have dropped out of Franklin's pocket."

"It might. But Franklin didn't carry his handkerchief in his pocket, you see, he kept it up his sleeve. Once I realised the significance of the nitrobenzene marks on Franklin's sleeve I looked for his handkerchief. When I didn't find it I knew I must be right. If Carr had been really efficient he would have substituted a clean handkerchief for the one he took, but he didn't think of it. You might say he was caught because Franklin had nothing up his sleeve."

A PRESENT FROM SANTA CLAUS

"I WANT to see Santa Claus," said Francis Quarles's nephew Jonathan. "Will he give me a present?"

"I expect so." They stood in the toy department of Merridge's among other late shoppers, on Christmas Eve. Children were experimenting with space pistols while their fathers longingly fingered electric trains. Balsa wood boomerangs curved gracefully through the air, monkeys performed trapeze acts over and over again, a woman demonstrator blew balloons out of the most unlikely looking material.

At one end of the department a sign said: "Children. Enter Aladdin's Cave and get your present from Santa Claus himself. One shilling only." A queue of children went in by the pay desk and came out holding small parcels wrapped in bright paper. Most looked delighted, one or two were snivelling, a small boy with fair hair swung his blue paper parcel by its tinsel string with an air of boredom.

IT WAS a cheerful scene, but Sir Wilfred Merridge, who had been showing Quarles round the store, looked worried. He began to talk about the thefts at Merridge's. "They began a fortnight ago as petty pilfering, but now they've gone far beyond that. At first it was fountain pens, scarves, cigar cutters, that kind of thing. Yesterday we lost a brooch worth eight guineas, an expensive bottle of perfume and a diamond-studded wristwatch among other things. More than fifty pounds worth of stuff altogether."

"And you're sure it's someone who works here, not customers?"

"Too regular for ordinary shop thefts. It happens every day. Must be a little gang among the temporary staff engaged for Christmas. It's not difficult to steal things, mark you. What we can't understand—my word, what's that?"

"You're dead." said Jonathan Quarles triumphantly. He had pushed into Sir Wilfred's back an oddly shaped red plastic instrument which screeched when he pressed a button. "Can I have this, Uncle Francis? It's a rocket detonator with atomic flame."

Quarles paid a beaming assistant. Sir Wilfred resumed. "What we

A PRESENT FROM SANTA CLAUS 153

can't understand is how they get the stuff out. I've had four times our usual staff of detectives keeping watch these last few days and they're convinced it's not passed to customer accomplices. And the staff don't go out in the daytime. We've got a canteen which everybody uses at this time of year when the lunch hour has to be short. For the last three nights we've asked all the staff to submit to a search before leaving—purely voluntary, of course. We found nothing."

"*When* can I get a present from Santa Claus, Uncle Francis?"

"In a minute. Go and look at the railway trains and see if you can buy a level crossing or signals or something that doesn't cost more than ten shillings."

When Jonathan had rushed away with the note in his hand Quarles said: "What's to stop the thieves from passing things to other members of the staff in the canteen?"

"They could do that, but it still leaves the problem of how they get the stuff out. If there were accomplice customers, our detectives would have noticed them hanging round one department or another. They've been watching particularly for anything like that."

"Trivial, but teasing." Quarles said. "What kind of size were the things stolen?"

"Small things, almost all of them. The biggest was a pair of solid silver candlesticks. If you're thinking of anything like secret pockets in clothing, I can assure you—"

"Nothing like that." Quarles said absently. "I say, whatever has that nephew of mine got now?"

"HERE'S something much better than signals and level crossings." Jonathan Quarles took out of a cardboard box a bright green parrot, wound it up and placed it on a counter nearby. The bird immediately began to flap its wings up and down and move along the counter squawking: "I've lost my buttons and braces. Hey, damn your eyes." Jonathan's own eyes were bright with delight. "Isn't it supersonic, Uncle Frances? Can I have it?"

"Certainly, my boy. Just the thing to appeal to your grandmother. Ask the assistant to wrap it up."

"And *can* I see Santa Claus?"

"As soon as you've got that bird wrapped up." He turned again to Sir Wilfred. "Is it literally true that everybody is searched?"

"Certainly."

"Are you searched, for example?"

Sir Wilfred went very red. "Of course not. Should I steal my own property?"

"I don't suppose so. I only wanted to point out that when you said everybody had been searched it wasn't literally true. In the same way your store detectives looked out for customers coming in contact with the staff, but I doubt if they thought of—"

"Can I see Santa Claus and get my present now?"

"Yes, you can." Quarles gave Jonathan a shilling. He paid it at the desk and joined the now dwindling queue. "What kind of things do they get?" Quarles asked.

"Little clockwork toys, cardboard cut-outs, that kind of thing. Splendid value. They cost us more than a shilling, but we do it to keep the youngsters happy." And to keep them in the Toy Department, Quarles reflected. Sir Wilfred said impatiently: "You've got nothing practical to suggest, then?"

"I'm not sure. Here he comes." behind the curtains they heard Jonathan pipe: "Merry Christmas," and the answering boom of Santa Claus: "And a Merry Christmas to you, my boy."

JONATHAN came out carrying a little box. Behind him came a small fair-haired boy who swung his green paper parcel by its tinsel string with an air of boredom. "That's the boy," Quarles said. He put a large hand on the fair-haired boy's shoulder. "Let's see what Santa Claus has given you."

"Let me go." The boy wriggled furiously but Quarles held him comfortably with one hand and tore off the parcel's paper wrapping to reveal a gleaming cigarette case.

Sir Wilfred gave an outraged exclamation and picked it up. "Solid silver. The little scoundrel."

Jonathan, who had undone his own parcel, said: "That's much better than mine. I've only got a jigsaw puzzle."

The boy suddenly raised his voice to a shout. "Bill, they've got me."

A moment later surprised shoppers in Merridge's saw Santa Claus emerge from behind his curtain and run as quickly as his long red cloak would permit across the room. At the department entrance two unobtrusive men gripped him by the arms.

"IT WAS absurdly simple," Quarles said, with a touch of mock modesty. "Probably there were four of them in it. Is that right?" he asked the boy.

"Yes. Bill's wife got a job in cosmetics and Harry Jones is in jewellery."

"They stole the things and passed them on to Santa Claus in the canteen at lunchtime. He handed them out as presents to this boy—the kind of customer your detectives never noticed coming into contact with the staff. I realised what was happening when I saw him going in three times in a few minutes. Not even your presents are such good value as that."

"Most observant." Sir Wilfred seemed quite overwhelmed. "I don't know how to thank you. Your fee—"

"No fee. I have only one request to make When you've got the stolen things back, don't make a charge." Quarles released his grip on the fair boy and ran a hand through his nephew's hair. "After all, it *is* Christmas Eve."

THE LINK

PROFESSIONAL soccer players in Britain are badly paid in comparison with American baseball stars, yet soccer is a remarkably honest game. The scandal was all the greater, therefore, when Billy Bissett, centre-forward in the Midthorpe Town team, was careless enough to say to an interested pub audience that they could all put crosses for Midthorpe on their pools forms that week because the team would be playing for a draw.

Bissett was questioned by the police. He revealed that he and two other Midthorpe players were sent a registered envelope with a cross marked on it when they were to play for a draw. After the match they received ten pounds each, in pound notes, sent in another registered envelope.

But it takes two teams to make a draw. Close questioning of Midthorpe's opponents in their drawn games revealed that players in these teams were engaged to play for a draw on exactly the same terms as the Midthorpe players.

By payment of sixty pounds a match the originators of this scheme made sure that they had six players, three on each side, working for a drawn game. They were generally successful in getting one.

Eight drawn games on this scale would cost four hundred and eighty pounds. That is a lot of money, but then if you can predict eight drawn games on the Treble Chance pool you may scoop the pool for as much as seventy-five thousand pounds, and that is a lot more money.

Who had won a lot of money on the pools recently? With the help of the pool companies the police traced a number of big wins to a professional gambler, backer of horses, and night-club owner named Gus Rankin.

Francis Quarles, the private detective, was with Inspector Leeds when he went to interview Gus Rankin at his Flora and Fauna Club. The gambler was a big, beaming man who offered them whisky and cigars. Both were refused. The Inspector came straight to the point by producing a list of thirty pools dividends of a thousand pounds or more that had been won by Rankin or people connected with him.

The big man nodded happily. "We got a little syndicate, had a run of luck. That's the way it goes. I tell you how many thousands I lost on the ponies last year you wouldn't believe me. What's up, Inspector?"

The Inspector told him. Rankin professed astonishment and disgust. "What, me bribe football players? I love the game, cheer my head off for our local boys every Saturday."

Inspector Leeds said slowly, "I'll tell you this, Rankin. Wherever we can trace that these players were approached directly, it was through Joe Dodge, the Laverham United centre half."

"Never spoken to him, never even seen him play."

The Inspector ignored that. "It's only a matter of time before we find the link between you and Joe Dodge. You'll make it easier for yourself, Rankin, by telling us the whole story now."

"Before you find a link between me and Joe Dodge, Inspector, I shall have died of old age. Because why? Because there ain't no such link." Rankin spoke with perfect confidence and serenity. He lit a cigar. "Mind the step, boys, as you go out."

THE essential link between Rankin and Joe Dodge needed by the police remained elusive. The Laverham United centre-half's story was that he had been approached first of all by letter, and that subsequent letters had told him what players to contact in other teams. He had destroyed all the letters, but said that they were typed and had a London postmark. Laverham is a London suburb.

Dodge, a big, shaggy, slow-witted man, could not be shaken from this story. After two lengthy interrogations he was released on bail, together with Mansell and Hartley, the two other Laverham players who had admitted taking bribes.

On being released the three men went straight back to the Laverham ground, where a half-hearted practice match was in progress. As they came on to the field the other players walked off without speaking to them. Mansell, Hartley and Dodge went to the dressing rooms after the other players had left them. There they were spoken to individually by the club manager George Noakes, who told them that they were indefinitely suspended, and would not be admitted to the ground again.

There was only one entrance to the dressing rooms, and an old groundsman named Tom Follett was working in the yard outside it. He saw Mansell and Hartley come out and go home, leaving Dodge alone in the dressing rooms.

Then Follett heard a sharp crack from somewhere around the back of the dressing rooms, to which he paid little attention. It was not until a quarter of an hour afterwards that he went in and found Joe Dodge on the floor with a bullet through his head.

INSPECTOR LEEDS was inclined to be cheerful. "This simplifies things. Somebody came up round the back of the dressing rooms and shot Dodge through the window. He knew too much, they were afraid of what he might tell."

Quarles reminded the Inspector that two days before he had expressed the view that Dodge was too stupid to be keeping anything back.

"So I did. He hadn't been killed then."

"Then again," said Quarles, "why choose Joe Dodge as contact man in the first place?"

"Don't understand you," the Inspector frowned. "Somebody had to be contact man, might have been one of half a dozen players."

"Perhaps you're right, but I have a feeling—." Quarles did not say what his feeling was. He went into the club's offices. Upstairs he found the club chairman, Topham Bentley, talking to the ginger-haired, freckled manager George Noakes.

"Anything fresh?" Bentley asked eagerly.

"The Inspector seems to think he's on something. By the way, had Dodge been in these offices lately by any chance?"

"Funny you should ask that," Bentley said. "Most extraordinary thing, a couple of days ago after the police first talked to him, I found him in my office here. He was at my desk, looking at some letters that were being sent out. Nothing special, just the ordinary club correspondence, but I sent him off with a flea in his ear, I can tell you."

Quarles digested this information and turned to go. He paused with his hand on the door. "Here's something that may interest you. The Inspector's found a couple of those notes that Dodge said he'd destroyed. May be nothing in them, but it does give some confirmation of his story."

AT half-past six that evening the policeman warned to stay on duty inside the club grounds saw a wisp of smoke coming out of the office window. He reached the fire before the paraffin-soaked rags had had time to do much damage. The typewriter, which had been piled round with rags, was badly burned, but the keys were still identifiable.

Quarles and the Inspector took the typewriter round to George Noakes's house. The freckles on the manager's skin seemed to stand out as he looked at it. "It's all up now, Noakes," Quarles said.

"I—I—" The manager seemed unable to speak for a moment. Then he said: "All right. It was that devil Rankin got me into it. I owed him betting money, and at first it seemed just an easy way to get out of paying it. Once I was in I got deeper and deeper. I was sorry about Joe, but the way he threatened me I couldn't do anything else."

"JUST as you said, there had to be a link somewhere joining Gus Rankin to the swindle," Quarles said to the Inspector afterwards. "And it wasn't Joe Dodge, who as you said yourself was too stupid to concoct a story like the one about the typewritten letters. Then why had Dodge, been chosen at all for the job of contact man? It seemed to me there was only one answer to that. The real link was someone who knew in the first place that Dodge would accept a bribe, and who was able to keep an eye on him. That meant someone connected with the club. Then came Dodge's murder. I couldn't see why Rankin should want to kill him, because he obviously had no fear of Dodge when we talked to him. It seemed much more likely that Dodge had at last found out who the link was, and tried to blackmail him. How had he done it? It could only be through the typewritten notes he had received. When I learned that Dodge had been looking at the office correspondence I guessed that he had been comparing the characteristics of the office typewriter with those on the notes he had received.

"Who was the link, Bentley or Noakes? It had to be somebody that Dodge had just threatened with exposure. Now, since he came back from the second police interrogation, who had Dodge spoken to? Nobody except his team-mates Mansell and Hartley, who were already involved—and Noakes. So it had to be Noakes."

"There's just one thing," said the Inspector. "Noakes said something about us finding some of the typed notes sent to Dodge. That was why he staged the office fire, to burn the typewriter and correspondence. We have found some of the notes since Noakes's arrest, in Dodge's lodgings, but we hadn't got them then."

"I knew they must exist," said Quarles, and coughed modestly. "I merely anticipated your discovery to get at the truth. It was what you might call detective's licence."

LITTLE BOY BLUE

THERE was a scarecrow in the field as Francis Quarles walked through it in the gathering twilight of a fine spring evening, a figure made out of ragged grey trousers, a shabby raincoat and an old Panama hat.

Quarles had reached the other side of the field and was out on to the main road when he heard the shouting, and turned.

For a moment it seemed to him in the twilight that the scarecrow had put on a trilby hat and was running towards him. Then the running figure changed direction as he saw Quarles. He had been concealing the scarecrow, but now it was visible again. At the far side of the field of peas other running figures could be seen.

What happened next happened quickly. The fugitive reached the edge of the field and jumped a barred gate. His foot caught in the top and he sprawled out into the main road under the wheels of an oncoming car. Quarles heard the screech of brakes, and then he looked away.

That was the end of a story. And the beginning of a puzzle.

IT was the end of the story for Little Boy Blue as Charles Maddox was called because of the wide innocence of his china blue eyes. He died two hours later in the hospital, of an internal haemorrhage caused by his injuries in the accident. His death created the puzzle.

Little Boy Blue was a leading member of a gang running a drug named zazurin, popularly known as zaz. The drug was a synthetic based on an obscure American plant, and its effects were much the same as those of hashish. There was the important difference, however, that zaz was invariably effective in producing intoxication and pleasant hallucinations, whereas hashish is uncertain. And only a minute quantity was needed, so that a cigarette box full of zaz was worth a good deal more than its weight in platinum.

Zaz was smuggled over from America, and the police had got on to Little Boy Blue's connection with it through the help of a stool-pigeon. On his advice they watched one of the stewards off a recently docked liner. The steward met Little Boy Blue in a Southampton pub and offered him a cigarette from a cardboard box. Little Boy Blue produced a similar box and suggested that the steward have one of his. Somehow he dropped his box and the steward bent to help him pick it up. The changeover was made adroitly, but the police watcher saw it.

Little Boy Blue could have been arrested then, but the police held off because they wanted to follow him and find out his sources of distribution. They picked up the steward, who confirmed that the box was full of zazurin. Little Boy Blue was followed unobtrusively, different cars taking up the job at various points on the road from Southampton to London.

Somehow the following wasn't quite unobtrusive enough. When Little Boy Blue spotted that they were after him he showed a fine turn of speed and a good sense of misleading direction. He led three police cars on a good chase through the Hampshire and Berkshire countryside. But southern England is not a good country for escaping from the police, not even in a car like Little Boy Blue's Cadillac. He was rarely more than half a mile ahead of the nearest police car. At last just outside the village of Lambert Condover, he blew a tyre, ran off the road into a ditch, and made his way across the field where Quarles saw him.

The puzzle was, what had happened to the box of zazurin?

It was not in Little Boy Blue's clothes, as they discovered when he was taken to hospital. Then they did the obvious thing, and asked the man himself.

"He's a kind of a joker," the narcotics man in charge said to Quarles. "And he's very tough, in spite of that innocent expression. I doubt if we shall get anything out of him."

LITTLE BOY BLUE was conscious, and he grinned at them. "Never thought I'd end up through careless driving. I hope the police are going to prosecute."

"You're finished, Maddox," the narcotics man said. "There's nothing that can be done for you. You know that, Where's the stuff?"

The other looked at him with china blue eyes, which had no emotion at all behind them.

"We shall get it soon enough, but you'll save us the trouble of looking. And you'll be doing good for once in your life, if that means anything to you."

"Nothing at all," Little Boy Blue said. "And I wouldn't lift a finger to save a copper from burning. You go ahead and look while I laugh. I hope it keeps fine for you."

He closed his blue eyes, and never opened them again.

THE police swooped quickly on the other leading members of Little Boy Blue's gang, but they badly needed the cardboard box of zazurin as evidence.

It was possible that the box had been thrown out of the car window when Little Boy Blue realised that he had been spotted, just out of Winchester. This seemed unlikely, because his natural instinct would be to hang on to such a valuable possession, but the roads were searched nevertheless. The search had no result.

While this search was going on, the Cadillac was painstakingly taken to pieces. The official theory was that there was a secret panel or recess in the car, and that when Maddox ran into the ditch he put the box of zazurin into it. Quarles shook his head doubtfully about this.

"Little Boy Blue impressed me as a really reckless man. I have the feeling he would have kept that box right to the bitter end unless he found a good hiding place for it. I don't think he would have abandoned it with the car."

He proved to be right. There were no fewer than three secret recesses in the Cadillac, but no cardboard box was found in any of them. Looking at the litter of the car, Quarles agreed that the hiding places it might have contained appeared to be exhausted.

"When he left the car he climbed a gate, ran across the field and got himself killed," the narcotics man said. "And the driver of the other car has been checked—he's an absolutely respectable local estate agent. There's only one possible answer. Maddox did throw the box out of the car window and we haven't found it. After all, the chase went on for twenty miles, and it's impossible to check every inch of the way."

THE next day, the fine spring weather, which had lasted for three weeks, broke. Rain poured down as though the sky were an upturned bucket. Looking out of his bedroom window, Francis Quarles remembered something Maddox had said. He began to laugh. He was still laughing when he picked up the narcotics investigator, and the joke amused him right down to Lambert Condover.

He stopped his car where Maddox had run into the ditch and said, "I shan't be five minutes."

He came back in less than that time with muddy shoes and a slightly sodden cigarette box. The narcotics man opened it, smelt the white powder inside, and said simply: "Where?"

"You told me Little Boy Blue was a joker. When I saw the rain this morning I remembered that he said 'I hope it keeps fine for you,' and I realised it might have been his way of saying he'd put the box somewhere where it might get wet. Little Boy Blue simply slipped it in his pocket as he passed."

"In *whose* pocket?"

Quarles led him to the edge of the field. In the middle of it stood the Panama-hatted scarecrow forlorn in the rain, with its old raincoat flapping.

AFFECTION UNLIMITED

NORMAN STRANGE said: "I should like to find my sister."

"So," said Francis Quarles, "would a great many other people." He opened the paper on his desk and pointed with a well-manicured finger at the headline: *Mildred Lancing Still Missing*. "If you find her," he added, "she'll stand trial. The police think she'll hang."

"She's innocent."

Quarles blew out his cheeks in a sigh. "Your sentiment does you credit."

"Will you try to find her?"

"For an adequate sum of money," Quarles said, "I am prepared to do almost anything."

FROM his friend Inspector Leeds at Scotland Yard, who was quite convinced of Mildred Lancing's guilt, Quarles gathered the details of the case.

The central figure in it was not really Mildred Lancing, but a man named Jeremy Bunn. Mr. Bunn was a not very successful traveller in cotton goods. He was 49 years old, he lived at Hammersmith, and he had a nagging wife.

Mr. Bunn sought for love by correspondence. He became a member of an organisation called Affection Unlimited, which offered to provide its clients with "varied introductions to congenial members of the opposite sex for the purposes of matrimony and friendship."

On his application form Mr. Bunn made a false statement that had serious consequences for him. In the space provided for the word "Married" or "Single," he described himself as single.

On the records of Affection Unlimited Mr. Bunn was shown to have been given the names and addresses of five ladies.

The fifth woman was Mildred Lancing. She had been the wife of a civil servant who spent most of his life in India. When he died suddenly of a kidney complaint, he left her with his pension, a small annuity, and a handsome young son named Richard.

The pension and annuity were enough to keep her from starvation, but not sufficient to enable her to live comfortably and educate Richard. She went to live with her bachelor brother Norman, a fairly prosperous manufacturer of children's toys, and had lived in his house for five years as a kind of unofficial housekeeper at the time she met Mr. Bunn. Richard was then nineteen.

Mrs. Lancing was a fair, slightly faded woman of forty two, with babyish features and a small, puckered mouth. She had been passionately devoted to her son Richard, who resembled her in colouring and features. Now she became devoted also to Mr. Bunn.

It is almost certain that by the time he had known Mildred Lancing two or three months Mr. Bunn was regretting that rash description of himself as a single man. It had helped him to win Mildred's love, but it had also exposed him to a little quiet blackmail on the part of Mr. Jack Cade, the proprietor of Affection Unlimited.

Mr. Bunn, who had originally paid a guinea for up to a dozen introductions, found himself paying £10 a month to keep his shabby little secret. And he was not a rich man.

In his dilemma, Mr. Bunn made a bold attempt—it was probably the boldest thing he had done in his life—to escape from all his difficulties and preserve his new-found love. A letter from him found in Mrs. Lancing's jewel box, proposed in fervent terms elopement, marriage, a new life, and, most significantly, a new name.

On Friday, the 17th of February, Mr. Bunn left home as usual. He told his wife that he would be away on a five-day trip. He withdrew the whole of his bank account, which amounted to nearly £2000.

Mr. Bunn travelled down to the seaside resort of Southbay, and registered there at the Good Resolution hotel in the name of B. N. Jeremy. He told the booking clerk that his wife would be coming at about six o'clock.

At half-past seven, apparently in much perturbation of mind, he ate his dinner and retired to his room, after having made another inquiry at the reception desk.

NORMAN STRANGE was at his office that Friday. During the day an important client named Morland, who lived at Brightside, some fifteen miles from Southbay, asked him to come to dinner.

When he arrived, Strange found that Morland had been suddenly taken ill with some form of food poisoning. He insisted, however, that Strange should stay the night.

The toy manufacturer, like Mr. Bunn, ate a lonely dinner. He then went for a drive in his car, returning at about half-past ten. He saw no reason to telephone his home, because it was quite common for him to be away occasionally.

THE shock of discovering the letter left by Mrs. Lancing fell, therefore, upon young Richard, when he returned home late that evening from a day spent in London at art galleries and the cinema.

Upon the dining-table he found the hurriedly scrawled, tear-stained letter left for him and his uncle. Mildred Lancing's letter said that life had offered to her for the first time a chance of personal happiness, and that she felt bound to take it.

They must both try to understand how she felt. She was going to be married—secretly—it was almost an elopement, she added with an exclamation mark. She would write again later on, after the marriage. If they wanted to wish her good luck, a telegram sent to the Good Resolution at Southbay would reach her.

Richard Lancing, who, by his uncle's account had returned his mother's passionate devotion, did not send a telegram. He went, instead, for a long walk on that dank February evening, and at half-past eleven appeared, distraught, at the house of a friend, where he spent the night.

The movements of Mildred Lancing had not been difficult to trace. Woodlands, where she lived, was about twenty-five miles from Southbay, and there was a good train service from Woodlands station.

For some reason, however, she took a train from Gearley, the next station down the line, where the ticket-collector remembered her as a fair woman, wearing a veil and carrying a suitcase. She arrived at the Good Resolution about nine o'clock, and said to the reception clerk: "I believe a gentleman is expecting me."

"Ah yes," said the reception clerk, beaming. "Mrs. Jeremy, isn't it? Your husband is just calling from his room to know if you've arrived."

He held out the telephone receiver. Mildred Lancing took it and said: "Mildred here." The clerk heard a babble of excitement from the other end of the line.

Mrs. Lancing said: "I'm coming up now," and replaced the receiver. The clerk said: "Room 43, madam, third floor." As Mrs. Lancing turned away from the desk she laddered her stocking on the leg of one of the small tables in the reception hall. She looked down at it ruefully, and then hurried across to the lift.

By the time it came down three young girls were also waiting for it, and when the gate was opened by the liftman, Mrs. Lancing showed an extraordinary hesitancy to enter it.

The girls, too, hung back—after all, Mrs. Lancing had been there first—but at last they got in and she followed them.

The liftman let her out at the third floor. And that was the last anyone saw of Mildred Lancing.

That evening, too, saw the end of Mr. Bunn's quest for romance. In the morning the chambermaid found his body. The face was purplish, the tongue lolled out. Examination proved that he had been hit over the head and strangled while he was unconscious. The two thousand pounds he had drawn out of the bank had vanished.

QUARLES spent a day in London and Southbay after digesting this information—a day during which he saw, among other people, Mrs. Bunn, Jack Cade and the reception clerk and liftman at the Good Resolution.

Then he went down to Woodlands and saw Norman Strange. The toy manufacturer lived in an opulently ugly gabled Victorian house with a driveway in front of it and a rock garden behind. Behind the rock garden was a square lawn, at the back of the lawn a large lily pond. Strange was anxious. "Is there any news of Mildred?"

The detective's bulky figure was enclosed in a teddy bear coat. He stared at the lily pond, then turned his back to it and looked at the house. "A large house for two people," he said. "Are you going to stay here?"

"I don't think so." Strange shivered. "Unpleasant memories. But Richard doesn't want to leave. He's taken it rather badly, I'm afraid." He paused. "Do you think Mildred was guilty?"

"I think she was foolish."

In a sitting room full of family portraits Quarles met a fair, slight young man with red-rimmed eyes of deep blue. "This is Richard." Strange put a hand on the young man's shoulder. "He has had a shock and he's going away soon for a holiday. Eh, Richard?"

"I'm staying here," the young man said fiercely. He ran out of the room. Norman Strange shook his head gloomily and Quarles held up his huge hand. "What was that?"

"I didn't hear anything."

Turning suddenly towards the garden window Quarles knocked over a vase of flowers. Dirty water spilled onto his teddy bear coat. He looked at it with distaste and said severely, "Clumsy."

Strange, although the accident had been none of his making, felt impelled to hurry out to the kitchen and get a cloth to wipe Quarles's coat. By the time he had returned the detective had recovered his elephantine equilibrium. "I should like to come down again tomorrow," he said.

"I shall be here."

"And Richard?"

Shaking his head Strange said, "I wish I could get him to leave the house."

Quarles went again to Southbay and then returned to London. There he saw grizzled, gritty-voiced Inspector Leeds. "And what have you been playing at?" the Inspector asked cheerfully. "Nothing for you to exercise that great brain on here. We know *who*—Mrs. Lancing. And we know *why*—she found out somehow that Bunn couldn't make an honest woman of her. The only thing missing is the lady, and as soon as she tries to pass one of those fivers from Bunn's bank we shall have her."

"Perhaps," Quarles said, "I can help you to find her a little sooner than that."

QUARLES and Inspector Leeds confronted the toy manufacturer in his sitting room. He looked bewildered. "I don't understand. Who are these two other gentlemen?" The two other gentlemen, looking very uncomfortable, sat on the edge of a sofa.

Quarles raised his voice. "They have found Mildred Lancing for us," he said.

Upstairs a door opened. Feet ran quickly down the stairs. The pale face of Richard Lancing peered into the room. "Did you say ..." he began. Then he saw the two men sitting on the sofa, turned and ran up again.

Quarles leapt after him, but by the time they reached the top of the stairs they heard a key turn in a door.

Immediately afterwards there was a shot. When they broke down the door Richard Lancing was dead.

"THERE was a little guess-work," Quarles said modestly, "And some excellent deduction. As soon as I asked myself whether the person at the hotel could have been someone other than Mrs. Lancing, all the questions in the case were answered.

"Why didn't Mrs. Lancing get on the train at Woodlands? Because she was too well known there for an impersonation to be risked.

"Why did she say on arrival at the hotel, 'I believe a gentleman is expecting me,' instead of 'I am Mrs. Jeremy?' *Because she didn't know the name of the man she was to meet*. And so she used that extraordinary form of greeting, 'Mildred here.'"

"Wouldn't you expect a woman three hours late to say 'Hullo, darling, sorry I'm late,' or something of that kind? But of course the impersonator had to use the name of Mildred to make sure that Mr. Jeremy was the right person. Then it wasn't Mrs. Lancing at the hotel. Was it a woman at all? 'Mildred here' is a man's form of speech, rather than a woman's. And would a woman go up to meet the man she was running away with before trying to mend a laddered stocking? But the conclusive point was the lift."

"What about the lift?" the Inspector asked.

"The reception clerk thought Mrs. Lancing was hesitating on the brink of some decision. But in fact the impersonator had temporarily forgotten his assumed sex, and was showing the well-known courtesy of gentlemen in allowing ladies to enter a lift first.

"But all that was simply useful corroboration, for in fact only one person could have impersonated Mrs. Lancing. That was the person who had features and colouring that resembled her own, the only person who saw the note that said where she was going. 'Mrs. Lancing' vanished after the death of Bunn because he took a change of clothing in that suitcase. He entered Bunn's room as a woman and left the hotel as a man.

"All this was suspicion, you may say. But when, through a little stratagem with a vase of flowers. I was able to steal a photograph from your sitting-room and take it down to the hotel, suspicion became certainty. I brought the liftman and reception clerk back here to identify him, and when he saw them Richard Lancing knew the game was up."

"Then what really happened?" Mr. Strange sounded dazed.

"That we shall never know exactly. But Richard must have returned home at five o'clock, just when his mother was leaving, after she'd written her note. They quarrelled—remember his passionate devotion to her, and the jealousy he must have felt at being replaced in her affections—and, by accident perhaps, he killed her. Then, partly to preserve his own skin, partly to avenge his mother, he embarked on that mad adventure which ended in the death of Mr. Bunn."

There was silence. The Inspector said: "Two things you haven't told us. First, where's the money?"

"Lancing took it as a blind. I don't doubt that he's hidden it somewhere in the house, probably in his room."

"And where's Mildred Lancing?"

"From a cursory look around the grounds," Quarles said with one of his heavy sighs, "I should say that you will almost certainly find her in the lily pond."

They did.

THE WHISTLING MAN

APPLE-CHEEKED young Freddy Bannister wriggled uncomfortably in his seat in Francis Quarles's office. "You'll think it sounds a lot of nonsense about this whistling man, but it's got Uncle Herbert and Aunt Miriam really worried."

"Tell me."

"The first thing happened three weeks ago. Some people we know had come in for drinks—John Meiklejohn the singer, Edgar Williams who writes film scripts. Arthur Gillespie and his wife Nora. He's an Australian, used to be some sort of big shot variety artist, retired now. We were all in an upstairs drawing-room, with Uncle Herbert and Aunt Miriam and a guest of ours named George Peart, who's over here from India—when there was a crash, and then the sound of somebody whistling a few bars of The Blue Danube. The crash and the whistling both came from downstairs. Aunt Miriam went down to see what had happened. A rather valuable vase had fallen down from a shelf where it had been standing safely for years. That was the first thing, nothing in itself. Four or five days later our ginger cat Timmy was missing. Aunt Miriam heard somebody whistling The Blue Danube out in the street. She looked out. Nobody was there but a small parcel lay outside the front door. Timmy was inside it with his throat cut.

"A week later Uncle Herbert and I were going to the races with George Peart and the Gillespies. Somebody pushed Mrs. Gillespie so that she almost fell on to the railway line. I caught her arm and we all heard The Blue Danube being whistled some way back in the crowd."

It was a hot day. Freddy Bannister wiped a forehead that was gleaming with sweat. "That's all. It may not sound much, but believe me there's something eerie about that disembodied voice whistling The Blue Danube."

QUARLES grunted. "Do you know of anybody with a grudge against your family? You don't. What about George Peart?"

"Uncle Herbert has an export business and George Peart is agent for a firm of Indian tea traders. They've done business for years, but this is the first time Peart has been over or that Uncle Herbert has met him. Peart treats the whistling man as a joke, keeps saying it reminds him of his old friend Harry. Lord knows what he means, John Meiklejohn did a tour in India," Freddy added helpfully, "and I believe Arthur Gillespie has been out there too."

Quarles grunted again. "Either this is some sort of practical joke, or the stage has been carefully set for something else to happen. What it is I don't know, but the next time you hear the whistling man watch carefully to see where everybody is. That might be informative."

WHEN the Gillespies gave their little party the following evening, Freddy Bannister was on the alert for something queer to happen. Under the pressure of dry Martinis and general conviviality, however, his attention relaxed. When the thing did happen he was as unprepared as everybody else.

They were playing a version of the old game Celebrities, which involved one of the party going into the next room, and looking up details of a historical character in the *Encyclopaedia Britannica* which had been placed ready to hand.

When he came back primed with information the others had to guess his identity.

Nora Gillespie had been guessed quickly as the Queen of Sheba. Herbert Bannister as the engineer Brunel had deceived them for some time. When George Peart went out, the rest of them stood at one end of the room round the fire, talking and drinking.

John Meiklejohn said that Peart was a long time, and Nora Gillespie suggested that he had chosen Napoleon and was reading the whole entry of several pages.

Arthur Gillesple handed round sausage rolls that he had just brought in from the kitchen. Then they heard a scream, high-pitched and sharp, from the next room. The scream died to an indistinct mutter. It was followed by the whistling of a few bars from The Blue Danube.

Freddy Bannister was standing by the window. He was able to swear that nobody left by the front door of the house. After an instant of paralysed immobility Meiklejohn ran over to the door between the two rooms. It was locked. They had to go round through the kitchen and the corridor outside.

They found George Peart in the room, with a long stiletto-like blade buried deep in his back. He was dead. His body sprawled across closed volumes of the *Encyclopaedia*.

Freddy Bannister telephoned the police. He also telephoned Francis Quarles.

WHEN the house had been searched. Quarles, accompanied by a grim-faced Inspector Leeds, came into the room where the party now sat, hushed and uneasy.

"To detect a crime is always easier than to prevent it," Quarles said. "When Freddy Bannister came to see me I told him that the stage was being carefully set for something to happen. I had an inkling of the way it was being done, and I told him to watch carefully where everybody was placed the next time he heard the whistling man—a piece of advice which he unfortunately neglected. But I had no idea of the victim's identity. Now we know that it was George Peart. Somebody hated George Peart enough to kill him. We have no idea of the motive, perhaps we shall never know it. We do know that George Peart had lived most of his life in India, and that the secret must have been connected with the past. Mr. Meiklejohn, you've been in India. So have you, Mr. Gillespie. Have either of you ever met George Peart? Had anybody here met George Peart before his visit to Mr. Herbert Bannister?"

Nobody spoke. "Now which of you is lying?" Quarles said softly. "Who killed George Peart?"

"The whistling man," said Freddy Bannister.

"Ah, yes, the mysterious whistling man, the man George Peart so oddly said reminded him of his old friend Harry. It struck me when I heard about the whistling man that the things he did could have been done quite easily by any of you.

"Any of you could have put a vase right on the edge of a shelf so that with any luck, it would tip over, or have killed a cat, or have given Mrs. Gillespie a little push, enough to send her off her balance, but not to push her off the platform.

"Those incidents set the stage for what happened to-night. They established the whistling man, and the purpose of the whistling man was to give the murderer an alibi.

"You were all together in here when you heard the scream, weren't you? But Peart was dead when you heard it. He had been killed a couple of minutes earlier—before he'd even opened the *Encyclopaedia*—by somebody who slipped out of the kitchen, along the corridor and into the room, stabbed Peart, locked the door communicating with this room, and then returned—carrying, perhaps something to eat or drink."

Quarles tapped the parcel in his hand.

"The game's up, Gillespie. You really shouldn't have left Harry lying around, you know. Disgracefully careless. Tell me, what was the motive?"

Gillespie's teeth were chattering, "I was married out in India. I met Peart out there once with her. We'd been separated for years, and I thought she was dead when I married Nora.

"Peart found that she was alive and came over here to blackmail me. I couldn't let Nora ..." His voice died away.

"But I still don't understand," said Freddy Bannister. "How did he arrange the whistling and the scream? And who is Harry? And why did you ask me where we were standing when we heard the whistling?"

"I'll answer those questions in reverse order. I wanted you to check where people were standing because the man who was doing the whistling would have taken care to stand apart from the rest of you. As for Harry, here he is."

He unwrapped the parcel in his hand. A dummy dressed in a cutaway blue coat with brass buttons smiled with his clapper mouth, stared boldly at them out of boot-button eyes.

"And this answers your last question," Quarles said. He held up a theatre bill. There was a photograph of Arthur Gillespie with Harry on his knee. The bill said:

ARTHUR AND HARRY. The famous whistling ventriloquist demonstrates his amazing powers of voice control and transference. The greatest ventriloquist act in the world.

PARTY LINE

THE parties given by Lady Muriel Jape, that well-known patroness of the arts, were on a high social level, and yet upon a high—or at least fashionable—artistic level, too.

On his arrival at this one Francis Quarles saw women in great glossy furs emerging from great glossy cars. Within, deferential servants were taking charge of furs that seemed even glossier. In the large drawing-room upstairs there were plenty of diamonds, plenty of pearls and, as accompaniment to them, a great many port-winish looking men in evening clothes.

But there was another element, too. Quarles saw. That grand old man of art, Gustavus James, boomed out his views about life and society, wearing a patched sports jacket and a pullover. Armand Balatone, whose one-man show of thought paintings was the nominal reason for Muriel Jape's party, giggled quietly in a corner with several friends in fancy waistcoats.

Quarles fought his way through a considerable crush to meet his hostess. She gabbled something unintelligible at him.

A harassed little man, whom Quarles recognised as Muriel's husband Sir Jasper, caught him by the elbow. "Want you to meet ..." he said. "Mr. Smiles ... Mr. Burton ... dramatic critic. ..."

"My name's not Smiles." Quarles said to the uneasy-looking young man. "Is yours Burton?"

"Driscoll," the young man said.

"And are you a dramatic critic?"

"Art critic."

"For what paper?"

"I'm in the provinces," the young man said gloomily, and sipped his drink.

"What are you going to say about Balatone's show?"

"Lot of rubbish." Driscoll sounded fierce. "Why don't they get some English painters to boost if they want to boost anybody, instead of all these Frenchmen—Picasso and that lot."

"Frenchmen?" Quarles said surprised.

174

"Balatone's French, isn't he? Said so in the catalogue. Thought paintings my eye."

"You prefer the English impressionists perhaps—someone like Ben Nicolson."

"I like an English painter," Driscoll said. He looked at his watch and then at the door. People were still coming in, the red-coated man at the door was booming their names like a foghorn.

"But there's something to be said for the French, surely." Quarles pursued the matter rather persistently. "The water-colours van Gogh painted in his Aries period—wouldn't you say they are very fine?"

"I only like English painters," Driscoll said angrily. "Pardon me." He walked away from Quarles, and stood by the door.

Quarles pushed through the crowd until he found Sir Jasper again. "That man you introduced me to says his name's Driscoll, not Burton."

"Does he? I suppose he ought to know."

"Do you know him personally?"

"Not from Adam, my dear fellow. Better ask my wife."

Lady Muriel was talking to Balatone. "The effect of imagination projecting outwards through space," Quarles heard her say. With some difficulty he obtained her attention, pointed to Driscoll, and asked if she knew him.

"Never seen him before in my life. But then I've never seen you either. Yes, I have, I invited you, but I can't remember your name, isn't that funny?"

"Immensely. But you really don't remember that man?"

"No. I'm sure I've never seen him. Probably Jasper asked him. If not he's a gatecrasher. Always get a few gatecrashers, you know."

Quarles looked again at Driscoll, who stood by the door sipping his martini and not speaking to anyone. Then he left the party to make a telephone call.

Half an hour later what Quarles had expected happened. There was a confused noise downstairs, a scream quickly cut off, which penetrated to the door of this noisy upper region. The red-jacketed man at the door heard it and moved to go downstairs. He found his way barred by the young man who called himself Driscoll.

"Don't nobody get worried, and nobody won't get hurt," Driscoll said ungrammatically. He showed the man a small pearl-handled revolver. "Just you stay in there. Won't be five minutes."

The red-jacketed man gasped like a fish, and looked behind him for help. But the sound had not reached people farther inside the room.

Francis Quarles, standing at his side, watched with some amusement. "Don't bother to try any heroics," he said. "I've telephoned the police."

There was a sound like a bump from downstairs, the noise of a car starting, and then shouts from the street.

"Do you hear those, Driscoll?" Quarles asked amiably. "The coppers were all ready waiting for your friends."

Driscoll stared at him, said one impolite word, threw the pearl-handled revolver at Quarles, and ran down the stairs into the arms of a burly policeman at the door.

Quarles paused long enough to make sure that the revolver was unloaded and then followed him. Two men were struggling in the grip of policemen. On the pavement were some forty more or less valuable-looking fur coats.

"All safe, you see," Quarles said to the man in the red jacket, who had come down with him. "Not a mink lost. You'd better go back again and make sure than none of the guests knows about this. Let joy be unconfined."

"I am eternally grateful to you. Mr. Quarles," Muriel Jape said: "There would have been a mild panic if a robbery, even an attempted robbery had been suspected. I promise that I shall never forget your name again. But I don't understand, even now, why you thought Driscoll, was anything more than a simple gatecrasher."

"It's very simple. When I was introduced to him I was rather persistent in asking questions. He said he was an art critic. Then he made a remark which showed that he thought Pablo Picasso was a Frenchman instead of a Spaniard. That was an odd mistake for an art critic to make, so I gave him two howlers in as many sentences. I called Ben Nicolson, the best-known abstract artist in England, an impressionist, and I talked about the watercolours in van Gogh's Aries period, when he was painting in oils."

"When he listened to those two remarks of mine without turning a hair, and then stood by the door obviously waiting for something to happen. I thought it would be a good idea to telephone the police."

WHO KILLED HARRINGTON?

WHEN Charles Harrington, the detective story writer, was found shot dead at his desk his murder presented some unusual features.

There was, first of all, the book that Harrington was writing, a sheet of which was in the typewriter at the side of him when he died. This was a story called *Who Killed Charteris?* and as bright young Inspector Merrilees read the half-completed typescript he became excited, for he traced easily enough in the suspects characters known to Harrington himself.

Briefly and skilfully *Who Killed Charteris?* sketched the detective novelist Charteris himself, keen, intelligent and witty.

Then it showed us the people who had a motive for killing him—first, Charteris's wife and his best friend, who were carrying on an affair under the writer's nose.

Then his son, who had become thoroughly involved with gamblers, and had appealed to his father for help which had been refused in the son's best interests.

And finally his doctor, an old school friend who hated Charteris because of some unrevealed incident which had occurred years before.

THESE were the principal characters, and they were all recognisably drawn from life—they were, in fact, Harrington's wife Pamela, his son Felix, his stockbroker friend George Bentham, and his physician, Doctor Winter. One or two other minor figures like a housemaid and a first-class golfing bore were also obviously the Harringtons' housemaid, Elsie Withers, and their neighbour, Colonel Chubb.

On the evening of his death Harrington had particularly urged his wife (so she said) to go to the pictures, and she had, in fact, gone with George Bentham. Felix Harrington had been out visiting some friends. Dr. Winter had done evening surgery and had then been called out on an urgent visit. Elsie Withers had had the evening off and had also gone to a cinema.

Harrington had thus been alone in the house working when, about nine o'clock at night, he was killed by one shot through the head. There was no indication of forced entry to the house, and since Harrington was sitting down he had presumably known his visitor.

The revolver, which belonged to the dead man, was kept in a desk drawer in his study. It was found about ten feet away from his body, near the wall. There were no prints on it.

"THERE'S the case," said bright young Inspector Merrilees to private detective Francis Quarles while they were on their way to the Harringtons' house in Hampstead. "Now, which one of them did it?"

"Which of them was the criminal in Harrington's story?"

Merrilees shook his head. "I don't know. Can't find any trace of how it was to end. If Mrs. Harrington's to be believed he always kept the plots in his head. But they all agree that he was very pleased with this new story, wouldn't tell them what it was about, and said they'd get a surprise when they read it.

"Naturally they all deny the accusations in the story. Mrs. Harrington admits she's friendly with Bentham, but says there's never been anything more to it than that. Felix did get into some financial trouble when he was at Oxford, but his mother settled it for him. Winter flatly denies he ever had a grudge against Harrington. So far we haven't turned up anything to disprove their stories. Can't give anybody an alibi, either. They'd all have had time at a pinch to nip home and murder him."

"What do they say about Harrington?"

"Nobody seems to have loved him. The doctor says he was malicious, and the son says he was mean. Notice that it was his mother, not his father, that he went to when he was in debt. Mrs. Harrington told me that so far from her taking a lover the reverse was true. She says Harrington could never keep his hands off a woman, and that she'd have divorced him long ago if she hadn't been a Roman Catholic. It does seem that he wasn't a nice character. Shall I tell you what I think?" Inspector Merrilees was plainly bursting with the desire to confide in somebody. "*One* of those stories Harrington put into his book is true. Find out which one it is, and we shall know who killed him."

With apparent irrelevance. Quarles said: "Have you read any of Harrington's other detective stories?"

"No time for such stuff."

"He was a devotee of the plot in which the most unlikely person is the murderer."

The Inspector snorted contemptuously. "I've told them all to be there, waiting for us," he said. "Then it's a matter of interrogation and waiting for somebody to make a slip."

BUT none of them made a slip. Elsie Withers, the neat little maid, let them in and for half an hour the Inspector fired questions at Mrs. Harrington, a plump and pretty woman in her early forties, at tweedy, pipe-smoking George Bentham, who managed to convey that he thought the whole thing an outrage, at pleasant-faced Felix Harrington, who was in his early twenties, and at short-spoken Winter.

Quarles sat almost silent while the Inspector tried unavailingly to shake their stories.

He broke in only once, when Mrs. Harrington was fervently denying the accusations in her husband's book about George Bentham. "No, no," she cried. "It was Charles who was unfaithful, not I. And he was clever in the way he did it. He would hide things from me and then produce them when they would hurt me most."

Quarles spoke. "Mrs. Harrington, would you say, your husband was a cruel man?"

Her hands were clasped together in her lap. "He was like a cat. He loved to play with his victims."

"If you had known the kind of book he was writing, would you have expected it to end in some very disagreeable surprise?"

She looked startled. "I hadn't thought of it like that. But—yes, I should."

"That would be in keeping with his character?"

"Very much so," said Mrs. Harrington bitterly.

FROM the sitting-room, where they had been talking, the Inspector and Quarles went into the study. The doctor and Bentham accompanied them, but Felix did not come, and Mrs. Harrington excused herself with a shudder. "It's silly, I know, when Elsie was in there this morning giving the room a thorough cleaning, and I don't know why I should feel like it, but—I can't go in."

George Bentham took his pipe out of his mouth, patted her arm and made reassuring noises. Inside the room the Inspector explained the murder in pantomime.

"Harrington is sitting at his desk typing." The Inspector sat down in Harrington's chair, and his fingers played over imaginary keys. "The door opens. He looks up."

The Inspector looked up, his gaze alert as a terrier's. "It's someone he knows. He doesn't bother to get up." The Inspector beamed upon the invisible guest.

Quarles broke in: "You might add that the visitor was an expected one, since he took some trouble to see that Mrs. Harrington was out of the house."

The Inspector looked a trifle disconcerted. "Well, maybe so. What happens next?"

What happened next was that a large, ornate clock on the wall opposite the desk struck the hour. A small mechanical dwarf advanced out on to a platform above the clock, raised his arm, and struck with a small hammer on an anvil.

Quarles cried: "What's that?" and caught the hammer with his hand. The Inspector jumped out of the chair and was across the room in an instant. A thin but strong piece of wire had been wound round the little hammer, and ran out through a hole bored at the back of the clock, where it was concealed by the clock body. The end of the wire was fastened in a loop.

The Inspector was excited. "A suicide trick. But how did it work?" His bright eyes glanced at various objects on the wall and settled in triumph at sight of a ledge with various knick-knacks on it.

He showed them that the wire reached just to the ledge.

"The revolver stands on the ledge," he explained, "tilted at an angle to shoot Harrington through the head, and supported by, say, a couple of book ends. Harrington loops the wire round the trigger. The clock strikes the dwarf comes out. As the hammer strikes it jerks the trip wire round the revolver trigger. The revolver goes off, shoots Harrington. Free of the trip wire it drops on the floor. And the wire, free of the revolver, falls back behind the clock. Neat."

THERE was silence. Then brusque Dr. Winter said, "Do you mean to imply, sir, that Charles Harrington committed suicide?"

"I certainly do. And then arranged it to look like murder, having provided us with a list of suspects. What's wrong with that?"

"It won't do." The doctor was emphatic. "Remember, I've known Harrington all my life. He was a thorough-going egotist, his health was perfectly good, he hated physical pain. I've never known a man less likely to commit suicide."

Quarles had been looking at the wire and the clock. "I'll tell you another thing that won't do, Merrilees. This little device never killed anybody. When the dwarf strikes with his hammer he does it so feebly that the wire hardly moves."

He put the loop round a small china ornament on the ledge and turned the clock so that it struck. The loop at the end of the wire jiggled slightly, but not enough to move the ornament. "No. I'm afraid this device was put here for us by the murderer."

The Inspector wheeled on Bentham and the Doctor. "Was it one of these two?"

"Hardly. They've had no chance to bore holes in the backs of clocks. They're visitors here."

"Mrs. Harrington, then? Or her son?" Quarles shook his head. "Then who—"

"I think the murderer is doing some carpet-sweeping outside the door now. She did a fine job of cleaning this room yesterday, including a little work on the clock."

Quarles went over to the door and flung it open. Elsie Withers was outside it with her ear to the keyhole. "It's no use, Elsie," Quarles said almost sadly. "The game's up."

"A SIMPLE little case, but not uninteresting," Quarles said afterwards to his secretary, Miss Inchborne. "Elsie Withers broke down and confessed as soon as she was interrogated. She had been Harrington's mistress, of course—a relationship Mrs. Harrington apparently hadn't fathomed—and Elsie made an arrangement to see him specially because she was afraid she might be pregnant. Harrington had got bored with her recently and kept out of her way. When she gave him her news he laughed at her and told her that far from doing anything for her he would make sure that she was dismissed immediately. He also told her that he had done her the honour of making her a murderess in the new book he was writing. That first put the idea of murder into her mind. She went to the drawer, got the revolver and shot him. It was all over, she said, in a minute. Then, when she heard of the incriminating material that Harrington had put into his story she rigged up the little device with the wire."

"Were any of the things in the book true, do you think? About Mrs. Harrington and the others?"

"I don't know, and I don't intend to inquire very closely. I'm too happy to know," Quarles said with a smile, "that the 'most unlikely person' that Harrington was so fond of making a criminal in his books killed him in the end."

MURDER IN REVERSE

THE light in Mrs. Trevor's bedroom was dim, but Charlotte Mansell was ready to swear to what she saw. She was not a particularly intelligent or observant girl, but nothing could shift her from her story.

"I was just passing by on the landing, see, on my way to vacuum the rooms upstairs, and Mrs. Trevor's door was open."

"How wide open?" she was asked, and went into a long explanation of the way in which the door swung almost halfway open, something to do with the hinges it was, if you didn't close it properly. That was what must have happened this time.

Inside the room Charlotte Mansell saw a figure pouring into a medicine glass the white liquid that Mrs. Trevor had to take every four hours. Then the figure shook some powder into it.

"It was Miss Pat," she said.

"What makes you so sure it was Miss Patricia Trevor? Could you see her face?" asked the Inspector in charge of the case.

"Well, no, I couldn't, she was standing sort of turned away from me, you see, but it was the way she does her hair, in a horse's tail at the back, you see, and then she was wearing her blue dress——"

"It was light enough for you to see the colour of her dress?" the Inspector asked sharply.

"No. She wasn't standing by the light, in the middle of the room, I suppose, or fairly near the bed. I could just see a corner of the bed. I meant I know the way the dress looks, you know. It was—well, it just was Miss Pat's dress, that's all. And then there was the brooch she was wearing. Near the shoulder it was. A sparkly glittery brooch, and it made her young man's name. Tim—that's Mr. Tim Williams, that she's going to marry."

"You know that Miss Trevor denies having such a brooch, that she'd never been seen wearing it, and that it can't be found among her things?"

"I can't help that," Charlotte Mansell said stubbornly. "She was wearing it when I saw her. I could see the letters ever so plain. T. I. M."

"And what happened then?"

"Why, then the door closed, and I went on along the passage. But it was Miss Pat. I'm sure it was."

The Inspector thought that Charlotte Mansell was telling the truth, and so indeed she was to the best of her belief. He arrested Patricia Trevor. For old Mrs. Trevor's medicine that night had been heavily loaded with a barbiturate, and under its effect the feeble ticking of her old heart had stopped.

FRANCIS QUARLES came into the case through Patricia's brother, Maxwell Trevor, a big tweed-suited man with a face which normally was ruddy, but was now pale.

"It's preposterous to think that Patricia would do such a thing. She wouldn't hurt a fly."

"Flies are not involved."

Quarles sat back and tapped his teeth. "The police seem to think she had adequate motive. Four of you inherited a tidy sum—you, your eldest sister—"

"That's Mary Isabel," Maxwell Trevor said.

"Patricia and Maureen, who is twenty three, two years younger than Patricia. All of you lived with your mother. By the terms of the will you were none of you to marry during her lifetime. Anyone who did so would be cut out of the will. Years ago Mary Isabel had wanted to get married, but the young man broke if off when he discovered that she would come to him without money. Like Mary Isabel long ago. Patricia had asked permission, and been refused. Nevertheless, she apparently intended to get married to young Mr. Williams. She would have suffered considerable financial loss. That is the police case as far as motive is concerned."

"But it's preposterous," Maxwell Trevor said again. "Pat goes to commit a murder and leaves the door open so that anyone passing by can see her. Then she obligingly puts on a brooch with her lover's name on it, to make sure there's no mistake. It's nonsense."

Quarles shook his head. "One mustn't get too subtle. Murderers do make ridiculous mistakes. They wipe off fingerprints—there were none left in this case—but they leave the door open. Things like that are not unknown. However, if you want me to investigate. I will. You realise, of course, that nobody outside the four of you who live in the house had any obvious motive for wishing your mother dead."

"I realise that," Maxwell Trevor said. "But I know I didn't do it, and I don't believe Patricia did either."

"WHERE were you standing?" Quarles asked Charlotte Mansell, and she showed him her position on the landing. Maureen Trevor, wide-eyed, and the eldest sister Mary Isabel tight-lipped and grim-faced stood watching him. Maxwell was there, too.

Quarles opened the bedroom door. The hinges were binding, and it stayed almost halfway open. Quarles placed himself beside Charlotte. He could see well into the left-hand half of the room. In the right-hand half stood the bed, with a small table beside it, and a chest of drawers. A large looking glass hung on the same wall as the door.

"Where was the figure standing?" he asked.

Charlotte was vague. "About here, I suppose." She indicated a spot near the centre of the room.

"But you said—" Quarles stopped himself, thanked Charlotte Mansell, went into the bedroom and closed the door firmly.

HIS subsequent researches occupied two days, and when they were completed he talked to Inspector Grading, who was in charge of the case. Grading went with him to the Trevor home, and the family assembled to greet them. The Inspector wasted no time.

"Mary Isabel Trevor. I have a warrant for your arrest on the charge of—"

Mary Isabel's thin mouth turned down. "You'll never prove it. Charlotte saw Patricia—"

Quarles interrupted her. "What Charlotte saw was what she was meant to see, a reflection in the looking glass, which had been brought from its proper place and put against the wall where it would reflect what went on in the other side of the room. I realised that when Charlotte said she'd seen a corner of the bed, which was quite out of her range of vision. That's why Charlotte was so vague about where the figure had been standing. In the looking glass she saw Mary Isabel, wearing a frock exactly similar in style to her sister's (we've traced the dressmaker who made it), and with her hair done in a horse's tail, pour out the medicine and add the barbiturate. Then the door was closed."

"But why the looking glass?" Mansell asked.

"The criminal's usual love of over-ingenuity. I should guess that Mary Isabel wanted to make quite sure that Charlotte identified the figure as Patricia in the dim light. She happened to possess a brooch that said T.I.M., Tim, when Charlotte saw it in the glass, so she wore it. I should imagine that it gave her great pleasure to build a case against her sister by use of a lover's name, because of her own frustrated love in the past."

"You mean she bought a brooch?" Maxwell asked.

"Oh, no. The brooch is almost the strongest point against her. The brooch was her own. A looking glass throws back a reverse image, so that the brooch she was wearing bore her own initials M.I.T.—Mary Isabel Trevor."

THE VANISHING TRICK

NEAT little Mr. Mott and his wife Evelyn lived in a neat little house with a neat little garden in the neat little suburb of Plumley. Wilfred Mott was a commercial traveller for a wholesale grocery firm, although as the neighbours said, you would never have guessed it to look at him.

If there is one thing you expect a commercial traveller to have, the neighbours said, it's personality. And personality was just what shy little Wilfred Mott seemed to lack.

His wife Evelyn, now, had personality enough for two. She was a fine big woman, with dark eyes which she could roll very effectively. With Mr. Mott away as much as he was more than a week at a time very often, everyone was agreed that something was bound to happen. And very pleased they were when something did.

First of all. Mrs. Mott started going out a good deal and coming back late at night. One night old Mrs. Pilkington, who lived opposite, distinctly heard Evelyn Mott's rich throaty laugh when a taxi drew up well after midnight.

And perhaps a week later, when it was growing dark, Mrs. Pilkington saw the man actually leaving the house. Unfortunately it was too dark to get a good look at him, but she could see that he wore spectacles, had carroty curly hair which he wore rather long, and used a stick to conceal a slight limp. She noticed also his jaunty air, as of a man obviously immensely pleased with himself. The man closed the door of the house, came down the little gravel drive, and tapped away jauntily down the road.

"Well," said Mrs. Pilkington. She lost no time in spreading the news.

During the next three weeks the man was seen several times, coming out of the gate or walking down the road. Once Mrs. Pilkington met him outside the gate. "That's Mr. Mott's house," she said. "You don't live there, do you?"

The man looked at her from behind thick pebbled glasses. She noticed a thick, whitish scar on his cheek that made her avert her eyes. "No," he said. "Do you?"

Soon after this Mr. Mott came home and Mrs. Pilkington felt it her duty, as a good neighbour, to tell him what she had seen. In his mild way Mr. Mott gave her to understand that he had perfect confidence in his wife.

That night Mr. and Mrs. Mott walked out together arm in arm. Three days later he went away again.

THE MAN with the limp did not reappear, but very late one night Mrs. Pilkington saw somebody leaving the Motts' house with two large cases. She could not be quite sure whether it was a man or a large woman, since she caught no more than a glimpse of the figure in a dim light.

It was four days later that Mrs. Pilkington noticed the growing number of milk bottles on the front porch, and telephoned the police.

Her more gruesome hopes were disappointed. The house was in perfect order, except that most of Mrs. Mott's clothes had gone—just about as many as you might expect to be carried in two large suitcases.

Mrs. Mott had left a note for her husband in the living room. It was dated, and there was no doubt about it being in her writing.

The note said that she had fallen in love with another man, who was a real man, even though he might have a scar and a limp from honourable war service. She no longer loved her husband and was leaving him for ever.

She asked him not to try to trace her, and signed her name with a bold flourish: "Evelyn."

SUCH were the facts told by Wilfred Mott's brother, Charles, to private detective Francis Quarles. The detective lit a cigar. "Your brother needs a divorce lawyer."

Charles Mott leaned forward. "Wilfred had disappeared."

Quarles stared at him, "What?"

"I live in Manchester, but I was in London on a business visit, and thought I'd call on Wilfred and Evelyn. When I heard the neighbours' story I got in touch with the police, but, of course, it isn't really their business if a man's wife runs away from him. Then I spoke to Wilfred's chief, Marples, who told me that he'd sent a note to Wilfred at the hotel in Broadstairs where he always stayed. The police had told him the situation, and he'd sent a note of sympathy. I went down to Broadstairs. The note was there all right, but Wilfred hadn't been seen at the hotel. So I came to you."

"Were your brother and his wife happy?"

"Wilfred was madly in love with her." Charles Mott hesitated. "He looked mild enough, but he was very jealous."

"Had she any special friends—women, not men?" Quarles learned that she had one, named Adela Ricks. Then he got up. "I'll do what I can for you Mr. Mott. Give me the name of your hotel."

"I KEEP myself to myself," Mrs. Ricks told Quarles. "But I'm not surprised she's gone. He wasn't the right fellow for her, and that's a fact."

"Did she ever speak to you about anyone else?"

Mrs. Ricks looked coyly at her red fingernails. "As a matter of fact, she did. Never told me his name, but said I'd fairly scream if I knew it. Said he was big, strong and handsome."

Quarles mentioned the man with the limp. Mrs. Ricks shook her head doubtfully. "Doesn't sound like the same fellow to me. Perhaps she had two of them on a string. Wouldn't put it past Evelyn." She began to laugh.

MR. WILLIAM MARPLES sat behind his desk and listened in silence to the story Quarles told him. He was an ox-like man, coarsely good-looking, with a shock of fair hair and an engaging grin. Just now he looked worried.

"The private lives of our employees aren't our concern, though I like Wilfred and his wife, and I'd be sorry to see them split up. But there's something else in this case. I'm not surprised to hear Wilfred wasn't at Broadstairs. He's been playing this trick before."

"What trick?"

"Our travellers have to send in their reports three times a week, giving details of the firms they've visited. Wilfred's been sending in reports lately giving details of visits he's never made."

Marples pushed some letters across the table, with half a dozen typed reports. "Here's his report from Broadstairs, which came in this morning. Phoney, I suppose, like half the others."

"Have you got the envelope this last report from Broadstairs came in?"

Marples called in his secretary and asked her to try to find it. While they were talking, the light flashed on his desk intercom. He pressed down a switch and a girl's voice said: "Your house-keeper on the line, Mr. Marples."

"Tell her I'll call back." Marples frowned at his shoes. The girl brought back the envelope. It had a Broadstairs postmark for the previous day.

Quarles got Marples's private address, took the letters and the typed reports, and left.

Back in his office, he spent an hour in making telephone calls to various numbers in Broadstairs before finding what he expected. Then his own telephone rang. It was Marples, and he sounded excited.

"Wilfred's just rung up, and we've had a fair flaming row. He turned the job in before I could sack him. Said something about starting a new life, that he was through with being a salesman and through with Evelyn, too. What do you think of that?"

"I think he was perfectly right." said Quarles.

TWO hours later, Quarles and his friend, Inspector Leeds, searched the Motts' house.

The Inspector was inclined to be sceptical until he saw the loose stones in the cellar. Under the stones, with a little earth shovelled hastily on top of him, they found the body of Wilfred Mott.

He was not immediately recognisable, because of the scar painted across the face and the carrot-coloured wig that had fallen askew on his head. He had been killed by a blow that had cracked his skull.

When Quarles and the Inspector rang the bell of Marples's house, the man himself opened it. The Inspector thrust a foot inside while Quarles said: "We want to see your housekeeper."

"She's out," Marples said loudly. The Inspector pushed past him and caught the woman who was running down a passage to the back door.

She scratched him before he got the handcuffs on, and then turned to them a face of such furious and passionate despair that her friends would hardly have known her as Evelyn Mott.

"IT was a vanishing trick that failed," Quarles told Charles Mott afterwards. "Wilfred found out that his wife was having an affair with Marples. He decided to kill her, and hit on the ingenious idea of creating an imaginary lover so that when she disappeared it would be thought that she had left him. He faked his reports so that he should have time to let the lover be seen in disguise. Unfortunately he overdid it—a carroty wig, pebbled glasses, a scar and a limp is altogether too much of a good thing. Marples and the woman realised what he was doing pretty quickly, and decided to give him a surprise. They came in one night when Wilfred had entered the house in his disguise—of course, he only showed himself when he knew his wife had gone out. They thought they'd make a fool of him, but by Marples's account Wilfred was like a madman. He started to strangle Evelyn. Marples hit him on the head with the poker, and killed him. That's their story, and it may be true.

"Then they tried a vanishing trick of their own. They buried Wilfred, left that note, and Evelyn went to live in Marples's house. They meant to move Wilfred's body at night, but thought it was too dangerous when you started making inquiries. Then Marples tried to prove that Wilfred was still alive. He faked a report, and got it posted from Broadstairs by putting it in a letter to a customer and then telephoning to say the report had been included in error and asking them to post it back. But their real mistake was the letter she left."

"Why?"

"She said she'd gone off with the man with a limp. Once I realized that the limping carroty-haired man was Wilfred in disguise, I felt almost sure he was dead and she'd been party to his murder. But what a nerve she had. To bury her husband in the cellar, and then sit down and write him a letter. I wouldn't call myself a highly imaginative man. Mr. Mott, but I shudder to think of it."

THE IMPOSSIBLE THEFT

IT was an impossible theft, as private detective Francis Quarles said when he told the story afterward in the club; and like all impossible crimes it was really simple. The way the crime was committed, and the identity of the criminal, were obvious once you knew his occupation.

"And of course you guessed it," one of his listeners said sarcastically.

"Not guessed, deduced. That's the point of the story."

It began when Ossie Gregory—who was always called Ossie for some reason, although he wasn't an Australian and his name was not Oswald but Dick—came to see him. Gregory also was a private detective, of a humble kind. After a couple of drinks he would tell you that he had been a professional boxer and a bodyguard, had worked in a casino and a circus, and had even been a cowboy on the biggest ranch in Texas.

Just now Ossie Gregory was worried.

"It's Solly Raven's daughter, she's getting engaged. You know Solly Raven?" Quarles nodded. Raven was the flashiest bookmaker in London. "Solly likes to put on a show, you know that, so he's bought her this rope of pearls as an engagement present—cost him I don't know how many thousand quid. Nothing'll do for him but the pearls must be on show at her engagement party for everyone to see. So he'll take 'em out of the case, put 'em round her neck, and everyone yells hurrah for Solly, right? He's hired me to be there—to keep an eye on 'em and on everything in general. Get it?"

"It sounds straightforward enough," said Quarles.

"Should be, but then yesterday he got this."

"This" was a sheet of paper on which words cut from newspapers had been pasted. They read:

TEN O'CLOCK YOU'VE GOT YOUR PEARLS TEN FIFTEEN YOU HAVEN'T

Quarles raised his eyebrows. "Nice of him to tell us in advance when he's going to take them."

"It's just about when Solly's going to put them round his daughter's neck. I don't like it, Mr. Quarles. A straightforward job, taking care of toughs, that's okay. But something like this needs more in the upper story than I've got."

Gregory then added wistfully, "I don't suppose you would come along? Two heads are better than one, especially when one of them is yours."

That was why Quarles attended Roberta Raven's engagement dance at London's newest hotel, the Lanchester.

THERE were at least two hundred guests, many of them looking uneasy in their dinner jackets. The pearls were in a showcase at one end of the room and Solly Raven, with the biggest cigar Quarles had ever seen stuck in his red face, led guests up to them with pride.

Ossie Gregory stayed near the showcase, his face set in a look of dogged suspicion. Quarles ate canapes, turkey, and iced strawberries, and reflected that although some of the guests might pick pockets, they did not look up to stealing pearls.

Solly Raven came up to him. "Enjoying yourself, Mr. Quarles? Got all you want to eat? Seen what I'm giving to my little girl? And she deserves it, let me tell you." He put a large arm round the shoulders of his pert, pretty daughter. "Nothing's too good for my Roberta."

"Does that mean you think I'm not good enough?" That was Roberta's young man, James Barry, dark and self-assured. He was wearing a conspicuous emerald-green double-breasted dinner jacket. Raven merely grunted, evidently not delighted by the prospect of having James Barry for a son-in-law. But now he turned to greet a small gray-haired man who had just arrived.

"Professor Burtenshaw, this is a real honor. You know my daughter—and Mr. Quarles."

"We're old friends," Quarles said. Burtenshaw was one of the greatest British experts on precious stones—in particular, on diamonds and pearls.

"Hey, Gregory," Raven called out. The detective nodded, obviously knowing what he had to do. He unlocked the showcase, carefully took out the rope of pearls, and handed it to Solly, who passed it on to the Professor.

Quarles looked at his watch. The time was exactly 10.01.

"BEAUTIFUL," Burtenshaw said. "Perfectly matched. And such luster. Quite beautiful, I must say."

"I'm not going to tell you how much they set me back." Raven looked as though he would have been very willing to tell if he were pressed.

The pearls went from hand to hand in the circle of a dozen people

THE IMPOSSIBLE THEFT 193

surrounding the bookmaker. James Barry murmured something about them matching their wearer, and passed them on. Ossie watched their progress with unconcealed anxiety, sweat on his forehead, until they came back to him. Then he returned them to the showcase, locked the case, and sighed with relief.

"Oh, no, you don't," Barry cried out suddenly. He turned on a small foxy-looking waiter just behind him. "You had your hand on my wallet! Come on, turn out your pockets, and show us what else you've got."

The waiter protested innocence, and shook off Barry's hand. Everybody was looking at them.

"Please, darling," Roberta said. "You've still got your wallet, after all. Don't spoil the evening."

Reluctantly Barry subsided. Harmony was restored. Solly Raven clapped his hands. "And now, ladies and gentlemen, your attention for a moment, please. Gregory."

Ossie unlocked the showcase again, and then paused before touching the pearls. He looked frightened. The veins on his neck stood out like cords.

He said in a strangled voice, "Mr. Raven, Professor, Mr. Quarles. These pearls don't look right."

Professor Burtenshaw took out the rope in the showcase, examined it, and said, "These are not the same pearls. They're the crudest sort of paste."

Raven howled with anger. Roberta began to cry. Quarles looked at his watch again.

The time was exactly 10.15.

AT this point Quarles stopped, and beamed at his club audience. Somebody urged, "Go on."

"That's all. The problem is: Who stole the pearls and how was it done?"

"The police searched everybody?"

"Everybody. And everyone who had touched the pearls when they were passed round was searched and stripped, even Raven and Gregory. They searched the room, too. No good."

"That expert, what's his name, Burtenshaw," said an accountant named Sanders, who claimed to solve every detective story he read. "He was a fake."

"No. I told you I knew Burtenshaw. Everything he said was absolutely true."

Sanders was thinking hard. "That row Barry had with the waiter must have had something to do with it. The waiter was an accomplice. Barry stole the pearls and slipped them to the waiter."

"Barry had nothing to do with it. But you're right about the waiter being an accomplice. His job was to create a diversion so that the thief could hide the pearls."

"Solly Raven stole them, for the insurance?"

"No."

Sanders' brow wrinkled. "You're not going to tell us it was Gregory?"

"Yes. It was he who wrote the warning letter, who arranged the whole thing."

"But he called you in himself."

"He wanted a respectable witness, and thought he could fool me. That was his only mistake," Quarles said modestly.

"You told us he'd been searched, and there was nothing on him."

"He was searched, and there was nothing on him."

"He hid them somewhere in the room? Under the showcase, with chewing gum?"

"He didn't hide the pearls in the room."

"But that's impossible! Where were they?"

"When the real pearls were handed back to Gregory, he palmed them and put the paste ones in the showcase. Then he got rid of the real ones."

"But how?" Sanders cried. "How?"

"What was Gregory's occupation? I told you that was the point of the story."

"Why, you told us he was a private detective."

"And what was he before that? I told you he'd worked in a circus, and I told you he was called Ossie. I put two and two together, and realized what Ossie might stand for."

There was silence. "Come on then," Sanders said. "What did it stand for?"

"The name of his circus act. He was a swallower. He used to swallow live frogs and rats, and bring them back alive. A string of pearls was nothing to him. They called him the Human Ostrich."

FINAL NIGHT EXTRA

FRANK SEDGEHAM finished his game of squash at the club, bought an evening paper and walked home. The walk took him ten minutes. Just before he opened the door of his family's small, pretty house in a Kensington square he looked at his watch and saw that the time was half past four.

When he opened the door a policeman confronted him. Frank stared. "What are you doing here?"

The policeman did not answer this question. He simply said: "Your name, sir?"

"My name's Frank Sedgeham, and I happen to live here. What's wrong?"

Before the policeman could reply, the door of the living-room opened and his sister June came towards him, arms outstretched.

"Frank, Frank," she cried. "Step-father's been murdered. And it was I who found the body. Such a shattering experience." June was training to be an actress, and it was obvious that she regarded this as her first big part. She added with a kind of gurgling sigh: "The police are making their investigations. They suspect us all."

Frank went into the living-room. There he found his mother, her fair hair beautifully set, lying on the sofa with a hand over her eyes. His step-uncle, John Tapscott, paced up and down the room with mincing steps, pulling nervously at his ear.

"You here, Uncle John," Frank said. "How did you know about this?"

"He saw it in the paper, you fool," shrieked his sister. "Haven't you looked at the paper?"

"As a matter of fact, I haven't."

She snatched the paper from his hand. It was the *Evening Standard* Final Night Extra edition. "Is it in this one? Yes, it's the same as Uncle John's. Look."

Her finger pointed to a paragraph about the death of the wealthy industrialist Andrew Tapscott. It said that his body had been found by his step-daughter Miss June Sedgeham, that he had been shot through the head, and that the police were making investigations. Mrs. Tapscott moaned from the sofa, and John Tapscott spoke to her sharply.

"Don't be a hypocrite. You won't fool anybody, not even yourself. You know very well that you're glad to see him go."

"How can you say such a thing?" Mrs. Tapscott said, and burst into tears. "And in front of the police, too."

Frank Sedgeham became aware that there was another person in the room. This was a grizzled, square-headed man who so far had merely been listening to what they said. Now he introduced himself to Frank as Inspector Leeds from Scotland Yard.

"It doesn't seem to me that any of you are heartbroken," he said dryly. "I'd just like to go through the course of events again. Mrs. Tapscott, you went out at half-past twelve, leaving your husband alive and well. There was a cold lunch set for him, and he apparently ate it. Miss Sedgeham, you came home at half past one after having an early lunch with a friend. You went into the room your step-father used as a study, and found him sitting in a chair. He had been shot between the eyes."

"Was the gun there?" Frank asked. "Couldn't it have been suicide?"

"It was his own revolver, but if he shot himself he rubbed his prints off the barrel afterwards, and dropped it on the other side of the desk," said the Inspector.

"A stranger, it must have been a stranger," said Mrs. Tapscott faintly from the sofa.

"No, ma'am. Your husband sat at his own desk, and the murderer used his revolver, which you tell me was kept in a cupboard in the study. The murderer was somebody who knew the revolver was there. Now, let's continue. You came home at three o'clock, Mrs. Tapscott, after lunching out and having your hair done. Before that time—soon after she found the body—Miss Sedgeham had telephoned the police, and also telephoned the newspapers. Why did you do that, Miss Sedgeham? Could it be that you wanted to see your name in the paper?"

"If you like to think so," said June defiantly.

"You didn't know what hair-dresser your mother had gone to, or where your brother was, so you couldn't get in touch with them. Why didn't you telephone your step-uncle?"

"Because he isn't on the telephone."

"I abhor the instrument," John Tapscott said. "I am by nature a recluse, and find the telephone a distraction from my work. Since I retired from the civil service I have occupied myself with a scheme for turning water into petrol. The results of my experiments are near completion." There was a fanatical light in his eye.

"Not too much of a recluse to buy a paper." The Inspector picked up the paper John Tapscott had brought with him. It was another Final Night Extra edition of the *Evening Standard*.

"I live in Croydon, and take a constitutional after lunch," John Tapscott said. "I occasionally buy a paper from the newsboy at East Croydon Station. I bought this paper today at 2.15, and, when I saw the news, got straight on to a train. I caught the 2.45 train to Victoria."

"He was here by half-past three. Afraid of losing his share of the spoils, no doubt," Mrs. Tapscott sneered.

John Tapscott stopped his pacing, and faced the Inspector. He was a little man, neat as a sparrow. "There is something you should know, Inspector. My brother was a hard man. I grant you, I had no great love for him. But this woman is a harpy who married him for his money, and has never ceased trying to screw a little more than her generous allowance out of him. And what about her children? June has spent three years at an academy of dramatic art. She recently achieved a walking-on part—silent, of course—in a play put on by a local amateur dramatic society. Frank is reading for the Bar. What was he doing this afternoon?"

"Playing squash," Frank said, and muttered something about the need for keeping fit.

"Playing squash. You see how seriously he takes his studies. He has failed his examinations twice, and is likely to be eligible for the old age pension before he passes them. A pretty crew—"

"Liar, liar," June shrieked. "I've got three lines to speak."

At the same moment Mrs. Tapscott got off the sofa and tried to claw John Tapscott's face. Frank Sedgeham said: "If you were twenty years younger …"

The Inspector restored order, took statements from them, and left.

"THEY certainly are a pretty crew," the Inspector said to Francis Quarles afterwards, "And John Tapscott's as bad as the rest of them. He's been pestering his brother lately for money to back this crazy invention of his."

"Was there much money to get?"

"Yes. Tapscott was a wealthy man. John Tapscott gets £20,000 outright, and Mrs. Tapscott has the income from the rest after providing £500 a year each for the step-children. At her death the money is divided between them. They all had motives for murder, and none of them has a watertight alibi. It's a toss-up between them."

"Oh, surely not," Quarles said. "You've got reasonable grounds for making an arrest on suspicion. After all, one of them told an obvious thumping great lie."

Which of the Suspects Lied?

SOLUTION

THE LIAR and murderer was John Tapscott. The earliest time a Londoner would buy a Final Night Extra Edition of the *Evening Standard* would be 2:35 and then only in areas near Fleet Street. It was therefore quite impossible for him to have bought a copy at a quarter past two outside East Croydon Station.

APPENDIX: THE CASEBOOK OF FRANCIS QUARLES

The following includes all known Francis Quarles stories. For stories first collected in this present volume, as well as still uncollected stories, we include information on first publication.

Murder! Murder! (London: Collins Fontana paperback, 1961) contains 21 Francis Quarles cases:

"Centre Court Mystery"
"Test Match Murder"
"The Grand National Case"
"The Case of S.W. 2."
"The Unhappy Piano Tuner"
"A Pearl Among Women"
"Credit to William Shakespeare"
"Meeting in the Snow"
"The Wrong Hat"
"The Absent-Minded Professor"
"Each Man Kills"
"Time for Murder"
"The Case of the Frightened Promoter"
"Picture Show"
"Sailors' Hornpipe"
"The Hiding Place"
"Airport Incident"
"The Plaster Pekingese"
"Comedy in Venice"
"The Invisible Poison"
"Little Man Lost"

200 JULIAN SYMONS

Francis Quarles Investigates (London: Panther paperback, 1965) contains 15 Francis Quarles cases:

"Strolling in the Square One Day"
"The Archer"
"Out of the Mouths"
"Thirty Days Hath September"
"The Woman Afraid of October"
"Blue Paint"
"One Little Letter"
"The Santa Claus Club"
"Hot Summer Night"
"Coffee for Three"
"Four Letters"
"Kidnap Plot"
"A Matter of Dentistry"
"By the Sea"
"Ace of Spades"

How To Trap A Crook and 12 Other Mysteries, ed. Ellery Queen (New York: Davis, 1977) is a mixed collection of Symons' stories including one previously collected in *Murder! Murder!* and two in *Francis Quarles Investigates*. The following Francis Quarles case however is first collected in this book:

"How to Trap a Crook"

The Detections of Francis Quarles, ed. John Cooper (Norfolk, Virginia: Crippen and Landru, 2006) contains 42 Francis Quarles cases:

"Red Rum Means Murder." *Evening Standard*, 15 May 1952
"Death in the Scillies." *Evening Standard*, 13 March 1951; *Ellery Queen's Mystery Magazine*, March 1954, as "Life and Death in the Scillies"
"Poison Pen." *Evening Standard*, 15 September 1952
"An Exercise in Logic." *Evening Standard*, 8 September 1952
"Summer Show." *Evening Standard*, 21 August 1954; *The Saint Detective Magazine*, September 1955
"The Desk." *Evening Standard*, 29 September 1950); *The Evening Standard Detective Book*, series 2 (Gollancz, 1951)
"Mrs. Rolleston's Diamonds." *Evening Standard*, 10 August 1950

"Murder—But How Was It Done?" *Evening Standard*, 29 October 1956
"Ancestor Worship." *Evening Standard*, 3 November 1956
"Iced Champagne." *Evening Standard*, 19 October 1953; also published as "Ten Thousand Dollars a Dance," *Nero Wolfe Mystery Magazine*, March 1954
"No Use Turning a Deaf Ear to Murder." *Evening Standard*, 1 June 1964; *The Saint Mystery Magazine*, January 1966
"The Duke of York." *Evening Standard*, 27 January 1953
"Double Double Cross." *Evening Standard*, 25 September 1952
"Tattoo." *Evening Standard*, 16 September 1953
"Jack and Jill." *Evening Standard*, 19 September 1953
"The Conjuring Trick." *Evening Standard*, 28 January 1953
"Happy Hexing." *Evening Standard*, 19 September 1950
"No Deception." *Evening Standard*, 29 January 1953
"The Second Bullet." *Evening Standard*, 31 October 1956
"Preserving the Evidence." *Evening Standard*, 18 September 1952; *John Creasey's Mystery Bedside Book 1970* (Hodder & Stoughton, 1969)
"Death for Mr. Golightly." *Evening Standard*, 22 December 1952
"A Man with Blue Hair." *Evening Standard*, 31 January 1953
"The Two Suitors." *Evening Standard.*, 15 September 1953
"Airborne with a Borgia." *Evening Standard*, 28 September 1955
"Art-loving Mr. Lister Lands a Fake …" *Evening Standard.*, 13 March 1963; also published as "A Taste for Art," *The Saint Mystery Magazine*, January 1964
"The Collector." *Evening Standard*, 18 September 1953
"Ghost From the Past." *Evening Standard*, 1 October 1951
"The Swedish Nightingale" *Evening Standard*, 14 September 1953
"The Barton Hall Dwarf." *Evening Standard*, 16 August 1954
"The Pepoli Case." *Evening Standard*, 2 February 1952
"Nothing Up His Sleeve." *Evening Standard*, 23 September 1952
"A Present from Santa Claus." *Evening Standard*, 24 December 1954; *The Saint Detective Magazine*, January 1956
"The Link." *Evening Standard*, 30 January 1953; *John Creasey's Mystery Magazine*, August 1957
"Little Boy Blue." *Evening Standard*, 20 August 1954
"Affection Unlimited." *Evening Standard*, 10 July 1950
"The Whistling Man." *Evening Standard*, 9 July 1952
"Party Line." *Evening Standard.*, 30 October 1956
"Who Killed Harrington?" *Evening Standard*, 28 November 1950
"Murder in Reverse." *Evening Standard*, 2 November 1956

"The Vanishing Trick." *Evening Standard*, 28 July 1952

"The Impossible Theft." *Ellery Queen's Mystery Magazine*, January 1966; the story was copyrighted 1964, but its previous appearance, in *Evening Standard* or elsewhere, has not been located.

"Final Night Extra." *Evening Standard*, 3 September 1955; solution published 5 September 1955

The following stories remain uncollected:

"A Cup of Tea." *Evening Standard*, 12 September 1950

"The Clue in the Book." *Evening Standard*, 5 May 1952

"Murder Too Perfect." *Evening Standard*, 19 July 1955

"Death of an M.P." *Evening Standard*, 29 August 1955; solution published 30 August 1955

"Dial 999." *Evening Standard*, 30 August 1955; solution published 31 August 1955

"The Claimant." *Evening Standard*, 31 August 1955; solution published 1 September 1955

"Mr. Longden Had a Diary." *Evening Standard*, 1 September 1955; solution published 2 September 1955

"The Briefcase." *Evening Standard.*, 2 September 1955; solution published 3 September 1955

AFTERWORD BY KATHLEEN SYMONS

Julian was a Londoner—born and bred—although during our long marriage we made several moves to the country we never stayed there very long and back we came to London. The exception was our last move to Walmer in Kent, a few miles from Dover, where Julian died in 1994.

He was the youngest child in a large family, the eldest being A.J.A., the author of the classic "experiment in biography" *The Quest for Corvo* who died tragically in 1941. In 1937 Julian founded *Twentieth Century Verse*, which he ran single-handedly until the war and which published young poets including Dylan Thomas, Roy Fuller, George Woodcock and Gavin Ewart. He also had two books of poems published: *Confusions about X* in 1938 and *The Second Man* in 1943.

After the war Julian worked in advertising for nearly four years, leaving to become a freelance writer with the help of George Orwell who was a close friend for many years before his death in 1950. George wrote a weekly column called "Life, People and Books" in the *Manchester Evening News* and with the success of *Animal Farm* wanted to give it up. He persuaded them to give Julian, who was unknown to them, a trial and he wrote the column for ten years. During this time he also wrote many crime novels including *The 31st of February* in 1950, *The Narrowing Circle* (1954), *The Colour of Murder* (1957) and *The Progress of a Crime* (1960), which he thought were some of his best books.

It was at this time, from the early fifties to the early sixties, that he wrote many short stories introducing Francis Quarles, the rather unorthodox but very clever private detective who appeared in most of them and of whom Julian became quite fond. In fact he would be delighted to know that a selection of Quarles' previously uncollected stories were now to see the light of day in an elegant publication.

Julian succeeded Agatha Christie as President of the Detection Club in 1976 and was given the Grand Master Award from the Mystery Writers of America in 1982, two honours among many that he valued particularly. He also became a member of the Royal Society of Literature in 1975 and in 1990 he was awarded the Cartier Diamond Dagger by the CWA for a lifetime's achievement in the crime genre.

In 1975 we spent a very happy year at Amherst College where Julian was the visiting writer. His book *Bloody Murder—From the Detective Story to the Crime Novel* had been published in America in 1973 under the title *Mortal Consequences* to great acclaim on both sides of the Atlantic.

While we lived in Walmer Julian wrote one of his very best books—*Death's Darkest Face* published in 1990.

For many years he had been on tours for the British Council and in October 1994 he went on one to Spain. It was very successful and he enjoyed it but came home very tired and three weeks later he quietly died.

Some people on first meeting Julian found him rather cold and forbidding, but on getting to know him changed their opinion and delighted in his warm and witty personality. He rarely lost his temper but used devastating sarcasm instead. He could also, if in the company of good friends, be very very funny with a fund of amusing stories told with dry humour. If he liked you, you were a friend for life and nothing would change that. He as always fiercely loyal.

THE DETECTIONS OF FRANCIS QUARLES

The Detections of Francis Quarles by Julian Symons, edited by John Cooper, is set in 11-point Baskerville on 13-point leading and printed on 60 pound Natural acid-free paper. The cover painting is by Carol Heyer, and the Lost Classsics design is by Deborah Miller. *The Detections of Francis Quarles* was published in March 2006 by Crippen & Landru Publishers, Norfolk, Virginia.

CRIPPEN & LANDRU, PUBLISHERS
P. O. Box 9315, Norfolk, VA 23505
E-mail: info@crippenlandru.com; toll-free 877 622-6656
Web: www.crippenlandru.com

CRIPPEN & LANDRU LOST CLASSICS

Crippen & Landru is proud to publish a series of *new* short-story collections by great authors who specialized in traditional mysteries. Each book collects stories from crumbling pages of old pulp, digest, and slick magazines, and most of the stories have been "lost" since their first publication. The following books are in print:

The Newtonian Egg and Other Cases of Rolf le Roux by Peter Godfrey, introduction by Ronald Godfrey. 2002. Trade softcover, $15.00

Murder, Mystery and Malone by Craig Rice, edited by Jeffrey A. Marks. 2002. Trade softcover, $19.00.

The Sleuth of Baghdad: The Inspector Chafik Stories, by Charles B. Child. 2002. Cloth, $27.00. Trade softcover, $19.00.

Hildegarde Withers: Uncollected Riddles by Stuart Palmer, introduction by Mrs. Stuart Palmer. 2002. Cloth, $29.00. Trade softcover, $19.00.

The Spotted Cat and Other Mysteries by Christianna Brand, edited by Tony Medawar. 2002. Cloth, $29.00. Trade softcover, $19.00.

Marksman and Other Stories by William Campbell Gault, edited by Bill Pronzini; afterword by Shelley Gault. 2003. Trade softcover, $19.00.

Karmesin: The World's Greatest Criminal — Or Most Outrageous Liar by Gerald Kersh, edited by Paul Duncan. 2003. Cloth, $27.00. Trade softcover, $17.00.

The Complete Curious Mr. Tarrant by C. Daly King, introduction by Edward D. Hoch. 2003. Cloth, $29.00. Trade softcover, $19.00.

The Pleasant Assassin and Other Cases of Dr. Basil Willing by Helen McCloy, introduction by B.A. Pike. 2003. Cloth, $27.00. Trade softcover, $18.00.

Murder – All Kinds by William L. DeAndrea, introduction by Jane Haddam. 2003. Cloth, $29.00. Trade softcover, $19.00.

The Avenging Chance and Other Mysteries from Roger Sheringham's Casebook by Anthony Berkeley, edited by Tony Medawar and Arthur Robinson. 2004. Cloth, $29.00. Trade softcover, $19.00.

Banner Deadlines: The Impossible Files of Senator Brooks U. Banner by Joseph Commings, edited by Robert Adey; memoir by Edward D. Hoch. 2004. Cloth, $29.00. Trade softcover, $19.00.

The Danger Zone and Other Stories by Erle Stanley Gardner, edited by Bill Pronzini. 2004. Cloth, $29.00. Trade softcover, $19.00.

Dr. Poggioli: Criminologist by T.S. Stribling, edited by Arthur Vidro. 2004. Cloth, $29.00. Trade softcover, $19.00.

The Couple Next Door: Collected Short Mysteries by Margaret Millar, edited by Tom Nolan. 2004. Trade softcover, $19.00.

Sleuth's Alchemy: Cases of Mrs. Bradley and Others by Gladys Mitchell, edited by Nicholas Fuller. 2005. Trade softcover, $19.00.

Philip S. Warne/Howard W. Macy, *Who Was Guilty? Two Dime Novels*, edited by Marlena E. Bremseth. 2005. Cloth, $29.00. Trade softcover, $19.00.

Dennis Lynds writing as Michael Collins, *Slot-Machine Kelly*, introduction by Robert J. Randisi. 2005. Cloth, $29.00. Trade softcover, $19.00.

Rafael Sabatini, *The Evidence of the Sword*, edited by Jesse Knight. 2006. Cloth, $29.00. Trade softcover, $19.00.

Erle Stanley Gardner, *The Casebook of Sidney Zoom*, edited by Bill Pronzini. 2006. Cloth, $29.00. Trade softcover, $19.00.

Julian Symons, *The Detections of Francis Quarles*, edited by John Cooper; afterword by Kathleen Symons. 2006. Cloth, $29.00. Trade softcover, $19.00.

FORTHCOMING LOST CLASSICS

Ellis Peters (Edith Pargeter), *The Trinity Cat and Other Mysteries*, edited by Martin Edwards and Sue Feder

Lloyd Biggle, Jr., *The Grandfather Rastin Mysteries*, introduction by Kenneth Biggle

Max Brand, *Masquerade: Nine Crime Stories*, edited by William F. Nolan, Jr.

Hugh Pentecost, *The Battles of Jericho*, introduction by S.T. Karnick

Mignon G. Eberhart, *Dead Yesterday and Other Mysteries*, edited by Rick Cypert and Kirby McCauley

Victor Canning, *The Minerva Club, The Department of Patterns and Other Stories*, edited by John Higgins

Elizabeth Ferrars, *The Casebook of Jonas P. Jonas and Others*, edited by John Cooper

Anthony Boucher and Denis Green, *The Casebook of Gregory Hood*, edited by Joe R. Christopher

Philip Wylie, *Ten Thousand Blunt Instruments*, edited by Bill Pronzini

Erle Stanley Gardner, *The Adventures of Señor Lobo*, edited by Bill Pronzini

G.T. Fleming-Roberts, *Lilies for the Crooked Cross and Other Stories*, edited by Monte Herridge

SUBSCRIPTIONS

Crippen & Landru offers discounts to individuals and institutions who place Standing Order Subscriptions for its forthcoming publications, either all the Regular Series or all the Lost Classics or (preferably) both. Collectors can thereby guarantee receiving limited editions, and readers won't miss any favorite stories. Standing Order Subscribers receive a specially commissioned story in a deluxe edition as a gift at the end of the year. Please write or e-mail for more details.